Justice
Be
Damned

The
Tales of Flynn and Reilly

Rosemary J. Kind

Printed in the United Kingdom

First Printing, 2020 Alfie Dog Limited

The author can be found at: authors@alfiedog.com

Cover design: Katie Stewart, Magic Owl Designs
http://www.magicowldesign.com/

ISBN 978-1-909894-45-7

Published by
Alfie Dog Limited
Schilde Lodge, Tholthorpe,
North Yorkshire, YO61 1SN
Tel: 01347 838747

DEDICATION

To Chris - my rock.

AUTHOR'S NOTE

There are aspects of historical fact with which I have taken slight liberties. Despite attempts, I have not been able to find out the date of the Primaries in 1870. As a result, they have been dated to fit the story's needs, however they would probably not have been quite so late in the year.

NOTE:
The characters are all fictitious and any resemblance they may have to persons alive or dead is entirely coincidental. This book is not intended to suggest that the events portrayed happened in reality. It is purely a work of fiction, rooted in elements of real history.

"I will tell my daughter how proud I am of her mother and I will do whatever I have to do to make sure that my daughter is treated fairly and equally and is not persecuted for her sex."

Daniel Flynn, Unequal By Birth

"Throughout history, it has been the inaction of those who could have acted, the indifference of those who should have known better, the silence of the voice of justice when it mattered most, that has made it possible for evil to triumph."

Haile Selassie

"The dead cannot cry out for justice. It is a duty of the living to do so for them."

Lois McMaster Bujold

"There may be times when we are powerless to prevent injustice, but there must never be a time when we fail to protest."

Elie Wiesel

CHAPTER 1

Pierceton, Indiana, March 1870

"He said what?" William Dixon could feel his nostrils flaring as he tried to keep his voice steady.

"That he don't rightly think the fire was deliberate and that those boys shouldn't be tried for arson." The sheriff shrugged his shoulders, appearing to distance himself from his words.

"They damn near killed my sister and niece, and Ben died trying to save them. The Reese brothers should be tried for murder, never mind arson." William's hands were shaking and he took a deep breath to control his temper. He knew the sheriff was a good man and the words he was expressing were not his own, but by God, William would, at the very least, see those Reese boys behind bars. "What does Justice Warren say the charges will be?"

"Trespass," the sheriff said quietly. His eyes darted up to meet William's and looked back down just as quickly. "Given Reuben Reese confessed, Justice Warren can't try claiming they weren't at Cochrane's Farm. Story goes, they had their lamp with them and got lost on their way home from Marsh's bar, lamp spilled and the oil caught light, but by then they'd moved on, too drunk to notice."

William thumped the desk. "My sister's farm wasn't on their way home and those boys have lived around here long enough not to get as lost as all that. It was in the opposite direction out of town to their place, though I'll grant they had fields which bordered Molly's land." He snorted. This would be funny if it weren't so serious.

With the bad news delivered, the sheriff relaxed a little. "Why'd your sister have to go buying what was left of their land? They were sore enough over what their daddy lost to her. There's only one thing more trouble than an idle man and that's an idle man with a grudge."

"And don't I know it? Those boys will have all the time in the world to cause problems if they aren't in prison… or hanged." William got up from the side of the sheriff's desk and paced around the small office. It was only three paces across, so this proved more frustrating than calming. "I need some air, then maybe I'll ride out to Warsaw and see Justice Warren in person."

"He was friends with their daddy, you know. It won't do no good."

The sheriff couldn't meet William's eye and it simply served to make William more determined to see this through to a satisfactory outcome. What kind of world was it, where a man could be killed and a house burned down deliberately, and yet no one stand trial for those actions? Would Justice Warren see things differently if Ben hadn't been black, or if he'd been born in Pierceton as the Reese brothers had? William sighed.

"Good day, Sheriff." William nodded his head to the man, then marched out into the street, breathing deeply to fill his lungs with something good and wholesome as he went. There was still a chill in the air, in sharp contrast to being indoors, and the freshness was welcome.

The walk back to Dixon's Attorney's Office gave William time to think. Reuben Reese had confessed to arson, his intention was clear and a man had died. Yes, the brothers had thought there was no one in the property when they set it alight, but of course they must have known it was a possibility. William tried to consider what action his father would take if he were handling the case, and resolved to send word to him in Dowagiac as soon as he got to his own desk. He guessed his father had experience of life in a small town, with all the back-scratching that went on, but for William, all this was new. He believed in the rule of law and he wasn't ready to accept that justice wasn't available for all men, regardless of birth. He needed the established hand of a father figure more than ever, to introduce him in all the right places, and fervently wished there were someone in Pierceton who could take that role. Moving to a new town had been harder than he'd thought.

When he opened the street door to the office, Cecilia was deep in conversation with his sister's friend, Sarah Spencer. Given the appointment had been booked, William presumed the discussion was business and slipped quietly through to the back of the premises. Cecilia would no doubt update him later. He was proud to work alongside his wife. To his mind she was the better attorney, though he rather hoped she didn't realise that.

He went back to pondering the Reese brothers' case. The law failed so many of the people around him. His father had brought him up to believe that fighting for justice through the courts was laudable, but the more he worked, the more William saw that well-connected white men were the only ones who could truly find justice that way — if justice was the right term for a system which favoured their every move. It was worse than that. From what he could see, they'd got the whole political arena sewn up too. To make a name for himself he either needed to conform to the stereotype or blow it wide open, exposing it for what it was. He smiled, feeling his street-fighter roots rising to the surface. He'd not been scared to go head to head then, and he wouldn't be now. Admittedly, he had more to lose in reputation, but the difference was, this time, he had right on his side and Cecilia to support him. He could do this. Firstly, he needed to seek his father's counsel. He sat down behind the desk and took a sheet of paper from the stand.

He'd got no further than addressing the letter, when Cecilia came through and sat in the chair in front of him. He looked up at the grave expression on her face.

"Sarah's scared for her own safety and the safety of the children. It seems Joseph Spencer is a violent man."

William put the pen back in the stand and frowned. "Are we talking about the same Joseph Spencer? I always thought he was a better man than that. The Joe we know wouldn't raise a hand to either his wife or the children. Would he?"

Cecilia nodded slowly. "I don't think she knows rightly how far he'd go. He took his belt to her in front of young Henry for joining the women's rights protest last month." Cecilia shuddered. "She says it makes it impossible for her to bring up the child to see things any differently from his father."

William noticed the deep sadness in his wife's eyes. "This is one area where, thankfully, I have no experience. Granted, my father by birth was a drinker, but he never laid a hand on Mammy, not that I ever knew of, anyway." He paused, remembering back to his early life. He shook himself and focused on Sarah's situation. "The law does little to give her protection." He sighed heavily. "I've no more idea how we advise her than I know how to get the Reese boys tried for murder, or arson at the least."

Cecilia got up and stood behind the chair. "If Joe even knows she's been to the office to talk to me, I suspect she'll have a problem."

The two of them remained silent for a moment.

"I know it would be wrong for me to tell Molly I've spoken to Sarah, but I feel I should say something. One of us needs to offer her a safe home to move to."

William shook his head. "The whole point of talking to your attorney is knowing they won't repeat what you've said, even to your best friend. Besides, she knows Sarah a lot better than we do. I'd be surprised if we were telling her something she didn't already know, or at least suspect. For our part, we have to wait until Sarah's ready."

Cecilia nodded and began to leave the room. She turned back. "You said the Reese boys aren't being tried for arson…"

Before William had time to answer, the bell rang to acknowledge another client entering the offices and Cecilia reluctantly left the room.

"I'll tell you this evening," William called as she went out. He allowed himself a moment to smile and reflect on his luck in finding such a fine, intelligent and beautiful wife. Shaking his head, he took up the pen from the stand and dipped it in the ink.

Setting up an office here in Pierceton, where he could be close to Molly and her family, still felt as though it was the right thing to do, but he missed the wise daily counsel of his adoptive parents. Dowagiac was such a long way away, when you wanted to talk to someone.

He wrote as quickly as the pen permitted, trying to avoid any blots which would mask his words. If the State wouldn't bring a charge against the Reese boys, and Justice Warren was claiming there was no case to answer, what, if any, chance would there be of a private action? At best that would see damages paid, but it wouldn't see those boys behind bars. He mused for a moment on what other crimes they might be tried for, but that approach would take far longer.

By the time he finished the letter and took it through to the outer office for posting, the room was empty. The diary showed Cecilia was attending the American Woman's Suffrage Association meeting, which made William smile. At least one of them was making some progress on the political front. Underneath the diary entry was a note saying 'Dinner with Molly and Daniel'. William groaned. Of course, he did love spending time with his sister and his childhood friend, but he wanted to be taking them good news not repeating what the sheriff had told him.

He locked the office and walked his horse along to the Post Office before taking a gentle ride home to the Red House.

All was quiet except for Cady rushing to greet him. He'd grown fond of the little dog, although it had taken him a while to get used to having an animal around. He checked the hall clock. He'd got plenty of time. He and Cady could walk across the fields to Cochrane's Farm. Cecilia would no doubt take the carriage straight there from her meeting. It would mean they could all ride back together. He changed into stout shoes before he set off. The days were lengthening and his way would be easy to see.

As they approached the farmyard, Junior yapped with joy to have his sister for company and Cady ran to greet him. William smiled to see the two tumbling across the dirt as though they were still young puppies.

"Well, brother of mine, what are you looking so cheerful about?"

William pulled up with a start, seeing Molly framed in the doorway to the dairy.

She wiped her hands on her apron and came across to greet him. "Miss Ellie's in the house with the children. I was just finishing off here." She slipped her arm through his and walked up to the newly built farmhouse. "It looks kind of grand, now it's all finished." She smiled up at him.

He looked properly at the building and nodded. "It's a wonder Miss Ellie doesn't want it back, now it's a little more up to date."

"Then it's as well I had the best lawyer making sure the gift was signed over good and proper. Besides, these days she seems happier to be looking after the children than she ever was running the farm." She halted and turned to face him.

As William stood in front of Molly, she looked at him intently. He thought she could read every worry etched in his face.

"I know," was all she said.

William's shoulders let go of some of their tension. He was relieved that she must already have heard the sheriff's news and he wouldn't have to break it to her.

"It's not right," he said quietly.

"That it isn't, but there's little we can do to change it now. The insurance company has paid and Ben's been laid to rest."

Molly crossed herself, something William hadn't seen her do for a long time. They walked on in silence up to the farmhouse, but their reverie was broken by the sound of Miss Ellie talking to Mary and Thomas. William stopped in the doorway to watch his son earnestly licking a small amount of soup from a ladle which Miss Ellie was holding for him to try. He nodded seriously and kicked his legs in his chair. William smiled.

Thomas was beginning to put words together and pointed to his father. "Look, Da," he shouted, a broad smile breaking out across his face.

William kissed the boy and swept him into his arms, then held him where he could see him. "Have you been good today, Thomas?"

The boy nodded earnestly and William kissed him again before swinging him around, to squeals of delight.

"He'll be dancing a jig with you before you know it," Molly said, taking her daughter, Mary's hand in hers.

"Then we'll need Daniel to be singing for us." William put his son down, only to find the boy's arms raised toward him, wanting more.

"I could sing for yous, Uncle William."

Until he spoke, William had been unaware of John, sitting in the corner. He was about to say the boy didn't need to do that, but something in the child's face stopped him.

William remembered back to his own early days in Dowagiac, trying to fit in to a new family, and how hard adoption could be. He smiled and nodded to the boy. "I'd like that, John. Thank you. Perhaps you could sing while I get this little man to eat his food. Then he'll be asleep by the time we all sit down to our meal."

As Miss Ellie put plates of soup onto the table for Mary and Thomas, John began to sing. The sound sent a shiver through William. The boy's voice, still with its Irish brogue, was almost as haunting as Daniel's had been as a child and, not for the first time, he thought there was no better home John could have found than with Molly and

Daniel.

"And it's no nay never,
No nay never no more..."

As John sang, William quietly fed his son. It was as though the music had enchanted the children and they sat mesmerised, listening as they ate spoon after spoon of broth. It was only when John came to the end that the spell was broken and the children once again became restless.

The adults were sitting down ready to eat and the children were asleep when William finally heard the carriage coming into the yard. Moments later, Cecilia came rushing into the kitchen, unpinning her bonnet as she entered.

"I'm sorry I'm so late. I do hope you didn't wait for me."

William went over to his wife and kissed her, then moved her chair out so she could join them at the table.

"It's been quite a meeting." Cecilia's face was glowing as she spoke. "I've been asked to speak to the meeting about my legal studies and working with you in Dixon's Attorneys."

"Well, that sure beats where I got to with the sheriff. Well done. Maybe you should be the one arguing this before the court. I'm guessing Justice Warren wouldn't know what to do if you tried."

"That would be a fine thing, if Indiana officially recognised my training."

Miss Ellie's snort of derision made it clear what she thought of the State's unwillingness to recognise women.

"William," Cecilia said earnestly, and paused.

He stopped what he was doing and gave her his full attention. He was expecting her to say more about the events of the meeting and who had been to the office immediately prior to it.

"We need you to stand for Congress." She looked at him and then around the table. "I'm sure we'd all help."

He sat straighter. "Well." William looked around at the nodding faces. "You know I'd like to do that, but without mainstream support from the town, I can't see it happening."

"I know we don't have the vote, but the women at the meeting today are all ready to give you their support. We need men who are sympathetic to our cause to represent us in Government, if there is to be any change." Cecilia smiled across to Miss Ellie. "It's such a shame you weren't there today. You would have been so proud to hear the speeches and the discussion which followed. We really are making progress. The ratification of the 15th Amendment without our inclusion only seems to have served to make everyone more determined. It's all well and good, giving men of all races the vote, but now it's time for women." She turned back to William. "So will you start a campaign to stand?"

William looked first to Daniel, who shrugged in his gentle way, then to Miss Ellie's cousin James, who appeared totally confused. He turned back to the eager faces of the women. It was seeing his wife's eyes, shining as they had when he first met her in Iowa, which made up his mind. For a moment, he wondered exactly what he was letting himself in for, and pondered if the support of the women's suffrage supporters could possibly be enough, but then he nodded.

Would he live to regret what he was about to say? "You know I hate injustice, and taking no heed of half our population is one of the biggest injustices we have. That, and no one atoning for Ben's death. Will you help me to see those Reese boys behind bars first?"

Cecilia got up and wrapped her arms around him. "Of course I will. Now, where do we start?"

CHAPTER 2

It was good to be back in the rebuilt farmhouse with space around them. Daniel Flynn stretched as he came in from milking and breathed in the smell of the eggs cooking on the range. "No Molly?" he asked Miss Ellie as he cleaned up in the sink near the door.

Miss Ellie pointed the spatula to the far side of the kitchen where Molly was sitting alone at a small table in the corner.

Daniel went across the room in his stockinged feet. "You seem quiet this morning — is everything all right?" He looked at Molly's furrowed brow and her tongue held between her teeth. He sat on the wooden chair beside her and waited for her to finish transcribing some figures into the ledger.

After a moment or two had passed, she turned suddenly, as though surprised to see him. "Did you say something?"

"I was wondering what ailed my wife. You haven't been yourself since last night's dinner. Is it the farm?"

She put her pen down. "No." She said the word in a measured tone. "I know William wants to fight for justice for Ben, and for that matter for you and me, but do you think he's going to make matters worse for us all? If he's working with the Woman's Suffrage Association too, there are going to be people who will want to see him fail." She put her hand down on the open book. "We're back on our feet after all that happened last year, but…" Her voice trailed off.

"I thought you believed in the movement? That's what the protest last month was all about. It's about fighting for Mary to have the rights and opportunities that you've been denied." He got up and paced the room, running his hand through his hair. He was confused to hear his wife talking like this. Only a few weeks ago she'd been prepared to be arrested while standing up for women's rights.

He looked at her, and Molly smiled.

"Oh, don't you worry, husband of mine, I'm as determined as I ever was. I just need to think about what's best for us all. When I was in the general store, Joe was saying he'd heard those Reese boys were threatening to do to William all they've done to us, if we don't leave things be."

Daniel turned and, screwing up his eyes, stared into her face. "Are you saying you don't want to fight? You want to let the bullies win?"

Molly shook her head. "No, we just need to be cleverer than they are in the things we do and not try to give them an easy target. We've not even finished rebuilding the farm; the last thing I want is for them to destroy us all over again. Besides…" Molly's voice became quiet and a gentle smile played over her face. She got up and came across the room to Daniel. Taking his hands in hers, she said, "Not everything is bad news."

He searched her face for clues to what she was saying and noticed a rosy glow to her cheeks, unusual so early in the year. Realisation dawned on him. "You mean…?" He dropped to his knees and put his ear against her belly.

"I do indeed mean!"

He got up and took her in his arms. "Oh, Molly, that is

wonderful news. How long?"

"Four months, I think. I didn't want to tell you until I was sure. And before you say anything, yes, I promise to take care. I'm not ready for another fight with those Reese boys, though I would like to see them behind bars for a long time."

"We know that wouldn't make a great deal of difference. That family has more arms than it takes to bring in the harvest. Even if they aren't around themselves, there'll always be a cousin or two to spare. I don't know what to think. Do you want to go away for a few months, to stay with the Dixons, perhaps? Of course, taking care of our family has to come first, but I can never forgive what the Reese brothers did to Ben." His shoulders dropped as he thought of his dear friend, who'd died saving Molly and Mary from the fire.

"Nor would I ask you to." Molly hesitated. "You do know they could hang if they're found guilty of arson, don't you?"

Daniel took a step back. "Wouldn't they just be imprisoned?"

Molly shook her head. "Not from what William was saying."

Daniel sat heavily and looked down. "Hanging's not what Ben would want. I thought... Well, I assumed..." He shuddered.

"I'm sorry, I shouldn't have said anything." Molly sat next to him and took his hand. After a few moments where neither of them spoke, she went on, "I don't doubt you could manage the farm quite well without me here, but you should know me well enough by now to know I don't run from trouble. And I guess that includes those Reese boys! Besides, we've John to think about as well. He needs a mother around as much as any other child of ours. Maybe we just need to trust William, though we know he can be impetuous at the best of times."

They both laughed.

"Now, come on," Molly said, in her more usual matter-of-fact tone, "you need to get some breakfast inside you and John will be waiting for us. We've said we'll finish the last of the painting together. Once it's done, this farm will be as good as new. Mary's going to spend the rest of the morning with Miss Ellie down at her log cabin and I do believe she's big enough to show an interest in her own little cabin playhouse."

Daniel noticed a tear in Molly's eye and looked at her quizzically.

"Oh, don't mind me. I was thinking how much Ben would have liked to see her starting to enjoy the things which he and James built for her." She waved him away and dabbed her eyes. "I'm fine."

Daniel knew better than to say anything further, and simply followed Molly across to the kitchen. He looked hungrily at the buckwheat pancakes Miss Ellie was turning out onto a plate and was relieved to find they were for him, as the rest of the family and the farm workers had been provided for. He ate quickly, watching as Molly tidied things away.

Once all was done, they went out into the yard, where John was waiting, as Molly had said. He already had the brushes and paint and was eager to begin.

They worked side by side on the new fences, which ran around the house and yard. Whilst the old house had fencing to the side, it hadn't been enclosed and separated from what lay beyond. This fence was as much symbolic as serving a real purpose. After rebuilding the house,

Molly needed to create a barrier and Daniel had no objection. With this finished, the farm would be complete. Removing the physical traces of the fire was one thing, but the memory of it ran deep, especially for Molly.

Daniel still felt guilty for being away that night, and would never forget the sight of the farm on his return. More importantly, he would never forget the moment they found Ben's body. For Molly it was much worse. She still had nightmares, reliving her moments of not being able to get to Mary and of waiting for Ben to come out of the burning building.

Painting gave Daniel time to think and he used it to reflect on the past. Ben had been so kind as Daniel had grown up on Hawksworth's farm in Iowa. His only real friend through nine hard years. Quietly, as he worked, Daniel sang some of the songs Ben had loved to hear. He was brought gently back to the present by John joining in.

"Let the wind and the rain and the hail blow high
And the snow come shovelling from the sky
She's as nice as apple pie
She'll get her own lad by and by…"

As they reached the last stretch of fence, Daniel dipped his brush for the final time.

Molly stood back. "There."

"One moment." Daniel raised his hand for quiet. Then stiffly, as though on parade, he marched across, loosed the rope that held the gate open, and with a deep bow to Molly he continued his march across the yard until it was shut and the barrier complete. "Your sanctuary, ma'am."

Molly clapped her hands. "I know it's silly, as it's easy to climb over, but it does feel better. I do believe it's time for a celebration. Why don't we go and see what the others

18

are doing?" She slipped her arm through John's. "Pa and I have something to tell you all."

Daniel was delighted to see the spark back in Molly's eyes as they made their way over to the pail to wash before going down to the cabins.

"We can beat those Reese boys," she said to him quietly. "Ben wouldn't want me to walk away, would he?"

Daniel shook his head. "Indeed he wouldn't, though he'd not forgive me if I took chances with either you or Mary. But no, he wouldn't want us to give up."

Molly looked determined. "Then we'll do all we can to help William and trust his and Mr Dixon's judgement. I've as much right as any to run a farm, and those Reese boys had better remember that."

Mary toddled out onto the porch as they approached, and Miss Ellie was not far behind. Daniel scooped up Mary and put her on his shoulders as he sat on the bench seat. Molly remained standing and was fidgeting with her hands.

Daniel looked across to her to give her encouragement.

"We've got some good news," she said, almost shyly. "John and Mary, you are going to have another brother or sister. I'm expecting again."

"Oh, that's wonderful." Miss Ellie came forward and hugged her. "James, did you hear that?" She left Molly's side and went across to her cousin's cabin, still calling. "You're going to be a granddaddy again."

"I ain't rightly a granddaddy now," James said, beaming a broad smile and coming to shake Daniel by the hand. "But I'm more happy to answer to that than I am most names." He tickled Mary under the chin and the child giggled.

"There is one other thing," Molly said, having not

moved from the spot she was standing on. "We're not going to give up on justice for Ben." She looked across to Daniel and he nodded to her. "We're going to do whatever William needs us to, in order to fight back. I know there's a risk, but we can't forget what we believe in, and what those boys did wasn't right. There's folks in this town who know that and we need them to come forward. There, I've said it." She let out a sigh and went to sit by Daniel.

They were all quiet for a long moment. Daniel lifted Mary down onto his knee so he could rock her gently and let her fall asleep against his shoulder.

John was sitting on the rail in front of them with his legs swinging. Without turning to face them, he said, "P-p-p-p... pa?"

It was a while since John had stuttered, and Daniel felt unease wash over him. He nudged Molly and passed Mary to her, before getting up and going to stand close by John, so the boy could talk to him more easily.

"If you and M-m-m-m-ma h-h-h-h-h-have another ch-ch-ch-ch-child..." John broke off.

Daniel thought he could see where this was going. Hoping he was right, he cut in before the boy struggled further. "We will always love you, John. You are as much our son as any other child will ever be, and don't you ever worry otherwise. We adopted you in law and that makes you our son completely, but more than that, we love you in the same way we love Mary." He put his hand on the boy's shoulder and felt the tension fall away. John simply nodded but said nothing.

Daniel decided the best way to lift the boy's spirits was to get him singing, so he broke into a lively tune he knew John enjoyed.

"As I was going over the far famed Kerry Mountains

I met with Captain Farrel and his money he was countin'"

By the next part of the verse, John had left his place on the rail and was singing in harmony with Daniel, and a festive air overtook the party.

Once they'd all sat down again, John asked, "Pa, is there some way that I can help Uncle William?"

Daniel's first reaction was to say there wasn't, but he hesitated. There might be situations where John would stand out a little less than either he or Molly would and where they could obtain useful information. The boy was only ten, and not old enough to frequent the sorts of places Jacob and Reuben Reese could normally be found, but Daniel could see John wanted to be useful. "Let me think about it and maybe talk to Uncle William for his ideas. It's a worthy offer. I'm sure there'll be some way." Then he settled to thinking, happy that John was at least smiling again.

Daniel wasn't looking for revenge on the Reese brothers. He wouldn't want to see them hang. That would no more make him happy than it would Molly. He did want to believe his family was safe and he wanted to see some sort of justice for Ben's death — not an eye for an eye, exactly, but a recognition that Ben had been as important as any other man and but for those boys he would not have died. They might have finished rebuilding the farmhouse now, but without Ben, it would never be the same as it had been.

He was still deep in thought when Molly came and slipped her hand into his.

"It's not easy to see how William can get far with his political dreams, when we don't seem to fit around here."

Daniel looked at her, surprised. "But you've lived here much of your life. Surely you feel part of the place?"

Molly shook her head. "Belonging isn't just about being in a place. More than anything, it's about fitting in with what people expect and being comfortable with that. Miss Ellie always stood out as being a woman running a farm, and now it's my turn to do the same. William might be able to join one of the lodges in town, but I never could, and if you tried, well, I dare say you'd be more uncomfortable than a turkey being dressed for the table."

Daniel laughed. "You've got that one right. I'm a darn sight happier with animals than people, and overalls rather than a suit. Really, though, William's made for it, as long as Cecilia can keep him on the straight and narrow. He just needs to find other like-minded men who believe in doing what's right, even when it's unpopular. There are plenty of them around."

"And where might they be, Daniel Flynn?"

He scratched his head. "I don't rightly know. A few have found me over the years, but I've never known where to look. I'm guessing the women at the Suffrage Association will have a pretty good idea of who's on their side. That's probably as good a place to search as any." He grinned at her.

Molly turned to face him, her hands on her hips and a look of mock exasperation on her face. "And I'm guessing that's where I come in?"

Daniel leant forward and kissed her nose. "You, Miss Ellie and Cecilia. You're all going to have a part to play, if William is ever going to be nominated."

CHAPTER 3

William straightened his tie in the hall mirror. Satisfied, he looked around and listened carefully. Cecilia had already left for the farm with Thomas, and their housekeeper was visiting family. All was quiet. He brushed the shoulder of his jacket, coughed and stood back slightly, watching his reflection.

"It's a great privilege that the people of this District have bestowed upon me. I am sure…" He looked quizzically at his reflection, took hold of his lapels and stood a little taller. He nodded. "I am sure, with the support of my dear…"

"Sister?" Molly laughed.

William dropped his lapels and wheeled around to face her. "I, er… I was…"

"Oh, William, stop." She could hardly speak through her laughter. "I could see what you were doing. Let's hope you get to make the speech to someone other than a mirror before too long."

He grinned, feeling sheepish. "I didn't expect to see you."

"No, I can see that. I decided I'd bring the eggs and cheese over, as Cecilia forgot to take them with her. I guess they could have waited until later, but I needed some air." She followed him through to the kitchen.

"I'm not sure where they go," William confessed, looking around the spotless room. He pulled one of the chairs out from the table for Molly to sit down, then took another for himself. "Do you think there's any point in my trying to get elected?"

"Why ever not? You might be a little vain now and again, but you believe passionately in the things you'd be standing for."

"Is it enough? What if my opponents were to dig up my past and use it against me?" William put his head in his hands. "There's always someone ready to sell a story."

"Now you listen to me. There's no shame in being an Irish immigrant, or in having been orphaned, come to that. No shame at all."

As Molly spoke, William was reminded of their own dear Mammy all those years ago before she'd become ill, an angel made of solid iron. He smiled sadly. "I was a thief, Molly. Are you choosing to forget that?"

"William, we were starving and would have had no roof over our heads. When Mammy took ill, what choice did you have? Collecting rags wasn't enough to pay the rent. You only did what any man would do if their family depended on them. You found a way to provide for us and you were only ten years old." Molly's hand was shaking as she put it onto William's arm.

"Your Daniel never stole anything."

"My Daniel sang to draw a crowd so you could have your choice of pockets to pick. He knew how it worked. He was no more innocent than you were."

William looked into Molly's eyes for the truth of what she'd said, and nodded slowly. "Do you ever wonder what happened to Da, after he left us?"

Molly harrumphed. "You're forgetting he wasn't even my father, so I'm guessing he didn't feel any guilt on my account. Now…" She got up decisively. "Where am I to put this cheese?"

William sat at the table as Molly opened first one door off the kitchen and then a second, before appearing satisfied with where to put things. Once she'd finished, she came back to the table and stood in front of him with her hands on her hips.

"Now, you listen to me, brother of mine. You've never been afraid of a fight. Whether it was walking through streets owned by the Bowery Boys or standing your ground against the Reese brothers makes no difference. You already know not everyone plays by the rules and you've learned how to come out on top. I'm not saying you should adopt any approach you can't be proud of — none of us would want that, least of all Cecilia — but you're no coward. If they talk about your past, then be honest and tell people what life was really like. If they say you're adopted, be proud and have Mr and Mrs Dixon stand beside you. If they say you're Irish, show them your flame-red hair and use the gift of the Blarney that goes with it."

"And if they say my sister's married to an ex-convict?"

Molly's eyes flared and for a moment William thought he'd gone too far.

"Then tell them he's the bravest man you've ever known and he was defending himself from being recaptured by the brute who treated him as a slave and beat him to within an inch of his life. If I know my Daniel, he'll be willing to show them the scars to prove it. If we're prepared to go on standing up to the Reese boys after the things they've done to us, there's nothing that can be thrown at you we can't all face together."

William got up and hugged his sister. "Daniel's a lucky man."

Molly's face broke into a smile. "I'm the lucky one.

Now I guess I'd best be getting back."

"Will you walk with me into town or are you going back across the fields?" He got up and tucked the chairs back under the table.

"I've a mind to call into the general store on my way, so I shall be happy to walk with you."

As they walked, they talked of life in Pierceton. "You know, Jacob and Reuben Reese were at the hall we orphans were brought to, the day Miss Ellie took Sarah and me home. I think they were looking to take someone into their farm, but they wanted a boy."

William shook his head. "And no doubt he'd have been treated as badly as Daniel was by Mr Hawksworth. Thank God Daniel had Ben's friendship to see him through."

"And Mrs Hawksworth, come to that. Any child who'd been put to work by those Reese boys would have had no woman about the place to keep an eye on them."

They'd reached William's office and Molly stopped and turned to him before going on. "We were the lucky ones, there's no doubt about it. I don't suppose many who rode those orphan trains with us have ended up being nearly so fortunate."

William took his sister's hand in his. "Which is why, darling sister, I intend to use the fortune bestowed on me to make this country a better place."

Molly smiled at him. "And on that note, in my own small way, I shall try to do likewise."

William watched his sister walking away in the direction of the general store. He felt much lighter for sharing his fears about their past. He could have talked to Cecilia — there was nothing he'd kept from her — but Molly had been there and had lived through the harsh realities of street life. Her reassurance had given him the confidence to stand up, however he might be judged.

CHAPTER 4

Molly was kneading dough when there was a quiet tap at the kitchen door. She hadn't heard a horse so presumed it was one of the farm workers. She looked down at her dough-covered hands and, shaking her head, shouted to whoever was waiting, "Come in."

The door was opened slowly and Sarah stepped into the kitchen. "Is it all right if I...?"

Molly was stunned to see her friend, but the more so to immediately notice her tear-stained face. She abandoned the dough and went straight to the sink to wash her hands. "My dearest friend, come in, come in." Molly was rushing to clean herself up, as it was obvious Sarah was in need of comfort and the last thing her friend would want was dough patches on her clothes.

Sarah looked over her shoulder, her eyes wide with fear. "I don't think anyone's seen me come here."

"And what if they have?" Molly stopped short. "Sarah, are you saying Joe has forbidden you from coming to the farm? But this is the place you grew up, the same as me."

"Oh, Molly, it's worse than that. If he finds I've gone anywhere but to deliver the parcel he sent me with, well..." She paused as though searching for more words. Her eyes darted to the door once again. "... Let's just say he won't be pleased."

It was obvious to Molly that Sarah's smile was forced, and her heart jolted. How far was Joe going in showing his displeasure? Molly tried to keep the topic light. Sarah would talk if she wanted to, and Molly didn't want to drive her into being defensive of the Spencer family. "And how are the children?"

For a moment Sarah's face genuinely brightened, before a cloak of sadness passed over it again. "They're both well. Henry is very like his father." She looked down, fidgeting with the sleeve of her coat. "He follows Joe everywhere and…" Her eyes darted again toward the door. "…He tells his father everything we do. Everything!" She began to speak more quickly. "I couldn't bring him with me. Joe would have known as soon as we returned."

"And Jenny?" Molly wished her friend would tell her the whole story. She'd seen almost nothing of Sarah since she'd had the courage to stand with Daniel and sing outside the courthouse, when Molly had been arrested. Molly had dreaded what action Joe might have taken, but on her visits to the general store, Sarah, when she had been there, had said nothing.

"Jenny's fine. Her grandmother keeps a careful watch on her." Sarah hesitated. "Oh, Molly, do they really think at eighteen months old I can already influence her to be too independent minded? I know both you and Miss Ellie would love to see her, but Joe says I mayn't bring her here, and I cannot invite either of you into our home at the store."

It was as though the storm cloud had broken, and Sarah began to issue heaving sobs. Molly went to her side and put her arms around her friend as Sarah simply cried against her. As Molly held Sarah tight, she gripped her friend's shoulder and, despite the crying, Sarah flinched. It was obviously a reaction to pain, and, with sudden horror, Molly wondered just how badly Joe had beaten his wife. She bit her lip, knowing she needed to let Sarah speak when she was ready.

When Sarah did stop crying she looked across at the clock and started. "I should go. I've been away too long."

"You can't go anywhere looking like this. Did you walk here?" Molly reached a hand out to Sarah, who nodded meekly. "Come upstairs, I'll find somewhere you can wash and make yourself look presentable. While you're doing that, I'll call Daniel to get the cart ready." She saw a look of fear come over Sarah's face. "Now, don't you worry. He can either drop you long before the store or, better still, why doesn't he come to the store with our dairy supplies and say he picked you up as you were walking back from wherever it was you were supposed to be going?" Molly led Sarah toward the stairs. "It's not exactly your old room, as the house has been rebuilt, but we liked the old house well enough and we put most things in much the same place. I'll show you."

Molly led the way, and Sarah followed without a word. Once she'd opened the door to what would have been Sarah's old room and ushered her in, Molly went back to the kitchen to fetch warm water for Sarah to wash. While it was heating, she called Daniel to prepare the cart.

By the time Sarah came down, Molly had returned to the bread making and she was pleased to see her friend looking much better.

"Your room will always be there, if you need it," Molly said. She hesitated before adding, "There's enough space for the children too." Before Sarah dissolved into tears again, she quickly moved on to ushering her out to the waiting cart and her lift back to town. Molly had wondered about driving the cart, but she didn't trust herself to say nothing at the store when she got there. She guessed her intervention would only risk making matters worse. She sighed. Instead she worked the dough harder than usual and gradually felt her anger dissipate as she kneaded the bread.

By the time Daniel returned, the loaves were rising and Miss Ellie had brought Mary back up to the house. Molly raised an enquiring eyebrow to him, not wanting to ask any questions with Miss Ellie present. He shook his head in reply, a sad expression on his face, and Molly felt her shoulders drop.

As usual, Miss Ellie didn't miss a thing. "Did I see Sarah leaving in the cart earlier?"

"Sometimes," Molly said, taking cutlery over to the table, "I think you have an extra pair of eyes."

"I've needed them all these years, running this place and bringing up you girls. Now, are you going to tell me what's going on or do I need to work it out for myself?" Miss Ellie gave Molly her stern look, which was always hard to resist.

"I think you can probably guess most of it, or as much as I know with any certainty." Molly turned to check the children were not near enough to overhear. "I know Joe has told Sarah she can't see us, but it seems he's using force too." Molly shuddered and took a deep breath before adding, "He's beating her."

Miss Ellie nodded and sighed. "I feared that might be the case..." She narrowed her eyes and looked at Molly. "But what makes you think so?"

Molly told her how Sarah had flinched when her arm was touched and how she'd waited for Molly to leave, before undressing earlier. "I told her there's always a room here for her."

"You know," Miss Ellie said, smoothing down the front of her dress, "Liza Hawksworth might be a good person to speak to her."

"Now there's an idea," Molly said, pausing from what she was doing. "It's a wonder that wasn't my first thought. After the way her husband treated both her and Daniel, she must know a thing or two about what it feels like to go through something like this. I just hope Sarah has half the strength Mrs Hawksworth had in getting away from the man."

"We can't go pushing our way in where we aren't wanted and I dare say Joe would make it impossible in one way or another, but they know little of Liza's background and she might be able to strike up a friendship with Sarah or maybe even with Mrs Spencer." Miss Ellie looked thoughtful. "As there's no likelihood of Clara Spencer coming to any of the women's meetings, it would have to be by going to the store. Liza's been thinking of spending some time over here again, so this might be a good opportunity to write to her." Miss Ellie got up and walked around the room. "Of course, one thing which may hold Sarah back is those children. It will be bad enough for her, not knowing how she could support herself, let alone the shame of leaving, but I dare say Joe wouldn't let her bring the children if she did leave him, and that would break her heart. Unlike Liza Hawksworth, Sarah has no blood family to turn to, only you and me."

"She wouldn't go anywhere without those children, the more so for having been an orphan herself. She was always terrified of dying and leaving them without a mother. She's hardly likely to walk out on them." Molly thought back over all Sarah had said. "Although I think Joe is trying to turn young Henry against his mother, so maybe

I'm wrong."

"A mother has to be in very serious danger before she'll leave her children behind. Besides, she probably still thinks she loves Joe, despite his behaviour. Many women do. They even think what happens to them is their own fault. You won't change the way Sarah sees things until she's ready of her own accord." Miss Ellie picked up her hat from the peg. "I shall go and write to Liza now and see what she has to say."

Daniel had said nothing throughout the exchange.

As Molly prepared to move the bread to the oven she asked, "How did Sarah seem when you took her back?"

Daniel shook his head. "I did take her all the way to the store, but she was edgy long before we got there. I don't think Joe bought the story that I'd picked her up along the way. He practically barked at her to get indoors to the children, before helping to get things down off the cart. He was civil enough to me, but it wouldn't do to scratch too deep."

"She's been my friend for so long, I can't bear to think of her suffering. Why do men treat women so?" Molly was genuinely confused by what went on. "What issue do the Reese boys really have with us? Oh, Daniel, it's all so unfair."

"I don't rightly understand it myself. They're no better than caged animals some of the time, lashing out when they feel threatened, I suppose. Joe wants to keep control of Sarah. He doesn't want her making decisions for herself. As for the Reese boys, jealousy is an ugly bed-fellow." He shrugged.

Molly crossed the room to him. "Thank God I found you, Daniel Flynn. There's no better man out there."

"If that were true, I'd know what we should be doing

to counter those Reese boys, and I don't. I just wish it would all go away." He wrapped his arms around his wife.

"I know," Molly said quietly. "I'm so tired with it all. Now, on top that, I'm worrying about Sarah. I hope Mrs Hawksworth can come soon, though I'm not sure she'll be able to do much."

He tucked a strand of Molly's hair behind her ear. "It can take a long time before a person is ready to sort things out for themselves. I'm not sure whether Mrs Hawksworth ever would have done, if she hadn't had the courage to testify against her husband in my defence. Don't expect too much."

They were spared further discussion on the subject, as John came into the kitchen. "My that bread smells good, can I have some now?"

Molly broke away from Daniel and laughed. "John Flynn, I'll swear you have hollow legs. It's not even out of the oven yet and won't do you any good to eat too hot. Go upstairs and wash and it'll be ready by the time you come down. Take Mary to wash her hands too, and you can both have some."

John scooped Mary up from where she had been happily playing and headed toward the far door.

"They'll be back in no time. I'd better get the bread out." Molly went over to the oven and carefully took out the tins of perfectly golden bread. She looked up to see Daniel sidling over. "And don't you have work to do, husband of mine?"

He turned his mouth downward into a mock pout. "And isn't there a little crust for the man of the house?" He reached his hand out toward the steaming bread.

She gently slapped it. "And what are we going to be

eating later if you've all eaten it now?" She was laughing as she spoke. "Besides, it will be too hot to cut for minute or two, so you need to wait." She passed a butter knife to Daniel. "You can be ready and waiting to slather a thick layer of butter as soon as I do cut it."

A thought occurred to her and her face clouded. "Daniel, you don't mind I've told Sarah she always has a room here if she needs it, do you?"

"Oh, my darling wife, of course I don't mind. I'd expect nothing less. Sarah's family, and we'll always have room for family in our home, for however long she needs it."

CHAPTER 5

"I'm being proposed this week. Oh, Cecilia, what if they don't accept me for membership?" William brandished the letter in front of his wife. Both his proposer and seconder were the husbands of women known to Cecilia through the women's suffrage movement. William feared his not knowing many of the members directly might be a problem for him.

"And why ever should they not? You are an upstanding member of the community and will uphold their values. Now come, William, we already know the Odd Fellows are more sympathetic to our views than are some of the other lodges." Cecilia raised an eyebrow, which made William smile. He was always astounded by how much she could say without words.

"Besides," she continued, "whilst the Government might not be ready to trust us to vote, we women still have a fair amount of influence over our husbands." She smiled.

Cady jumped up and down with excitement at their voices. "Now will you look at that?" Cecilia said, scooping up the little dog. "Even Cady thinks they would be unlikely to refuse you." She kissed William and turned on her heel to go to tend to young Thomas, the taffeta of her dress rustling as she walked.

William took the letter through to his study, where he sat down intending to write a reply acknowledging his gratitude. Instead he found himself staring at the bookshelf, his thoughts turning once again to what action he could take to gain justice for Ben. He was still awaiting a reply to the letter he'd sent his father, but he remained determined the Reese boys should have to answer for their crimes. What would it take for those shielding the brothers to break ranks? William had no idea. The extended Reese family seemed to have branches in every activity in the town, all except the ones William was involved in. Regrettably, he seemed to have no influence whatsoever in any area which would be of use to them in this matter.

"Now, say goodnight to your father." Cecilia was standing in the doorway to the study with Thomas on her hip.

William got up and held his arms out to the boy. "And what would you do, Thomas? I've asked your grandfather's advice but maybe I'd be better asking you."

The boy's eyes were closing as William lifted him from Cecilia.

"I think he may be telling you to sleep on it." Cecilia laughed. "Here, let me take him off to bed and leave you to think."

"I've done nothing but sleep on it," William replied, kissing the boy and handing him back to his mother. He sighed. Then he slumped down into the armchair and picked up the newspaper to see what might have been happening elsewhere in the country.

He was reading an article about the goings-on of Boss Tweed's ring in New York City when Cecilia came back. She looked in at the doorway as she passed. William lifted his eyes from the newspaper. "It doesn't seem to matter where you live, there's corruption all about." He indicated the paper with his hand. "What would you do?"

Cecilia joined him in the study and sat down, looking

pensive. "It depends which problem you're asking me about. If you're asking whether you should go into politics, the answer is yes. It needs good men and women to be able to change how things are. If you're asking me how to bring the full weight of the law down on those Reese boys, that's by far the harder question." She got up and went over to the desk, then sat down, taking up a pen and dipping it in the ink. William watched as she drew two columns on the paper.

She looked at him, saw him watching her and blushed. She sat a little straighter and wrote at the top of each column, though he couldn't see the words.

"What facts do we have, which the court could not dispute?" She held his gaze intently.

"Both Reese brothers were drinking in Marsh's bar earlier in the evening."

As he spoke Cecilia added notes to the paper.

"Getting home from the bar, taking a direct route, would not have involved them turning in the direction of Cochrane's Farm or passing through any of its land."

Cecilia nodded. "You know," she said, "it really is as though we're talking about a completely different place than this house. We've changed it so much I can easily forget it was their farm before it had to be sold by the bank. I guess the fact we own it now won't make us any too popular with those boys and their supporters, even without the fact you're trying to get them prosecuted."

William sighed. He'd thought about that quite a bit and almost wished they hadn't bought the house. He focused back on the matter in hand and tried to think of pure facts. "We know the fire started by the steps at the far end of the farmhouse. The back of the house rather than the front. Even if they were lost, that's not the side of the house where they'd have ended up."

"Lost and drunk!" Cecilia said quietly.

He drummed his fingers on the brown leather of the Chesterfield chair. "We don't know exactly how they started the fire. We know there was some evidence of lamp oil, and they claim that's how it began accidentally, but we can't prove that, one way or the other. If they were lost, it's not likely they would have strayed around the back of the house away from the track." He got up and went over to the window, trying to picture it in his mind. "I know they claim they were drunk, but to get to the back they must have gone right through the yard… and through the small gate at the far end." He wheeled around. "I need to talk to the sheriff."

"Just sit down." Cecilia's voice was gentle but commanding and William obediently sat in the chair. "If we finish this list, we may have several points we wish to discuss with the sheriff. Let's complete the picture before we go rushing off. The bigger problem may be getting the judge to reconsider."

William nodded and tried to bring his thoughts back to the night of the fire. "Those boys aren't good at keeping their mouths shut. I'm guessing someone in Marsh's bar must have known what they had in mind. They'd been heard quite widely saying they planned to finish the job. We need a list of who was in the bar from the sheriff. It might be worth talking to all of them individually."

Cecilia made some more notes. "I'm guessing the sheriff will already have done that, but it may be worth doing again. Have you spoken to all of the farm hands from Cochrane's Farm? Were any of the casual hands out drinking that night?"

William sighed. "It's worth a try, but I'm guessing if

any of them wanted to talk, they'd have done so by now."

"It may be niggling away at a conscience somewhere." Cecilia paused and sat up straighter. "You know, it might be more effective for me to speak to their wives, if they have them. It might help their consciences along a little."

"I don't think many of the casual staff have wives, but it's worth asking. To be fair, I don't suppose many that waste their lives in Marsh's Saloon have a happy home life, but maybe I'm wrong." William went back to drumming his fingers as he tried to think of any other angle they might take.

They were silent for a while. William shook his head. "It's no use, if no one will talk there will be little we can do to prove the truth. It's not as though they're denying they were there at all."

Cecilia put the pen back on the stand and laid the piece of paper to the side. "There's little more we can do tonight." She went across to William and held her hand out to him. "Let's both sleep on things and tomorrow we can make a list of all the people we need to speak to. You can go to see the sheriff first thing in the morning."

William nodded. "I'll stay here a while first. I haven't finished thinking."

Cecilia sighed but left him in peace. Once she'd gone, William drafted the letter of thanks to the Odd Fellows and then sat staring at the paper Cecilia had written on earlier. Eventually he eased himself out of the chair and went up to bed. Cecilia was already asleep, and he wondered just how long he'd been sitting downstairs.

The following morning William rose early. Cecilia was already up with Thomas and was sitting in the dining room when he went in.

"There'll be little point in you going looking for the sheriff at this hour." Cecilia put the spoon for Thomas's food down on the table and he kicked his legs against his chair in complaint. "I shall be back in a moment, young man. I want to say my good mornings to Daddy."

William smiled as Thomas stilled his legs. He didn't know how much his son understood at this age and how much was simply the placating voice of the child's mother, but whichever it was had worked. He kissed Cecilia and she continued across the room to ring the bell to call for their own breakfast to be served.

William crossed to the window and looked out onto their garden, which was formerly the yard to the Reese family farm. "You know, I was thinking, what if there was someone who could spend some time in Marsh's Saloon and buy the regulars a few drinks? Might that be a better way to get the men to talk?"

Cecilia smiled and looked at him, very obviously from head to toe. "And how exactly were you thinking of blending in, dressed in your suit, William Dixon?"

William laughed heartily. He adopted a pained expression. "How closely have you looked at me recently, darling wife?" He tugged at a lock of his still-red hair. "Do you really think it's my suit that makes me stand out in a crowd?"

Cecilia returned to Thomas and continued to feed him, while confiding in a serious tone, "If we dressed your Daddy in green he could pass for one of those leprechauns that your cousin John was so excited about."

Her mouth twitched and William's heart missed a beat, even at her mocking his Irish roots. "How lucky I am to have you. As long as I have your guiding hand and your humour, I'll never be able to take myself too seriously."

Cecilia turned back to Thomas, now smiling broadly, and confided, "Which is a good thing."

"Is there not someone else who could go on our behalf?" William didn't want to let his idea go altogether.

His thoughts were interrupted by the serving of their breakfast, and by the time they were on their own again Thomas was demanding more of Cecilia's attention.

William ate quietly, thinking as he did so. He was aware of Cady resting her head on his shoe under the table. The warmth of it was comforting and he was careful not to move his foot.

He would have lingered a little longer, but he heard the sound of the post deliveries and left the table to see if there was a letter from his father. The box contained only one letter and it occurred to William that his father was more likely to write to him at the office on what was, after all, a business matter. He returned to the house briskly to collect his hat and coat, ready for his ride into town.

Cecilia had already disappeared with Thomas to prepare for the day, so he called up the stairs to her before setting off toward Pierceton. He would see her soon enough, once she'd taken Thomas to the farm for a day with his cousin, in the capable hands of Miss Ellie.

As he rode, he wondered what time was too early to see the sheriff and suspected Cecilia might be right that waiting until mid-morning could bring a better result. He had to ride past Marsh's bar on his way to Dixon's Attorneys, and mused once again as to who might be willing to talk and whether there was anyone, anyone at all, known to him, who could sit comfortably amongst the drinkers in the bar and not be noticed as an imposter.

As he arrived at his office, he was a little surprised to find a gentleman he vaguely recognised, waiting for him to arrive. William dismounted. "Good day to you, sir," he called in greeting as he tied the horse securely to the rail. He offered his hand and was greeted by a strong handshake in return.

"Charles B. Pritchard," the man said, handing William a card.

William glanced down. The name was familiar to him, but he couldn't place the man. The card informed him that Dr Pritchard was a doctor of medicine in the town, but not one William had had cause to contact.

"How may I be of service, Dr Pritchard?" William was intrigued by the man, who looked around fifty years of age and was grinning broadly at him.

"I rather thought I might be of service to you. Shall we go somewhere more comfortable and take coffee, perhaps?"

William looked at his pocket watch. It was still early and it would be a while before his absence from the office would cause issue. He was intrigued by the older man and yet still hesitant to accept too readily. His uncertainty must have been apparent.

Dr Pritchard was refastening his gloves as he said, "Would it help if I were to explain that our wives had a hand in my being here?"

William noticed his eyes had the same sort of twinkle as Cecilia's father's, and wondered for a moment if a slight eccentricity went with the medical profession. He nodded to the man, rechecked that the horse was securely tied and followed him across the street. If Cecilia had had a hand in this meeting, then William could only think it would be to the good.

"And please, call me Charles," Dr Pritchard said, falling into stride with William as they walked.

CHAPTER 6

Ellie Cochrane smiled as the front of the steam train came into view, approaching the station. She stood well back so as not to get covered in soot, but as the engine passed she breathed deeply through her nose. The smell of wood fire and the well-oiled engine, together with the regular chugging sound, conjured up happy memories of her own travels.

She ran her eyes along the length of the carriages to see which window held the face of her arriving friend, then swiftly moved forward to greet her.

"Well, am I ever pleased to see you?" Ellie reached out to take the small brown case which Liza Hawksworth passed to her. Liza lifted her skirts and stepped awkwardly down from the train carriage.

Ellie waved a hand in the direction of a porter. "If you can bring Mrs Hawksworth's trunk, I'd be grateful." She pressed a note into his hand. Then she picked up the small travelling case and linked her other arm through that of her companion. "Now, tell me, how was the journey?"

"You would think I'd be used to it by now." Liza shook her head. "I'm always happier to arrive than to travel. Although I must admit I do enjoy watching the fields go by. Somehow, the pattern of the land and the clackety-clack of the train are quite hypnotic. I'm sure I slept for more than half the journey. Now, I'm intrigued as to what it is you especially need my help with, and why you wouldn't include it all in your letter."

As they talked, they made their way out of the station to where James was waiting with the cart. Ellie looked first to James then back to Liza and, raising an eyebrow, said, "That, my dear Liza, will have to wait." She passed the travelling case up to James as the porter rounded the corner with the larger trunk that was Liza Hawksworth's main luggage. Ellie thanked him as he and James lifted the trunk onto the back of the cart. She turned back to her friend. "I'm pleased to see you're ready to stay a while. Something tells me we're going to need your expertise."

"Mine?" Liza sounded incredulous. "I don't rightly think there's anything much I could be described as an expert in." She was about to take James's offered hand to help her into the cart when she paused. "You know, I've been cooped up in that train for days. I think I'd like some fresh air and exercise, if it's all the same to you? Would you mind awfully if I were to walk back to the farm?"

Ellie smiled. "Why ever would I mind walking? As long as James doesn't mind us abandoning him with the luggage?"

He laughed good naturedly. "If it means I don't have to listen to you, cousin, I'm sure I can put up with it." He winked at Liza and geed the horses on before the women had time to respond.

"Now don't you mind him." Ellie began walking as she talked. "He gets more troublesome by the year. I thought he was bad enough, teasing me when we grew up together, but I guess getting old is a second childhood so I'm getting it all over again."

"I'm always surprised, when we meet him, that he's never married. He seems a pleasant enough companion."

Ellie looked at her friend quizzically. "Are you saying

what I think you're saying?"

Liza shook her head. "Good heavens no, and by rights I'm still a married woman anyway. Though I've no notion to ever see the man I'm married to again."

Ellie saw Liza shudder and wondered if this might be the time to tell her about Sarah's troubles and the reason for her being summoned to Pierceton. Before she got a chance to speak they began to pass Marsh's Saloon. As they did so, Franklin Marsh was coming around from the back door and into the street. Ellie was about to keep her eyes forward and pay no heed to his presence. She was surprised when he addressed them.

"Ladies." Franklin Marsh raised his hat and nodded to them as they passed.

"Franklin." Ellie nodded briefly, but frowned and turned to see Liza Hawksworth blushing ever so slightly. "I don't think that man's ever passed the time of day with me, in all the years I've lived here." She screwed her eyes up and looked more intently at Liza. "Whilst I heard what you said only a moment ago, I don't suppose you know something I don't, do you?"

Liza's eyes were wide with innocence as she responded, "I think I spoke to him briefly on my last visit, but I don't rightly remember." Then quickly she changed the subject. "Now I've got you on my own, what is it you can't talk to me about in front of James?"

They had left the centre of town and the frequency of the buildings had reduced. Now they were heading out to where Cochrane's Farm was sited, a mile or so further on. "That will need to wait until we're away from any prying ears, especially those belonging to Spencer's General Store." Ellie nodded further along the road, past the milliner's shop in the store's direction.

Once the general store was behind them and the buildings thinned further into open countryside, Ellie decided the time was right to explain. "We're fairly certain my other ward, Molly's friend Sarah, is being beaten by her husband. That's Joe Spencer; he runs the store with his mother. Molly seems to think it's pretty bad, but we've no idea how to help. We both thought…" Ellie trailed off, not wanting to say too much about the abuse she knew Liza had suffered.

Liza was quiet and Ellie wondered if she'd misjudged things. They continued to walk in silence but Ellie felt no desire to fill the void. She would allow Liza to think on things a while, as she herself was wont to do.

She could see the turn to the farm, off to the left, coming up ahead of them. These fields were given over to corn, but at this time of year you could see a good distance and the farmhouse itself was clearly visible.

Liza stopped and looked across in the direction of the farm. "Bullies everywhere are much the same. It's about power and control. Most of them are fairly inadequate in their own ways. They bully others to make themselves feel better."

She turned to Ellie, who noticed a tear in the corner of Liza's eye.

"Of course, I'll do what I can to help. It took me years to stand up to Ned, and if it hadn't been for what he did to that poor innocent boy I don't suppose I'd have had the courage to do it then." She paused and looked around her, then pulled herself up a little straighter, took Ellie's arm again and began to walk. "You know, when you go through something like that, you stop believing you're worth anything better. The worse it becomes, the more dependent you are on the abuser's praise, and the happier any small shred of recognition makes you. It sounds ridiculous now I come to explain it to you, but I hardly recognise the person I became, when I look back now. Young Daniel saved me from myself. When I saw what Ned did to him it opened my eyes to the fact these things weren't deserved. Daniel did no wrong. He was just in the wrong place at the wrong time. An easy target. It set me to thinking — if it wasn't Daniel's fault, maybe it wasn't my fault either." She sighed. "I'd spent so long defending the things Ned did, in my own mind if not to others, that I'd actually started to believe my own words."

Liza stopped talking abruptly, and Ellie looked around and saw Daniel coming across the yard toward them.

"Well, if it isn't the boy himself." Liza reached out her hands to take Daniel's.

Daniel quickly wiped his hands on his overalls before taking her hands in his. "Not so much a boy these days," he said, "but we sure are pleased to have you here again. Now, come inside and see everyone else."

Ellie was already walking ahead of them and in through the door of the farmhouse. Mary clapped her hands in delight, finding herself quickly the centre of attention as Liza went straight to her, before even greeting Molly.

"Nan nan," Mary cooed as Liza picked her up.

Ellie smiled. She knew all too well the joy of sharing in this small child, having had no children of her own, and was glad her friend could do likewise. They were an odd enough family, drawn from so many quarters, but no one would ever know that, looking from the outside. John came forward and hugged his adopted grandmother, as any loving child might, and the warmth of the welcome was far from wasted.

"I don't get much of a look-in these days." Molly smiled as she awaited her turn to greet their guest. "I've made up your usual room now you can be back in the house. That is to say, the one closest to it. Here, let me show you. You must be in want of a rest after your journey."

Ellie saw how happy Liza looked, surrounded as she was by Mary, Thomas and John, and stayed Molly's arm. "It looks to me as though this is the sort of rest Liza needs for now. We can show her upstairs when she's ready. Now, what can I do to help?"

No one came back to the reason they needed Mrs Hawksworth's assistance, that evening or on the following day. Instead, they spent time enjoying being a family together and catching up on the news from Iowa City. Liza had brought letters from Cecilia's parents, as well as news of the latest activities of the women's movement there.

The sun was gaining some warmth and Ellie sat outside her cabin while the children played about her. She couldn't be idle, it was not in her nature, so as they played she sewed a new pinafore for the ever-growing Mary. As she sewed, she mulled over what Liza had said on their walk. What would it take for Sarah to face the reality of her situation? Even as a young girl, Sarah had lacked self-confidence, so her now believing the image that suited Joe's ideas wasn't difficult for Ellie to imagine.

She heard gentle footsteps on the gravel approach to the cabins and smiled. "That's no workman's boots I can hear, children. Who do you think is coming down here to see us?"

"Nan nan," shouted Mary, pulling herself up using the rail of the deck around the cabin.

"Well, that's a pretty welcome." Liza scooped the child

up and carried her back to where Ellie was sitting. "I thought I'd have a little walk into town. Maybe take a look at that general store while I'm there. If I'm on my own, Mr Spencer is far less likely to think anything of it. I'm sure he's met me before, and this being a small town I'm guessing he already knows where I'm staying, but he needn't think so much if I call in for a few things and pass the time of day."

Ellie nodded. She could see the sense in that, although she did feel a little disappointed to be left out of the activity. "I guess I shall have to be patient and wait to hear what you think."

"There'll be plenty of work for you to do in all this, I'll be bound," Liza said, before kissing each of the children and setting off toward the town.

As Liza walked away, Ellie felt anything but patient. She turned her attention back to the children, wishing she didn't feel so torn between her role as carer and her desire not to miss out on the action. She was still deep in thought when another pair of shoes made a gentle approach. Ellie smiled and watched little Thomas to see when he would become aware of his mother's presence. "Hello, Cecilia. It's early in the day to see you back for this little bundle of trouble."

"William has heard from his father and wanted to talk to Molly and Daniel. I've come down to see if you'd like to join us up at the farmhouse."

"Oh, thank goodness. I need something to get involved in. I was starting to feel I wasn't good for any real work in all this." She lifted up Mary, leaving Cecilia to bring her own child.

Cady and Junior started barking as they approached the yard and Mary wriggled free to go to the dogs. Ellie was impatient to join the others, but she waited for the child to make her own way across the yard and, with the dogs circling them, to the house.

Now she was looking forward to finding out what Mr Dixon would advise them to do about those Reese boys.

CHAPTER 7

William was pacing the length of the farmhouse kitchen, waiting for the others to come in. The letter from his father was in his hand.

"Oh, do sit down, William. You're making us all nervous." Molly held a chair back from the table for him and went to sit down herself, with Mary curled up on her knee.

William ran a hand through his hair and moved to the chair as his sister had bidden him. He'd no more than perched on the edge of the seat before he got up again and went over to the window. He sat on the window seat, away from the group, but with the light giving him a clearer view of the letter. Once they were all seated he began. "If Justice Warren is determined to look at this only as a question of trespass, we still have to prove the brothers were in some way at fault. What they ended up doing is not enough in its own right. Besides, the best we can hope for is damages, rather than any other form of punishment." He looked up at Molly. "I'm guessing, if you do receive damages you might find the insurance company is the one who has suffered loss now, rather than you." He raised an eyebrow and sighed.

"I'll be surprised if those boys have a dollar between them, whether they need to pay Molly or the insurance company." Miss Ellie moved her chair back so she was turned more in William's direction.

"A good point, ma'am. If they can't pay, it's a shame debtors' prisons have ceased to be in use. It might have been the better way to put them behind bars. As it is, the chances are they will remain at liberty and not be able to pay their debts into the bargain. Anyway," William continued, "unless we can find some witnesses, and convince the judge to change his mind, they won't be tried for arson or murder."

"If they were tried for the real crime, what punishment do you think they'd get?" Molly asked, jogging Mary up and down on her knee.

William looked at his sister for a long moment before he answered. "They'd be hanged."

Molly stopped bouncing Mary. "We feared that. Is there no leeway?"

"Not if the law's followed." William shrugged.

A stony silence fell on the room as they took in the implication of the punishment.

Eventually and in a slightly shaky voice, Molly asked, "Is there anything they could be tried for which would not involve death?"

"I don't see it," William said, shaking his head. "The law is pretty unforgiving when it comes to major crimes. An eye for an eye and all that."

Daniel got up from where he was sitting and went over to a different window from the one William sat at. He rested his hands on the sill and peered out. He stood there a long moment before sighing deeply and turning around. "I've been thinking about it since Molly and I spoke a week or two ago. Ben wouldn't want that. He never was a man who looked for retribution. What's done is done. It's a bad affair, but the thing that's important here is they don't do it again, not that we take out some vile revenge."

William was surprised to hear such a long speech from Daniel, but then watched him cross the room again and slump into a chair as though the effort had left him spent. He paused to consider his own feelings on the matter. Until now, he had accepted the forms of punishment the law required, but if he wanted to go into politics he needed to consider what his own views were. He shuddered. How could it ever be right to take another man's life, even in revenge? More importantly, what about the times the law got it wrong? He knew it happened. He'd seen it.

"I'd hang the lot of them."

William was surprised by the strength of James's words and left a long pause, waiting to see if anyone would take up the argument. He looked back to his father's letter and felt a new weight of responsibility. He took a deep breath. Now, more than ever, he wished to see the words saying his father would be coming to them by train, but there was no such good news. Instead the conclusion of the letter sent his parents' regards to their son and George Dixon signed off. Everyone was looking to William to take the lead. There was no one else he could pass this on to. He took a deep breath.

"Thankfully, it's not for us to determine the punishment. That will be down to the judge. I think it right we interview anyone who might have been in Marsh's Saloon that night. Cecilia and I, with the help of the sheriff, have pulled together a list. We're going to work our way through it and ask them all a few questions. The place I'll find most of them is back at Marsh's, I guess." He looked over at Cecilia for approval and she nodded slightly. "I'd better make a start." He got up and began to make his way across the room.

"Oh, my dear child." Miss Ellie was on her feet in a

moment.

Under normal circumstances William would object to being called a child, even by Miss Ellie, but as she stayed his arm then turned him around with such gentle confidence he was grateful to accept.

"Firstly…" Miss Ellie spoke with resolution and, for a moment, William wondered whether it was she, rather than he, who should be representing people at the courthouse.

"Firstly, you are most certainly not going to Marsh's bar. In those clothes you'd need to be prepared for a fairly unpleasant audience. Secondly, after hearing what Daniel had to say, are we right to try to get the charges against them increased? Now, sit yourself down and let's agree the appropriate action between us. May I see the list of those you want to speak to?"

The idea they should hold back from the pursuit of justice was alien to William. He could see that hanging the Reese boys might not be the end of the matter and might make living in Pierceton the harder for the family's connections in the town. Before he handed the list over, a thought came to him. "Would you mind if I were to consult Dr Pritchard on what he thinks?"

"And what has this to do with Dr Pritchard, brother of mine?" Molly was frowning as she asked.

William looked around the room and saw the broad smiles on the faces of both Miss Ellie and Cecilia, which confirmed they had both been involved in setting up the meeting.

"Ah, so you've met Charles," Miss Ellie said. "Well done, my dear," she added, addressing Cecilia.

"Will one of you please tell me what's going on?" Molly was looking from one to the other in complete confusion.

William turned to Miss Ellie. "I think, ma'am, I'd quite like to hear your explanation too, if I may?"

Miss Ellie went across to the range and made a play of warming her hands. William presumed she was deciding how best to describe the process which had taken place. She turned back to them with a sheepish look on her face.

"Well… it was with William saying if he were going into politics here in Pierceton one of the things he would miss the most would be a… shall we say, more established gentleman, who might introduce him in the right places. I've lived in this fine town all my life and I know most of the folks who live here, so I set about thinking who might be able to take such a role in William's life. I'm sure there will come a day when it would be more than acceptable for me to make the introductions William needs. However, though I've run a successful business in this town, there's no getting away from the fact that I'm a woman and my voice is barely heard outside of this house."

They all laughed, and Miss Ellie looked gratified.

"Anyway," she continued, looking around them all, "I saw Mrs Pritchard at the women's meeting and explained the situation. I know Charles, of course, but I thought I'd have more success speaking with Dorothea first. I've known both of them since childhood. Then I took the opportunity to introduce Dorothea to Cecilia. They rapidly found common ground, with Cecilia's father being a doctor, and one thing led to another. I take it dear Charles has been to see you, William?"

"He most certainly has. I rather think I'm going to enjoy having his assistance. He's not quite as eccentric as Cecilia's own dear papa, but he has a zest for life which is no bad example to be in the company of." William looked to Molly. "Would you permit me to discuss the case with him and maybe invite him to join us one evening?"

Molly looked to Miss Ellie and smiled. "If he has Miss Ellie's blessing, I'm sure he will be a fine addition to our advisors. Perhaps we should invite both him and his wife for dinner."

"It's already done!" William slapped his thigh and laughed heartily. Seeing the look on his sister's face, he held his hands up in a gesture of defence. "Don't worry, I've not invited them here without asking. Cecilia has already issued an invitation to the Red House so we can talk about my political ambitions, and I was thinking we could make a bit of a party of it and invite you all. And before you say you've got nothing to wear" — William was reacting to the look of horror as much on Daniel's face as Molly's — "they are well aware you're a farming family and won't be expecting you to be dressed to the nines."

Daniel sighed.

William looked at his friend. "I could lend you one of my suits, if you prefer."

Daniel shook his head. "I'm sure I can find something. If I could smarten up for a bank manager, I'm sure I can do it for your chance in politics. Just don't go making a habit of it."

"That's the spirit," said William, slapping his friend on the shoulder. "Did I mention it would be tomorrow night?"

"William!" Molly shook her head, the image of mock exasperation.

William did feel slightly abashed to spring it on them all. "The thing is, I'm being proposed at the Odd Fellows lodge this week and Dr Pritchard, Charles, was going to run through a few things with me in preparation."

"We'll be there." Molly looked across at Daniel and

gave him a reassuring smile. "Now, about the list of those who were present in Marsh's bar…"

Molly held out her open hand and William realised she expected him to hand the list over. He sighed and did as his sister bid. There was little point in trying to argue with the women in this house. Besides, in his experience they were usually right when they had an idea.

Molly set the list down on the table and Cecilia and Miss Ellie joined her.

"We'll mark off the ones we can get to through their wives," said Molly.

Miss Ellie raised her eyebrows as she looked at the list. "Or mothers! I think we may find that to be the most effective approach, looking at these." She looked up at William. "The good news is, I know most of them quite well, at least for the Pierceton families. The ones who've moved here more recently I can do little about."

William left the women to work out how many of the men they could cover through their womenfolk, and instead picked Cady up and set her on his knee. He had to acknowledge there could be a lot of comfort in the company of a dog.

Daniel moved across and sat near to him. Quietly and out of hearing of the women, he said, "I don't think we should push for arson or, for that matter, murder."

"Why ever not?" William was surprised by the certainty in Daniel's tone.

"I don't think either I or Molly could cope with the Reese brothers being hanged."

"But Molly said herself, if they came back again she'd take a gun to them." William frowned in confusion.

"That would be different." Daniel paused, thinking. "I'd probably do it myself if they threatened my family again. That would be defence. Hanging them would be revenge, and I don't rightly think either of us holds with that."

William nodded slowly and sighed. The law didn't always take into account how the victims might feel. He wondered what to do for the best.

CHAPTER 8

William looked around at the dining room of the Red House. Cecilia had done them proud. This would be their first real dinner party and, as he noticed the china and silverware, he stood a little taller. Who would have thought, from his days as a pickpocket on the streets of New York, he'd end up here? He had always recognised precious metals when he saw them.

There would be eight of them at table. He checked the seating plan once again; a disproportionate number of women, but that couldn't be helped. He'd felt it would be going too far to include Miss Ellie's cousin James. Like Daniel, he'd be uncomfortable in the surroundings. Besides, they'd needed someone to look after the children and James had been more than happy to oblige.

"Will you stop fretting?" Cecilia swept into the room, carrying a decanter of port and stopped as she saw William straightening one of the knives. "We've got everything in hand. Now you go along to the sitting room and be ready to greet our guests."

No sooner had she spoken than the bell rang, and William started for the door. Then, realising he had put his papers down on the sideboard, he returned to pick them up.

Cecilia rested a hand on his arm. "There's no need to be nervous. You'll be fine. Besides, if you're this bad now, heaven help us when it comes to you being elected."

It was Miss Ellie who arrived first. "I thought you might appreciate a little moral support when Charles and Dorothea arrive, so I came on ahead of the others."

William smiled and shook his head in bewilderment. "As thoughtful as ever, thank you." He was unsure how to greet her on a formal occasion. She was family, but somehow, to kiss her cheek would be too intimate tonight.

"I believe you should take my hand and kiss the back of it," Miss Ellie said, seeing his discomfort.

She offered her hand and he took it willingly. No sooner had he done so than he heard the bell a second time and his eyes darted to the door.

This time it was Dr Pritchard and his wife, and William felt his hands go clammy. He tried to surreptitiously wipe them on his trousers as he went forward to greet his guests, turning first to the lady and bowing slightly as he took her hand, and then returning to Dr Pritchard.

William had barely had time to offer them a drink when Cecilia ushered Daniel, Molly and Liza Hawksworth into the room. William smiled to see Daniel looking smart but a little more awkward than usual. He knew better than to comment and greeted his friend as though dressing for dinner was the most natural thing in the world to him.

The half hour over drinks was spent with Dr and Mrs Pritchard being introduced to each member of the party and the usual small talk, whilst William longed to move on to the main business of the evening. He was, however, grateful that it was Miss Ellie who took the lead in these matters and, taking Dorothea Pritchard's arm, guided her to each person in turn, with her husband following indulgently behind.

"Isn't Mrs Pritchard's brocade dress beautiful?" Cecilia whispered to William, when the rest of the party was deep in conversation.

William had no idea what brocade was, so he simply agreed with his wife.

"And this," said Miss Ellie, making her last introduction, "is Liza Hawksworth, who I think you may have met once before. She's travelled all the way from Iowa City to be with us again. She knows Cecilia's parents, and of course her husband ran the farm Daniel worked on as a child." She gave Dorothea a knowing smile and it was clear to William that much of the detailed background had been conveyed prior to this meeting, quite possibly in order to avoid embarrassment.

Dinner was called almost as soon as the introductions were over, and William held the door while Cecilia led the way to the dining room. As William caught up, his wife was indicating the appropriate place for each guest. William took the head of the table and smiled to observe that Cecilia had seated Miss Ellie at the opposite end. What surprised him was how quickly and easily Daniel fell into conversation with Dr Pritchard on the opposite side of the table. Watching the two of them, William almost found himself feeling a little jealous.

As the dinner progressed, Dr Pritchard turned to Cecilia and said, "Can you face being a politician's wife? It's not an easy life, from what I can tell, and if you want to be together it can mean keeping two houses, one here and one in Washington."

None of this was any surprise to William and Cecilia. They'd already discussed it at length. While Thomas was still too young for formal schooling it would be easier in some regards, but it would make running the law office difficult, if Cecilia were to follow him about. William waited to see what Cecilia might reply.

"Being married to William, with him in Washington, couldn't possibly be harder than the first five minutes were. There can't be many brides who can claim to have been coated in manure before fully leaving the church steps."

"Ah yes," Dr Pritchard said, raising an eyebrow, "Ellie told me about that. Not the best start to a marriage."

"Besides," Cecilia continued, "my own political hopes cannot be achieved without a certain amount of sacrifice." She threw him a winning smile and the older gentleman appeared to be captivated.

Shortly after dinner, Molly and Daniel retired from the party as, like it or not, they would have an early start the following morning. Liza Hawksworth, who was staying in the farmhouse, took her leave with them, and to William's relief, he at last had the opportunity to talk more seriously of his political ambitions.

"I guess you can see this as your first campaign meeting," Charles Pritchard said as they moved toward the sitting room once again.

Cecilia made to lead Dorothea and Miss Ellie to the library, but Charles intervened. "I hope William won't mind, but I'd like the three of you to join us, if you would? However good this husband of yours turns out to be, I don't think he'll be winning any seats without your help."

Despite a twinge of disappointment that he would not have Charles's attention to himself, William saw the point of what he was saying and moved the chairs in the sitting room to enable them all to sit comfortably together.

"How much do you already know about standing for Congress?" Dr Pritchard got straight to the point. "It can be a long road and you're still mighty young."

As William relayed what he'd learned so far, Dr

Pritchard sat in silence, listening, and the women looked on.

"And what do you stand for?"

William knew these were all the sorts of questions he needed to be prepared for, but he hadn't expected them to start tonight.

"Sir, I stand on a platform of equality. Equality for all men and women, regardless of class, colour or creed. I believe this great nation has been made what it is by the labours of all races who make up the population, and there is nowhere more likely for any man to make his fortune by his labours than he might do here... and women, for that matter." He looked to Cecilia and Miss Ellie for reassurance.

"And what do you say to the man who calls you a nigger lover, and says your words threaten his livelihood?"

Dr Pritchard was unrelenting in his questions and William began to think if this was what it was like to address a friend, he had best be thoroughly prepared when he came to face his enemies.

"I would say, sir, here in America a man may make his own destiny and there is a good opportunity for any man to do so. One man's fortune does not limit that of his brother, and there are no grounds by which a man may only succeed by standing harshly on those who come after him, to keep them in their places." William swallowed hard. Had he been too forceful in the way he presented his views, and was his meaning clear?

"Bravo, young man." Dr Pritchard was calm in complimenting William, with only a hint of a smile on his face. "And what do you say to the 'gold-diggers' who want it all for themselves and don't believe there's more than enough to go around? No, worse than that, who believe there are men, and women for that matter, lower than they are in status, who should be at their disposal to enable them to make yet more money?"

"I say, sir, all men are born equal. It is our constitution and our right and they cannot be a true American and believe otherwise."

"And to those who say an uneducated man, or woman, cannot be allowed the same rights as an educated one, as they are not safe to exercise them?"

"To them, sir, I say many men have not been afforded the opportunity of education and we, as a nation, should ensure all our citizens are provided with the chance to be schooled beyond a level many might suppose their birth would suggest." William could feel his heart racing, and longed for a wider audience than he had within the sitting room of the Red House.

"Noble words indeed." Dr Pritchard got up from his chair and walked across the room, turning back to face the women. "Ladies, what do you think of our future Representative?"

"Well," said Dorothea, looking seriously at her husband and then turning a beaming smile on William, "I rather think that, with some hard work, I know many women who will canvass their husbands to support him."

Cecilia clapped her hands together. "If he goes on to stay true to his beliefs, I shall be exceedingly proud of him."

Charles Pritchard nodded and turned back to William. "We will need to rehearse your responses on matters of the economy, the law and so on, but I think you have the makings of an electable man." He turned his back and walked to the far end of the room. It was clear by his manner he hadn't finished speaking, and no one filled the silence. He stopped and looked up at the painting which hung on the wall. It showed a ship crossing a stormy sea, with dark clouds on the horizon. He gave a single nod and turned about. "You will need to be prepared for difficult questions and for those who wish to undermine you, or worse dismiss you, based on your early life."

William opened his mouth to speak, but Dr Pritchard held up a hand to stop him.

"I shudder at the thought of the things you may have had to do in order to survive during your New York days. Now, don't look at me like that. I'm not stupid. I know you were an Irish orphan and there's no point your trying to hide it. There's always someone prepared to come forward and use things against you, if it will serve their ends. Of course, I don't know the details of your life specifically and I don't ask you to tell me, but I know enough of what street life can entail to know what your opponents might try to say."

William felt his shoulders sag.

"All I'm saying is, you need to be ready for it and be prepared to be proud of your roots, but to make clear you are now a good American citizen and uphold all this country means." He came forward and held his outstretched hand to William.

William stood and shook Dr Pritchard by the hand.

"I'll be proud to work with you and do what I can to introduce you in the right places. We will need to win over Pierceton, but we'll need to go further afield too. You'll be making speeches from the balcony of the Kirtley Hotel in Warsaw, before you know it. Let's get you elected to the lodge first, and take it from there."

"Thank you, sir, thank you." William was too excited

to sit back down and wanted to be able to start right away.

Dr Pritchard waved his thanks away. "Don't thank me yet. It isn't likely to be plain sailing and some of your views will be unpopular. The road from here to Congress will be a long one, and most who start fall by the wayside, long before they reach Washington."

CHAPTER 9

"Are you in there?" Daniel was panting slightly, having run from the barn. He was loath to go into the dairy in his muddy boots. "Molly, are you there?" His eyes darted across to the house. Would he be better looking there? He was sure Molly had said she'd be finishing the cheeses. "Molly!" He heard footsteps hurrying across the main room of the dairy and breathed out.

"Whatever is it?" Molly was clutching a bowl in her arms that she was clearly in the process of working with.

"John's gone."

"Gone where? Now will you just calm yourself a moment and tell me clearly what's happening? Here, let me put this down while you catch your breath."

When she came back, Molly was still drying her hands as she walked briskly toward him. "Now, where has John gone?"

"James saw him heading toward the gate with Junior. He was crying and said we'd be better off without him and he was leaving."

"Do you know why?"

Daniel shook his head. "Not really. He said he was having problems at school again, but when I spoke to Mr Young he thought it was just boys doing no more than boys of that age do."

"We'll see about that." Molly's nostrils flared.

Whilst her voice was calm, Daniel was painfully aware

of how angry she was.

"Now, first we need to find that boy of ours, then I shall go to see Mr Young. It might be what boys of that age do, but bullying is never all right and they will not do it to our boy. We won't stand by while the next generation turn into the Reese brothers of the future. Daniel, saddle the horses whilst I go down to the cabin to see if Cady is there. Cady might find Junior faster than we could find John."

Molly marched across the yard toward the cabins. Daniel, as he headed to the stables, admired his wonderful feisty and practical wife. It would never have occurred to him that the dog might be able to help.

When Molly came back, Cady was trotting behind her, tail up and ready for whatever adventure lay ahead.

"When you ran away," Molly began, before she'd even reached Daniel, "did you run toward the town or away from it? And can you remember why you made that choice?"

It was a good question and Daniel searched his memory for times he had long since tried to bury. "The first time, I ran away from the town. The second time toward it." He hesitated, remembering why he'd made those choices. "The first time, I reckoned it was better to go where no one would see me." He paused. "The second time was different. I was older and knew the only way I'd get away from the town completely was with some sort of transport. I needed the town to find it. If I were John, I'd head away from town."

Molly nodded. "That makes sense. If he went toward town, he'd probably be safer anyway, and the sheriff would soon enough bring him home. "We'll go left out of the lane. You take the right of the road and I'll take the left. Being on horseback might help us see over the hedges, but if we have the horses walk, Cady will be able to keep up with us."

Daniel could feel his legs trembling as he mounted the horse and they began to walk along the lane to the road. When he ran away, he'd been running from a man who had beaten him almost to death. What had so upset John that he would run from a family who loved him? He felt quite sure John believed they loved him, but could he be certain? He looked across the edges of the field to his left, scanning in all directions for movement. John might hide, but Junior could rarely stay still for five seconds at a time. Daniel could see nothing. Cady seemed happy to trot along between the two horses in the middle of the lane, as Molly scanned the other side.

He was trying to think what was the maximum time John could have had as a head start. He could still be walking away from the farm, but boys didn't generally walk in a straight line, in his experience, and tended to find plenty to stop for along the way. Even at a walk, the horses were a little faster than John would have been on foot, so they must be making ground on him, if he'd gone this way.

Neither he nor Molly spoke as they rode. Both were concentrating hard on looking and the light was beginning to fade. They would have little more than another half hour before it became hard to see, then he had no idea what they'd do. He quickened the horse's pace, anxious to lose no time. He turned around a short while later to see Molly still working her way along the right of the lane, but no sign of Cady. He pulled up and turned about. Definitely no sign. He called her name — nothing. By now, Molly had caught up with him in the lane.

"Whistle, it'll carry further."

Of course! Why hadn't he thought of that? He took a

deep breath and gave out a long whistle. Suddenly, he saw not one but two shapes charging across the field from some trees a little way back. He spurred the horse through the open gateway and began to ride faster across the edge of the field toward the trees. Cady and Junior came around behind the horses and then ran on ahead, back to where they'd come from.

As he came close to the copse, Daniel slowed and dismounted. In the quiet he could hear his heartbeat pounding in his ears. He strained to listen and could hear sobbing as well. Leaving the horse where she was, he stumbled into the small wooded area, following the direction of the sound. John was curled up at the base of a large tree, hugging his knees to his body and rocking. Daniel didn't speak, but sat next to the boy and put his arms around him, waiting until John was ready.

Junior barked up at them, while Cady pushed her way between Daniel's arms and began licking at John's face. Little by little, the boy stopped crying and looked at the dog.

"Why, John?" Daniel asked.

The child was quiet, then, looking down, said, "He told me they'd kill Mary and Ma next time around if I said anything."

"Who did?"

"Freddie Hunter."

"Who is Freddie Hunter?"

"At school."

Daniel was aware he wasn't getting far and looked up at Molly, who was standing at the edge of the trees holding the reins of the horses.

"John," she said, keeping her tone even, "is he related to Jacob and Reuben Reese?"

John didn't speak, but Daniel felt his head move in a nod where it rested against Daniel's chest, and relayed the reply to Molly.

"John, no one is going to kill either me or Mary. What did Freddie Hunter do to you that you weren't to tell anyone?"

John remained silent, but Daniel felt fresh tears falling. This was no question of simple name calling, of that he was sure. What he didn't know was just how bad things were.

As Molly's gentle voice continued, Daniel wondered if there was a way for the two of them to change places and for him to hold the horses. While he was more than happy to embrace the boy, he didn't know what questions to ask to find out what had happened.

"John," said Molly, "how old is Freddie?"

This time, John looked up at Molly but said nothing.

Daniel quietly repeated the question.

Looking away, John mumbled, "I don't know. Older." He was staring away from his parents now, looking distant.

Daniel turned to Molly for guidance.

Deftly, she tied both the horses to the nearby tree and made her way over to them. She knelt down in front of John, but didn't try to look him in the eye.

"Did he make you do a very bad thing?" Molly asked gently.

Daniel felt the boy's body stiffen. John made no reply but simply stared down at the ground and began to rock again.

"John," Molly said, a little more firmly, "you need to tell us what happened."

John drew his knees still further in toward his body.

The light was fading rapidly and Daniel was conscious

they had no torches with them. They at least needed to get back to the road, if they were to make their way home. He took his arms from around the boy and gently lifted him up. It seemed unlikely they were going to get him to talk out here in the darkness, and they would all be better in front of a warm fire.

Molly sighed and nodded to him. As he carried John back across the field to the road, Molly untied the horses and led them the same way.

Once they were all on the lane, Daniel indicated to Molly that she should mount her horse, then he lifted John to sit in front of her, where she could hold him as she rode. She was by far the better rider, and with one arm around John and the other holding the reins she'd keep a straight and gentle pace even in the fading light.

When they returned, Miss Ellie, ever the practical one, was in the kitchen. A kettle was already boiled and the smell of fresh bread filled the air.

Daniel nodded to Miss Ellie, but said nothing as he carried John into the kitchen and placed him on a chair near the stove. Miss Ellie didn't ask any questions; she simply gathered up Mary and Thomas and led them out of the farmhouse and back toward her cabin.

Molly cut some of the bread and brought it to John, but he stared toward the stove. She sat beside him as Daniel made hot drinks.

"John, what happened?"

John began to rock once again. "He said they'd kill you if I told anyone."

"No one's going to kill me, John. You don't need to be frightened. What did Freddie do to you?"

John didn't turn to address his mother as he spoke, but looked vacantly into the distance and rocked. As Daniel watched him, it seemed as though John were seeing the events all over again.

"He made me go to the field behind the schoolhouse… he m-m-made m-m-me t-t-take…"

It took a long while for John to tell of the acts Freddie had made him perform. Daniel found it almost unbearable to listen to the worst excesses of the urges an adolescent boy might seek to fulfil by any means possible. No child should be used in such a manner, and his heart ached for what John must have gone through; what he must still be going through.

Both he and Molly remained silent as John stuttered out his story. Then Molly held John tightly and rocked gently with him until the boy stilled.

Never had Daniel felt so powerless. As he watched the depth and pain of John's humiliation, he would have done anything to be able to take those memories away from the boy.

"This isn't your fault, John. What Freddie did was very bad, but it's not your fault. We love you. You don't need to run away, and no one is going to come after Mary or me now you've told us."

Molly's tone was so gentle that even Daniel found it soothing as he stood in the kitchen, rooted to the spot by the anger he was feeling; anger that no one had stepped in to protect this precious child. A jumble of questions were going through his mind, but John was clearly in a very fragile state and now was not the time to ask them.

Would the problems they faced from the family surrounding those Reese brothers never stop? For the first time, Daniel started to think even hanging might be too good for those boys, and it saddened him he was thinking that way.

He would certainly need to go to the school the following morning to talk to Mr Young, but it was hard to see how John could return to his classes after this. He looked up at the rosary above the hearth. If ever there was a time they needed faith, it was now.

John eventually fell asleep, exhausted from crying and the exertions of the day. Daniel carried him up to bed and sat with him a long while, watching him sleep. How would John recover from this and what impact would it have on his life? Then he thought back to his own childhood and the different but gruesome traumas he had faced. He'd been saved by the kindness of Mrs Hawksworth and the love and belief in him Molly had shown. He hoped they could do the same for John, and prayed they would have enough love and strength to help him.

"It's a bad business," he said to Molly, when he finally returned to the kitchen.

Molly used her eyes to indicate that Mary was now back from Miss Ellie's and he should be careful what he said. He nodded his understanding.

"I know he loves the farm work, but he needs an education too. I just can't make him go back to that school, even once I've seen Mr Young." Daniel slumped into the chair near the fire, glad of the heat it threw out. He didn't feel he'd warmed through since coming back with John that afternoon. "And what do we do about what has actually happened?"

"I asked Miss Ellie if she knew the family and she does, but only by reputation and it's not a good one. It's going to be one child's word against another, and we couldn't make John repeat the story to anyone else, in any event. I feel sick to think of it." Molly rested on the arm of Daniel's chair and leaned in toward him.

"Perhaps it's time we had a bigger dog, as much to guard as for company. Although I grant it's unlikely to be any fiercer than Junior is if he feels his family's at risk."

They both looked down at the little dog, waggling his legs as he slept.

Daniel took breakfast in bed to John the following morning and told him he could work on the farm once Daniel returned from town. Then he took the horse and set off for the school house, to see Mr Young before classes started.

As soon as Daniel approached, Mr Young's face reddened and Daniel realised the teacher must already be aware of the situation.

"You knew," he accused Mr Young, "and you did nothing!" Daniel could feel the anger pulsing through him and balled his fists. "A defenceless boy — and you did nothing." He tried to block out the voice of reason in his head, telling him violence would only make matters worse. Right now, he wanted nothing more than to knock this man senseless for failing to protect his boy.

"I... I... you know what they're like. They burned your farm, for goodness sake. You know you can't beat them." Mr Young held his hands palm upward in a placatory gesture.

"You were a coward and you let the bullies win." But Daniel did know what it was like. He'd failed to protect his own family. He wasn't there to save Mary and Molly, and it had been Ben who lost his life. He was no better than the man in front of him, except... except he hadn't stood by deliberately. He hadn't been there. The voice in his head reminded him that he'd only said to William a short while ago that he didn't believe in revenge. He so wanted to hit this man. Standing there, wrestling with his conscience, Daniel felt he was losing. His anger was taking over and he could see or hear nothing except that moment of him facing Mr Young and his desire to lash out.

The spell was snapped when one of the children who had come in behind him, and of whom he had not been aware, suddenly spoke. "Sir, are you all right, sir?"

Daniel became aware that Mr Young was holding himself up with the support of a table and did indeed look unwell. Maybe his conscience was a more powerful opponent than even Daniel's fist would have been.

Daniel turned and walked away, leaving the children to tend to this weak and ineffectual man who was unworthy of their ministrations. For his own part, he would write to the School Board and ensure they were aware of Mr Young's failure in his duty to the children. He hoped William might help him to address the matter.

CHAPTER 10

Liza Hawksworth would have been far happier to turn and go in the other direction. If she could stand up in court and testify against her husband, she told herself she could do this. The problem was, it brought back all the memories of the past, things she would rather bury and never think of again. As she opened the street door and the general store bell rang, she steeled herself to fulfil her mission.

Taking a deep breath, Liza stepped inside. There was a certain look that fitted most general stores and this one was no real exception. It was tidily laid out with jars and boxes around the shelves, all neatly labelled; sacks set conveniently at floor level to the side of the counter, where a customer could fill whatever receptacle they brought with them. Of course, there were paper bags, although Liza could remember when they were a novelty.

The brass scales sat majestically on the counter, together with their tray of weights. Liza breathed in the scents and smells of the store as they mingled in the air, then walked over to a table on the far side, to take in the useful pots and cooking utensils displayed. Her mind turned to baking rather than the matter in hand. She picked up a cake tin and thought idly how she missed having her own home and kitchen and smiled, remembering the extras she would take down to Daniel when he was a child, when Ned had gone out with the boys into town.

"That's a fine tin," a man's voice said behind her, causing Liza to jump and return it to the display.

She had thought she'd timed her visit for an occasion when Joe would be out on deliveries, but clearly she'd been mistaken. She had no idea where to start a conversation with him, and distantly said, "Yes, I suppose it is."

"Were you looking for something in particular?" Joe was matter-of-fact but encouraging with it, and Liza suspected he made a good salesman.

All her carefully rehearsed lines went from her head and she struggled to think of a single item to say she was in need of.

At the point she thought all might be lost and her best option would be to leave, an older woman came through and said, "I'll look after this lady, Joe. I do believe you wanted to get the orders out."

Joe's tone changed. "Where's Sarah? Can't she do the delivery round?"

"I believe she's taken Henry and Jenny out for some air," his mother said gently.

Joe slapped his hand down on the counter but said nothing. Then he seemed to resume his salesman's manner. "Good day, madam, I shall leave you in the hands of my mother."

"Please excuse my son. Now, how may I help you? I think I've seen you before, but you're not local, are you?"

Liza smiled and began to relax a little. "No, I'm a visitor to these parts, but I'll be staying a while this time. It's difficult, with knowing so few people. I don't want to get under the feet of those who are kind enough to have me stay. They have their own lives to get on with. You know how it is."

Mrs Spencer nodded and sighed. "I feel that often times in my own home. My son, his wife and children all live with me here and whilst it's my home as much as my son's, I sometimes feel as though I'm in the way."

Liza began to ask Mrs Spencer about her grandchildren to find what common ground she could build on. Not having her own children made it harder, but she had grandchildren in Daniel's family, so she was safer there.

The conversation continued for a while, until the shop bell rang again and a young woman came in and wished them both good day before starting to browse the produce around the shop.

"Well, here we are talking so much, I've almost forgotten the things I came for." Liza began to gather together the buckwheat, sugar and other necessities she'd noted, with the intention of her visit looking as natural as possible.

As Liza paid, Mrs Spencer said, "Why don't you come over tomorrow afternoon and take tea with me? It will be nice to have the company of someone my own age, and Sarah will be in the store so I shall have some time."

Liza took her purse out and laid out the coins. "I'd like that. Thank you. Until tomorrow, good day to you."

Given how Joseph was vehemently opposed to women's suffrage, missing the following day's women's meeting to visit Mrs Spencer, should mean he was less worried about Liza developing a friendship with his mother. She wasn't used to being this devious, but she smiled to herself, realising she was rather enjoying it.

It was a fine day and Liza had no reason to rush back to the farm so she took a stroll through Pierceton toward the station at the far end of town. She paused to look in the window of the milliner's shop, as well as admiring a handsome carriage outside the hub and spoke workshop. She sighed; one of the hardest things about walking away from her old life was being left to the charity of her family and friends, with no expectation of its ever being otherwise. A carriage was something she would never afford. She laughed, reminding herself that had she stayed with Ned there would have been no likelihood of his allowing her a carriage, so in reality she was no worse off. That thought left a spring in her step as she continued along, and so it was that she came across Franklin Marsh once again, lingering outside his saloon, taking a little air.

As Liza approached, he raised his hat to her and called across, "Why, good day to you, ma'am. You're looking mighty pleased with yourself today."

She was feeling a little frivolous, so she stopped to answer. "And so I should be, sir. It's a fine day and I'm making the most of it."

"Well, that's pretty much what I'm doing right now too, though I need to get back to wetting the whistles of the ragamuffins who grace my bar."

Marsh had his head tilted and was eyeing her in a manner that made Liza blush.

"I thought you counted most of them as friends, from what Miss Cochrane told me." Liza knew she should probably be on her way, but she was having fun and well, why shouldn't she?

"Some days they're friends, some days they're family and some days..." Marsh didn't finish the sentence, but they both laughed.

"I could maybe take you for tea one day?" he continued, raising an enquiring eyebrow.

Liza's caution came back to her all of a sudden and she stood a little more stiffly. "Well, I'm not sure that would be appropriate for a single woman of my age."

"Better a single woman than a married one. I've no ties myself, so there's no one to complain that I'm missing."

Marsh, it seemed, wasn't going to be put off easily.

"I don't know," said Liza, hesitating.

The exchange was interrupted by a shout from inside the saloon. "Are you serving drinks here, Marsh, or do I have to help myself?"

He shrugged, looking much younger than his years as he did so, used his boot to push away from the wall he was leaning against, and raised his hat to her again. "Maybe another time. Good day."

As he turned to go back into the saloon, Liza could have sworn he winked at her and, feeling a little flustered, she turned and continued on her walk.

"You're looking mighty pleased with yourself," Miss Ellie said, as Liza got back to the farm later.

"You're not the first person to say that to me today. Yes, I've had a lovely afternoon." She unfastened her bonnet and laid the provisions she'd bought at the general store on the long wooden table.

"And who might the first person be?" Ellie stood with her hands on her hips, looking at her friend.

Liza was still feeling a little coy as she answered. "No one in particular, just someone I passed while I was out." Then she updated Ellie on the events of the earlier part of the afternoon at the general store, before she had the opportunity to ask further questions.

The following afternoon it was Mrs Spencer who met Liza when she entered the store. Sarah was nowhere in sight.

"I'm hoping Sarah will be down shortly, she's just…"

Mrs Spencer struggled to find words to finish the sentence. "Anyway, we'll have the children with us — I do hope that's all right. Perhaps we could take them out for a while? I'm sure the air would do us all good."

Liza felt a pang, thinking how much Ellie would like to spend time with her grandchildren, and hoped that her doing so would not cause upset. "Yes, of course," she said, trying to make her smile appear genuine. Having the children present risked limiting their conversation, but maybe she was getting ahead of herself in any event.

Before Liza said anything further, Sarah came into the store, and she jolted when she saw the red rims of the girl's eyes. Without question, she'd been crying, but from the matter-of-fact way in which Mrs Spencer addressed her, either she had not noticed, which Liza thought unlikely, or she was well aware of the cause and not disposed to intervene.

Liza swallowed hard, struggling not to comment or ask Sarah if she was all right. "Good day, dear. How nice to see you."

To begin with, Sarah's face showed no recognition of the visitor. Liza wasn't offended; they'd not met on many occasions and it was clear Sarah was in a state of some distress.

"Oh, why, it's Mrs Hawksworth, isn't it? Are you...? That is to say..."

Liza suddenly understood that Sarah didn't want to mention either Cochrane's Farm or the inhabitants there, so she quickly intervened. "I'm visiting for a while and trying to get to know a little more of Pierceton while I'm here. Your mother-in-law was kind enough to invite me to drop by this afternoon and, well, here I am." She threw her arms out to the sides and gave a little nervous laugh.

She followed Mrs Spencer through to the back of the shop before she could say the wrong thing, leaving Sarah alone behind the counter.

Henry, a serious-looking six-year-old was telling off his two-year-old sister for not paying attention to him. Liza shuddered, seeing the cycle starting so young. She had little doubt his behaviour was learned from a father who expected to be king of his castle.

Mrs Spencer did not reprimand him, but simply picked Jenny up to put on the girl's coat, ready for going out.

"I don't think I want to go, Grandma," Henry said when they were ready to set off.

This time, Liza was pleased to find Mrs Spencer brooked no arguments.

"I'm sorry you don't think that, Henry, but as we're all going, you don't have a choice in the matter." Her voice sounded weary as she addressed him.

"Papa should have taken me on his rounds. Then I wouldn't have to come."

"Yes," Mrs Spencer replied, "I rather think he should."

Henry made no further complaint, putting on his outdoor shoes for himself and stomping toward the door.

Mrs Spencer said nothing, but indicated for Mrs Hawksworth to go ahead of her and followed behind with Jenny in the child's wheeled chair.

Once outside, Henry was happy to occupy himself with running ahead and inspecting various objects he found in the dirt. Jenny was soon asleep in her chair and Mrs Spencer began, visibly, to relax.

"It takes me back to when my two were young," she said as they walked along. "Of course, I lost my Henry to the war. I've only Joe to think of now."

Liza had a vague recollection that Molly had been

going to marry Henry, and it was his death which had led to her trip to Iowa in search of Daniel in the first place. She thought it better not to bring Molly into the conversation, so she said nothing.

The afternoon progressed amicably in small talk. Henry climbed a tree along the way, causing Liza to hold her breath, thinking he would not get down safely. Clearly, however, he was used to such activities, and Mrs Spencer paid little attention to it. Liza wondered if that was how you became if you brought up boys.

Back at the farm later that afternoon, Liza was reflecting on the day as she talked to Molly and Ellie. "I'd be surprised to find Sarah isn't having the difficulties you spoke of, but I don't think Mrs Spencer is ever likely to criticise her own son. Sarah's on her own and no mistake. As for that son of hers — well, I reckon she's got her work cut out there. He's his father's child, and ruling the roost when his father's not around. And that at six years old." She shook her head. "I don't think there's all that much you can do, for the time being. Not until Sarah asks. I'll get to know Mrs Spencer more, if I can, but I don't think she'll say anything about it, however much I see of her."

Liza looked across at Mary and Thomas and hoped that, as they grew, they would stay as charming in their manners as they were now. She guessed a child learned most from the example they saw around them, in which case she would have little to fear.

CHAPTER 11

"You have to go." Cecilia had Thomas in her arms as she addressed William. "You would say exactly the same to me if it were the other way around."

"But what about campaigning?" William felt forlorn as he reread the telegram from his father.

"Your mother is more important than even politics. You have to go. We can mind the office, can't we, Thomas?"

Given the child was asleep and dribbling on his mother, William thought it highly unlikely Thomas was going to be any help in the matter, but nonetheless he once again appreciated the strength of this wonderful woman and the confidence she had as to the right thing to do.

"I'll need to see Dr Pritchard before I go and…"

Cecilia laid her free hand on his arm. "You will simply pack a bag and be on the first train tomorrow. I will see Dr Pritchard. I will write to you with everything that is happening, although I'll be bound you'll have other things on your mind. Once I've put this child to bed, I'll lay out the clothes you'll need, so you'll be ready. You pen a telegram to your father to say you're on your way." She kissed his cheek before leaving the study and making her way into the hall.

William stood where he was, not able to think. He remembered back to when Mammy had died, and it had been Daniel and not he who had been there for her and for

Molly. He couldn't deal with it then, and his instinct now was to run from, rather than toward, the problem. If time had taught him one thing, it was that he had to overcome instincts like that and face reality. Cecilia was right. He did have to go.

He sat back at his desk and first penned a line to send to his father and then began to make notes on the cases he was dealing with, for Cecilia. He wondered how his clients would react to dealing with his wife instead of him, but even if they weren't aware, William knew she was a more capable lawyer than he would ever be.

He had been elected to the Odd Fellows, but there had been no opportunity yet for him to make any impression on its members. That was something he was hoping to start doing in the coming weeks, but it would have to wait.

The following morning Cecilia took him in the trap to the station. He felt flustered as he said goodbye to both her and Thomas, and fervently wished they were going with him.

"I won't be away long. I'll write to tell you what's happening." He clenched his fists, trying to get his emotions under control.

"William." Cecilia's voice was calm. "You'll be as long as you need to be. We'll be fine. We've got Daniel, Molly and Miss Ellie to care for us here. Now don't you go worrying. I'll try not to lose all your clients at the office, too." She smiled her gentle smile and ran a soft finger down his cheek.

William turned toward the train. After a few faltering steps he turned back to see Cecilia and Thomas still standing there, watching him go. She blew a kiss toward him and William swallowed hard. Taking a deep breath, he nodded. He couldn't wave, as both of his hands were occupied with bags and there was no porter to be seen anywhere. Sighing deeply, he went to his assigned carriage and lifted his bags aboard.

As the train clicked over the tracks, William's thoughts became maudlin. He'd never undertaken the journey alone. Suddenly his mind went back to childhood, when he had first ridden the train to Dowagiac, in search of a new family and home. More especially, he realised how hard it must have been for Daniel, sent on from there on the train to Iowa, with no adult accompaniment. Streetwise as they were, it must have been a terrifying experience.

Hour after hour, the countryside rolled by, with William barely aware of his surroundings as he revisited the past. His thoughts turned to Jude McCaulay, his one friend at school. Whatever had happened to him? More than anything, he found himself praying that Ma would not have passed before he reached Dowagiac.

Memories continued to crowd in on him as the day passed, and the following day. It was almost as though the train were taking him to the past rather than a physical place. How would he feel if it were New York he was visiting, rather than Dowagiac? He shuddered. If he succeeded in going into politics, it was likely he'd have to go there one day. Perhaps he would be better to arrange a visit before it was essential. A chance to face the ghosts which rested there, but that was a journey he would not undertake alone.

When the train finally pulled into the station in Dowagiac, William looked along the length of the platform for his father. He gave a start when he saw Briggs, his family's old groom, standing there. This was a man he had treated badly, if ever there was one. His initial thought was

Briggs must himself be taking a journey or meeting someone from the train.

When Briggs saw him, raised his hat and came forward to assist him with his luggage, William was dumbfounded. "No, sir," he said, finding his voice again. "I cannot possibly expect you to carry my bags, when I owe you so much by way of apology."

It was Briggs' turn to appear lost for words, shaking his head and giving a slight smile.

"Where is my father?" William was still looking around, expecting to see him standing there.

"Firstly," said Briggs, "I think it best we put the past behind us. I am indeed glad you've had a change of heart, sir, but your father has looked after me and my family well, so you've no need to worry."

"That is extremely kind of you. I've learned a great deal about myself in the years that have passed, and I hope I'm the better person for it."

"That's good, sir." Briggs paused. "As to your father, it's a bad business. Your ma cannot be left unattended. My wife offered to sit with her, but your father won't leave her side. You need to be prepared."

William was at a loss what to say. He'd been dreading arriving to news his mother was already gone, and now quickened his pace at the thought that he would not be too late to see her.

Briggs said nothing further. He simply helped William to stow his luggage and then took the reins of the trap and set off at a brisk pace toward the house.

"I'll bring the bags," Briggs said, when they pulled up at the house. "You go straight up."

"Thank you." William realised what a great injustice he'd done this kind man when he was a child and had caused him to take the blame for Bounty's lameness. He walked briskly up the steps and, as quietly as he could, let himself in through the front door, across the hall and up the staircase to the landing. He turned toward his parents' bedroom. His father looked so gaunt as to be barely recognisable, as he came onto the landing, closing the door quietly behind him.

"She's sleeping," his father said, by way of greeting.

William stopped where he was, unsure what to do now. "May I see her?"

Pa smiled a sad smile and nodded slightly. He reopened the door, and noiselessly William made his way into the bedroom and stood by the side of the bed.

Ma's face was all but white and her breathing laboured as she slept. He wanted to reach down and take her hand, but so as not to disturb her he would wait until later. For now, he'd content himself with the fact she was still there. The dear woman who'd taken him in and given him so much love. His ma. He felt a tear track down his cheek as he stood looking at her. How could such a strong woman be reduced to this? Why couldn't the doctor treat her?

He went out of the room again and headed down to his father's study. The door was open, but William still knocked before he entered. His father had poured two glasses of bourbon and they were waiting on a tray for William to join him.

William looked carefully at his father. The greyness of worry spread from his hair and across his whole countenance. The lines were deep-etched and he seemed smaller than when they'd last met.

"I don't think she'll be with us much longer." His father fell silent for some time, swallowing repeatedly.

William had no idea what to say.

His father looked at him, his eyes glistening. "Thank God she's made it until you arrived. The doctor has given her laudanum to ease the pain, but he thinks it's unlikely to be long."

William was used to this man being his rock and his guide, and yet here he was looking broken. "Sir, is she sleeping much?"

"When the pain's controlled she sleeps. When it gets too much she wakes again. It's not easy to watch. I'm grateful it's progressed so quickly and she won't suffer for an extended time. Although what I'll do without her, I simply don't know. It's impossible to imagine." He closed his eyes and sat swirling the drink around the glass.

When his father resumed, he spoke quietly. "We couldn't have children of our own, as you know. I thought I'd failed her. My beloved Margaret being childless was unbearable to see." He paused and took a drink from the bourbon. "When you came into our lives, I have never seen her so happy. It was almost as though she really believed she had given birth to you herself. Oh, I know the connection of the red hair helped with that. You looked so like her, and even more like her own father, when he was your age. People have short memories and it didn't take long for neighbours and acquaintances to forget you hadn't always been part of the family. You've made us so proud."

Again, his father went quiet, but William had no idea what to say and left the silence intact.

It was a long moment before his father spoke again, and when he did his voice cracked as he said, "It was her dying wish she should see you one last time. She'll be so happy that you're here." He looked at this pocket watch. "We should go up again in about twenty minutes; she's likely to be waking then."

"I should perhaps go and wash," William said. "I'm somewhat in need of it from my journey."

Abstractedly his father waved a hand and nodded. William replaced the crystal glass on the tray and quietly left the study to go to his room.

He took little time to get washed and changed. His clothes had been neatly laid out for him and warm water was ready. He smiled, appreciating the thought that had gone into things he'd taken for granted when he was growing up.

Within fifteen minutes he was back on the landing, heading for his parents' room, and he found his father waiting there ready for him. They went in together. His father moved a second chair to the side of the bed, next to the one he had clearly been using these past days since Ma had been bed-ridden. He indicated for William to sit on the one which would be in Ma's line of sight when she awoke. Then they sat wordlessly, waiting.

William watched his mother's chest rise in stages as she struggled to take the breath she needed, and then fall again as though the effort had used all the strength the breath had given her.

It was some while before she opened her eyes. Her face was contorted with pain when she did so, and she took a while to focus. "William?" she said, as though having difficulty believing what she saw.

William wondered if the drugs were causing her to hallucinate at other times. He smiled and reached for her fragile hand. "Yes, Ma, it's me."

"My son." Her eyes closed again and she dozed for a while, until pain brought her back to her senses. William was still gently holding her hand and waiting.

"I'm glad you came." The struggle of putting a few words together had exhausted her and she lay back.

Pa moved around to rearrange the pillows and so he could see his wife's face. "You can have more laudanum soon, my love," he said, in barely more than a whisper.

The next two days passed in something of a blur for William. He and Pa took turns to sit by Ma's bed. He took on giving her the medication when required, but Pa did most of the care for his wife. Each day Ma was a little more distant, and the intervals between her being in pain grew shorter. Her appetite was almost nothing, beyond the drops of water they could get her to take, and she seemed to be disappearing before their eyes.

When the doctor came on the morning of the third day he was grave when he spoke to Pa and William. "I've increased the doses of laudanum for Mrs Dixon. That should help with the pain. I'll call in again this afternoon. However, I'd be surprised if she takes many more doses. I think it's her time. That will at least relieve her suffering, though I doubt it will help with yours. I'm sorry, George." He clapped Pa on the shoulder and quietly withdrew.

Pa and William didn't speak. Without need of explanation they went and sat in the room with Ma. This time it was Pa who took her hand and William who sat slightly to the side.

They both sat in silence, watching.

William didn't know the exact moment Ma had left them. One moment, her chest rose a little, and the next, the movement had stopped. He looked across at Pa and, from the tears tracking down his cheeks, knew his father had seen the same. The silence between them continued, but while it had been watchful, now it was leaden.

Neither of them moved until William heard the bell and went out to greet the doctor.

"Ma passed about an hour ago. Pa's still with her. I don't think he knows quite what to do."

The doctor nodded and patted William's shoulder. "I'm sorry, William. I'll go up to him."

"Thank you, sir." William turned and went through to the sitting room to find a table where he could sit and write to Cecilia.

CHAPTER 12

April 21st 1870
Dowagiac, Michigan

My dearest Cecilia,

It is with a heavy heart I must write to you on the death of my mother. I am only happy that I was able to be with her at the end, which was her dying wish.

My father is more lost than I would have thought possible, although on reflection, now I have you, I know the same depth of love and would feel much as he does.

Cecilia could read no further through her tears. She wished she could be there to support William, but was glad he could at least be there for his father. The clock indicated she should be setting off for the office, but her feet felt heavy with the weight of grief, as much on William's behalf as her own.

She folded the letter carefully and resolved to read the rest of it in a quiet moment, once she'd opened Dixon's Attorneys. She was sad Thomas was still too young to have known his grandmother, and for a moment felt a pang for her own parents, who she'd not seen for a while.

By the time she'd taken Thomas to Miss Ellie and arrived back in Pierceton, there were matters demanding her immediate attention. The diary said she was expecting a Mr Edwin Steinmann in the office at ten o'clock, but made no reference to what the matter related to. Cecilia went through to William's office and looked first through the pile of papers on the desk, but could find nothing of relevance there. She went through the legal files housed in the drawer to the left of the desk which held William's current matters. When she found nothing, she started to feel a little concern. It was proving hard enough to get some of their clients to accept a woman working on their papers, without her having to admit she'd no knowledge of what they wished to consult upon.

The clock stood at a quarter to the hour. Cecilia took a few calming breaths. Why would there be an appointment which William had left no notes about? Perhaps he didn't know the nature of the call. If it was an initial meeting then quite possibly there was no file yet. Cecilia convinced herself that was the case and began to tidy the office ready to receive Mr Steinmann. She was lifting an old newspaper off the armchair when underneath it a file came to light, bearing the name Steinmann. Cecilia cursed herself for not having looked there previously. However, no sooner had she picked up the file than the bell rang and she needed to go out to greet the visitor. She laid the file open on the table, trying to make it look as though she'd been acquainting herself with the matter, and went through to the outer office.

The first thing Cecilia noticed was that Edwin Steinmann had an extremely bulbous nose. For some reason, probably linked to the relief of finding the file, she really wanted to laugh. She gritted her teeth to stop herself as she approached him. "Mr Steinmann, how good of you to come in." She stretched out her hand to shake his.

"Well, thank you, young lady." He handed her his hat and umbrella rather than taking her hand in return. "Shall I go straight through to Mr Dixon's office?" he asked, showing signs of impatience.

"Let me show you through," Cecilia said, now gritting her teeth for different reasons. She hung the hat and umbrella on the stand as she passed it. "Shall I take your coat?"

Mr Steinmann seemed more reluctant to remove his coat and Cecilia could only presume he didn't plan to stay long. She was certainly starting to hope that was the case.

She opened the door to show him through and indicated the chair on the opposite side of the table to the open file. She then proceeded to take her own seat.

"Now, Mr Steinmann, I'm afraid Mr Dixon has been called away on an urgent personal matter —"

Before she was able to continue her sentence, the visitor cut in. "Why didn't you say so at the door and save me the trouble of removing my hat?"

There was steel in Cecilia's voice as she replied, "Mr Steinmann, please sit down and allow me to continue."

As though responding to a parental instruction, Mr Steinmann sat meekly back at the table.

"In his absence, I am managing Mr Dixon's files. I am his wife and I too am a trained lawyer. Your affairs are perfectly safe in my hands." As she spoke, Cecilia was trying to scan the document in front of her to get the gist of what they would be talking about, if Mr Steinmann managed to cut his bluster and continue the meeting.

"But you're…"

"A woman, Mr Steinmann."

He looked shocked at her bluntness.

"Yes, I most certainly am. Mrs Cecilia Dixon." She stuck her hand out once again for him to shake, and this time, after some hesitation, he took it. Cecilia smiled; the first hurdle was out of the way.

"But this state doesn't recognise women attorneys. You can't…"

"Sign the final papers," Cecilia said, finishing his sentence. "How right you are, Mr Steinmann. Mr Dixon will need to be the final signatory. Now," she said, glancing back to the notes and scanning the words as fast as she was able, "I believe you were consulting my husband in the matter of a business you have offered to purchase."

Edwin Steinmann spluttered, "Yes, that's correct."

Again Cecilia gave him no chance to divert from the detail of the meeting and, having had the chance to scan further, she added, "I'm pleased to say the present owner's attorney has accepted your offer on his client's behalf and I am now in a position to draw up the necessary papers for your purchase of the hotel. Shall I send word to you, as soon as they are ready for you to come in to sign? I believe you already have a loan agreed through the bank in Warsaw, so the matter should be able to progress quite speedily."

Edwin Steinmann's mouth was opening and closing, but no words were ushered forth.

"Will there be anything further, Mr Steinmann? As you can appreciate, I'm very busy and, if we have concluded all you came in for, I will get on with the paperwork." Cecilia was itching to smile, having turned the impatience back on the man.

In a moment he recovered himself, thanked her for her time, took his hat and umbrella from the stand and, shaking his head as though in disbelief of what had taken place, made his way toward the door.

As the bell rang, signalling his exit, Cecilia gave in to a smile and set about making some notes on the file.

According to the diary, she had two hours before her next appointment, so she took the opportunity to take out William's letter once again. She was reading the details of the funeral, which would take place the following day, after which William hoped, his father's own health permitting, he would be able to return to Pierceton. The bell rang, indicating a new arrival.

Given that she was struggling with her composure on reading the letter, Cecilia was relieved to find Dr Pritchard standing in the office.

"How are you, my dear?"

She got up quickly and folded the letter. Then, realising it might be better for Dr Pritchard to read it himself by way of explanation, she handed it to him. "From William today," was all she could say.

Dr Pritchard put his coat and bag down and sat in the visitor chair in the outer office to read the letter.

Cecilia, suddenly coming back to what was happening said, "I'm sorry, won't you come through to somewhere more comfortable?"

He smiled at her. "I'm fine here, don't you worry." Then he continued to read.

He didn't look up until he'd finished the letter.

"A difficult time indeed. Our sincere condolences, my dear." He bowed his head to her and was silent for a moment.

"Thank you. It seems strange to be trying to continue as normal, but I must. There's nothing else I can do to help." Cecilia sighed.

"And how well are the community of Pierceton coping with a woman attorney?" He had a twinkle in his eye as he asked.

Cecilia laughed and enjoyed the release it gave. "I'm

handling it exactly as we discussed and it's going rather better than we feared." She recounted the reaction of Mr Steinmann earlier that day, and Dr Pritchard was happy to join in the laughter.

"I do know the man, although he's not a patient of mine. If you've impressed Steinmann, I imagine a fair few people will hear about it and it won't do you any harm at all. Now," he said, picking up his outer things, "I've visits to make, but I'll drop by tomorrow and check all is well."

"Thank you," Cecilia said, showing him toward the door and wishing he could stay longer. Today of all days, she felt she needed moral support.

Before she made a start on the work for Mr Steinmann's business purchase, she set about writing a reply to William. Drafting the legal documents would seem easy in comparison.

The next visitor to the office was considerably more straightforward than the first, given it was one of Cecilia's own clients. Mrs Jackson wanted Cecilia to draw up a will for her — a relatively standard matter, were it not for the fact she was cutting her eldest son out of her estate entirely. "If he's not going to visit his old mama from one year's end to the next, I'd sure rather leave my money to those who keep me company once in a while," had been her words of explanation.

Of course, Cecilia never expected to ask a client's reasons. She was simply there to ensure their wishes would be carried out, however strange, or, as in this case, reasonable, they seemed to be.

The day was generally going well, until an older gentleman came in mid-afternoon without an appointment. "I needs me an attorney and I needs one now."

Cecilia got up from her desk to welcome the man to Dixon's Attorneys. "I can certainly take a break from what I'm doing for half an hour. Now, how I can be of assistance, Mr…?"

"Taylor Irving," he replied automatically. Then, as though what she'd said had just registered with him, "You say 'you' can see me now? But you're a woman. I can't discuss my private affairs with no filly. Where's there a man I can talk to?"

Cecilia took a deep breath. Much as she was tempted to make a clever retort, it would help neither herself nor their law practice, let alone William's chances of being elected to Congress. "I'm sorry you feel that way, sir, but I'm fully trained and perfectly capable of undertaking your business."

Taylor Irving let out a loud guffaw. "Well, I've heard it all. Where's Dixon? I presume there is a Mr Dixon, being Dixon's Attorneys an' all."

"Mr William Dixon is out of town for a few days. He'll be back sometime next week. I'm Mrs Cecilia Dixon."

"Then it's a good job there are other attorneys in town. Good day, ma'am."

"I'm sincerely sorry you feel that way, Mr Irving. Good day to you."

Once Taylor Irving had left the premises, Cecilia slumped down in the reception chair, brought her balled fists down on the desk and let out a scream of frustration.

The scream must have been rather louder than she intended. A small, lean, bespectacled man who was passing the street door stopped, turned about and entered.

"Are you all right, ma'am?" He was wringing his hands as he asked.

Cecilia looked up in embarrassment and smiled. "Oh,

I'm sorry, yes, I'm fine. It was just that some people simply won't take a woman seriously. I don't know you, do I?"

The man, whose suit hung as though it belonged to a man two sizes larger, blinked repeatedly. "No, I don't believe you do." He held out his hand to shake hers. "Frederick Carter. I'm the accounts clerk at the sawmill." He blinked several more times.

"Cecilia Dixon," she replied. "It's a pleasure to meet you."

"If you were talking about Mr Taylor Irving, ma'am, it's not just women he doesn't like. It's pretty much everyone. From what I hear, yours is not the first attorney's office he's walked out of and I doubt it'll be the last. He's not local and can't understand why no one around these parts has heard of him. I don't rightly know why they should have done, but I guess some people are like that. Made his money down in California and thinks everyone should know it. If you ask me, you're probably better off without him. There, I've probably said too much. I just wanted to be sure you were all right." He made to turn around and leave.

"It was indeed kind of you to drop by, Mr Carter. You've made me feel much better. Thank you."

He scurried out of the door almost as quickly as he'd come in and for a moment, Cecilia wondered if he'd been there at all.

She began to tidy the office ready for the end of the day. She might have time in the evening to write a longer letter to William. Perhaps, if she were to recount the stories of what had happened, they might give William a little light relief.

CHAPTER 13

William sat at the breakfast table, his head in his hands. He had no appetite for food. The last few days had passed in a whirl of arrangements for his mother's funeral. There had been so many people coming to the house to pay their condolences, he'd barely had five minutes to himself. His father, stricken with grief, had taken to his bed, leaving William to manage the house and those calling.

William had written a eulogy to give the following day, but wished he could rehearse it with either his father or Cecilia. He thought he'd covered all that needed to be said about the wonderful woman Margaret Dixon had been, but would have been happier to be given reassurance.

A knock at the breakfast room door brought him to his senses. Briggs was there, as he had been so often over the preceding days.

"What is it, Briggs? Please tell me it's not another caller at this hour." William glanced at the clock, which said twenty minutes past the hour of eight.

"No, sir, but if you've finished eating, I thought you might like to come and see something."

William sighed. He'd made his peace with Briggs for the awful way he'd treated the man when William was a child. He'd caused him to both lose his job and be sent to fight in the Civil War. He'd been grateful to find his father had not only continued to pay Briggs throughout that time, but had brought him back into the household once

William moved away. His father was wiser and more patient than any man William had met, and he hated to see him laid so low by the loss of Ma.

William rose, laid his unused napkin on the table and followed Briggs out of the room.

Briggs led him out through the side door of the house and around to the stables. William frowned, looking down at his suit trousers and polished shoes, but resolved that any cleaning could be dealt with later.

"Here, sir." Briggs had stopped before a stall in which a beautiful chestnut mare was happily eating from a net of hay.

She looked up as they approached, her brown eyes showing a depth that jolted William's heart. He looked enquiringly to Briggs.

"She's Bounty's girl."

William's smile could not have been wider as he went forward to stroke the mare's flank. "And what of Bounty? Is she still alive?"

"She is indeed, sir, though she's retired now and put out to pasture. I thought, sir, it might do you good to get out for a ride. She's a good horse and knows the routes around here."

Without mentioning the incident when William had brought Bounty back lame, William knew Briggs was gently reminding him where not to take her, and felt he deserved no less.

"I've brought no suitable clothing with me, Briggs, otherwise you're right. That is most likely exactly what I need."

"Everything is laid out for you in your room, sir. I'll saddle her ready for when you come down." Without further word, Briggs opened the door to the mare's stall and began to prepare her for riding.

"Just one thing before I get ready, Briggs, other than of course to thank you for all you've done — what's her name?"

"Brandy, sir." Briggs continued to work as he answered.

"Well, Brandy," William said, gently stroking the girl's nose. "I'm really very pleased to meet you, very pleased indeed. Which field is her mother in? May I see her too, while I'm here?"

Briggs smiled. "I'll bring her down to the stables for when you get back, sir."

William's step was by far the lighter as he crossed the yard back to the house. He looked up and saw his father at the window of the bedroom. He waved, but there was no response and William wondered if Pa had even seen his son.

Once William was changed and ready to go, he led Brandy out of the stables and through the yard. "Your mum and I were great friends when I was young. She taught me how wonderful it was to ride a gallop across open land. What do you say that you help me blow away some of the pain of the last few days?"

He kissed Brandy's neck before mounting. When they were both ready, they trotted out toward the ridge. Though he rode regularly, these days it was mainly of necessity rather than pleasure and being somewhat older he had learned just a little sense. They took things at a steady pace until they were both warmed up. Then he encouraged Brandy to lengthen her stride and rode along the ridge, enjoying the sense of freedom it had always given him. Ma had been there to greet him back that first time he'd ridden Bounty, and he was only sad she wouldn't be there on his return this time. Perhaps she was there, though, in the wind which blew gently as they galloped, and in the trees which graced the far end of the ridge. He pulled Brandy back to a trot and finally stopped, looking out across the land.

"Thank you, Ma," he called to the breeze, "wherever you are, for taking in this poor waif and making me your own. Thank you."

It was hard to work out which were tears and which was sweat running down his face as he returned at a steady pace to the house. Brandy knew her way and carried him safely, despite the fact he could see little of the path through his stinging eyes. He was glad of the towel Briggs had left for him at the stable when he returned. Unlike in his childhood however, he didn't simply leave Brandy for Briggs to tend to while he went into the house. This time, he lovingly washed her down, putting her comfort before his own. Once she was settled with hay and water and he'd spent some time with Bounty, he went in to find fresh clothes. Now, he felt ready to eat breakfast.

He was surprised when he went back into the breakfast room that not only did he have no need to ring the bell, but Pa was there, washed and dressed himself.

"How good to see you, sir." William didn't presume to take what would have been Ma's place at the table, but sat the other side, even though he could not then see out of the window.

Though he was still very pale and looked to have lost an amount of weight, Pa's voice was nevertheless strong when he spoke. "Did you enjoy your ride, William?"

"I did indeed, sir. If anything, Brandy is a yet finer horse than Bounty."

His father nodded. "Yes, I think you're right." He

paused and looked out onto the garden. "Watching you going out with her somehow reminded me life must go on. Ma would have loved to watch you riding out on the next generation and so I want to be there to watch the next generation of our family and see your Thomas growing up. I'd rather Ma was here to see it too, but she wouldn't want me to give up."

William went to speak, but Pa raised a hand to indicate he wasn't finished.

"It will take me a long time to come to terms with what's happened, but I need to take the first steps, and taking to my bed won't do that."

William nodded. He was unsure what to say in return, but was saved the trouble by cook coming in with some fresh warm pancakes. William breathed deep, savouring the smell as his stomach growled its welcome. "Thank you," he said, and promptly fell upon eating them, enjoying their flavours as though he had not eaten for days.

As William went about the final preparations for his mother's funeral the following day, he didn't see anything further of his father. Pa disappeared off to his study after breakfast and remained in there for much of the rest of the day. William could only hope the decisions he had made would meet with his father's approval.

The day of the funeral was overcast. It seemed appropriate. William's mother had died too young and he was in no mood to treat this as any sort of celebration. As he prepared himself for the day, in his black suit and waistcoat, he once again wished Cecilia could be there to give him support, but with a couple of days' travelling each way, it had been impossible to arrange.

He rode to the church in a carriage with his father, who

was showing less of the determination that had come to the fore the previous day. Leaving Pa here when he returned to Pierceton would be hard.

When they arrived at the church, it was already filled with mourners. Many were women his mother had known through her work with the women's movement, but some were there in support of his father and for that William was grateful. He couldn't take in all the faces. There were many he didn't know.

Although his eulogy was more important to him than any political speech he might give, strangely, William didn't feel nervous. Instead he felt peace. He thought of his mother's strong but gentle nature, and as he spoke he followed her example. He reached the end of his piece and looked around the congregation before returning to his place, he felt a jolt as he noticed Jeanie Makepeace, the congressman's daughter, sitting right at the back of the church. He'd not seen Jeanie since she broke off their engagement, when William's early life on the New York streets had become known. He hoped he might talk to her after the service. He bore her no ill feeling. He was so happy married to Cecilia that Congressman Makepeace's prejudice had turned out to be a blessing.

When he returned to his seat, Pa rested his hand on his son's arm and squeezed it slightly. William didn't need words to know his father was telling him he'd done a good job.

When William finally made his way to the back of the church, Jeanie was nowhere to be seen. He was disappointed, but perhaps it was for the best. He was caught up in a whirl of people offering sympathy and telling him how much his mother had meant to them. He thanked each one in turn and tried to find his father amongst the throng.

He wrote to Cecilia again that afternoon.

My darling Cecilia,

Today went as well as I could have hoped. It is fair to say, these events have taken their toll on Pa and he is struggling. I have asked him to come back with me to stay with us a while. I felt sure you would not mind my doing so. However, he is insistent he must stay here and attend to Dixon's Attorneys in Dowagiac, and will not be persuaded otherwise. Perhaps he is right.

I do not feel I should leave him for at least a day or two, but plan to take a train, to begin my journey back to you, early next week...

Once William had finished writing, he was left unsure what to do with his time. He'd seen nothing of his father after the funeral, so he took up his coat and hat and decided to walk into town to the Post Office. Did his childhood friend Jude McCaulay's family still live in the same house? He resolved to detour on his walk to find out.

When he arrived at what had once been the McCaulay homestead, he was surprised to find the march of progress had razed it to the ground and in its place a new road had been built, with buildings either side. He shook his head in wonder and walked slowly along the road, looking at the clapboard structures, each neatly laid out.

The Post Office would likely as not know where the family had gone, and he would ask when he went in.

Before William got as far as the Post Office, he was surprised to see lights on in his father's offices. He went up and tried the main street door and found it open. Raising an eyebrow, he went inside. There was no one in the outer office, but the door to his father's room was ajar and light spilled out from within. William went and tapped gently, before pushing the door a little wider and seeing his father at his desk, deep in concentration.

He coughed and his father looked up suddenly.

"I'm sorry, Pa, I didn't mean to startle you. I wasn't expecting to find you working today."

His father waved him in distractedly. "Si' d'n," he slurred.

It was then that William noticed the bottle and glass. He took a deep breath. He brought a chair around in front of his father and sat facing him.

"Th'rs w'k I…" His father gesticulated in the general direction of his desk.

William sighed. Having a logical conversation with a drunken man was never easy, but William knew he had to try. He moved the bottle out of his father's reach and took the half empty glass away.

"Firstly, your work is built on your reputation, and there is nothing in that which will be improved by alcohol."

His father's elbow slipped off the desk and he hiccupped before resuming his position.

"Secondly, you are the father I look up to. My father by birth was a drunken idiot. He left Mammy with Molly and me and went off, supposedly to work the railways. That was the last we saw of him, which was probably for the best. Drunken men are never the best of company for those around them, and whatever ill has driven them to it, they cause the more trouble for those whom their behaviour affects." For a moment, William felt as though he were the parent and wondered if any of what he was saying was having an effect. "I will not stand by and watch you go the same way my good for nothing da went. I'm taking you home."

He looked around for his father's coat and found it on the floor. He had no idea if, when his father sobered up, he would remember any of this conversation or whether he would need to have it all over again, but he did know that he cared too much about Pa not to try.

Once he'd got his father into his coat, he took him into the outer office and found another chair. "Now I want you to wait here while I go to the Post Office."

His father's chin had already fallen to his chest and he was clearly asleep. William wasn't prepared to take any risks, so he went back for the bottle and glass and tipped their contents away, before taking the letter he'd written to Cecilia, for posting. Now all he needed to do was work out how to get his father home.

CHAPTER 14

"Well, indeed!" Dr Pritchard handed the latest letter back to Cecilia. "What that man needs is a purpose. Would you allow me to write to him?"

Cecilia was a little surprised, but only because he asked permission before doing so. "Why, of course, we'd be grateful for any help. I fear William will either wish to stay longer or return almost immediately, unless help is found for his dear pa."

Dr Pritchard nodded. "There's something you might find it helpful to know, my dear. Dorothea is not my first wife." He waved away her surprise. "I was young." He looked away into some imagined distance as he spoke. "My first wife died long before her time. Influenza. I was barely more than the age you are now, when I found myself a widower. I nearly gave up on everything, but Dorothea, who had known me since childhood, believed in me and had her reasons for thinking me a good doctor. Not being able to save Alexandra had shaken my confidence, you see. Anyway, let's just say that Dorothea gave me a reason to carry on. I think William's father needs a purpose."

"I can't see him marrying again." Cecilia was frowning.

Dr Pritchard laughed heartily. "Oh, I'm not thinking he would be looking for another wife, but I do think I might have an idea that would make him feel of use."

Cecilia noticed the wonderful twinkle in Dr Pritchard's

eyes and was disappointed he didn't elaborate. Instead he picked up his dispensing bag and almost skipped back out into the street. Cecilia smiled and shook her head. At times like this, he did rather remind her of her own father.

The contracts needed one final check, ready for Edwin Steinmann to sign later that afternoon, but before she got back to them, Cecilia was expecting another new client to come to the office. Mrs Woodrow had asked for an appointment and was due in twenty minutes. Cecilia decided to use the time while she was waiting to write back to William, but chose to make no reference to Dr Pritchard's plan. After all, she didn't know what it would entail.

She was still writing when Mrs Woodrow came in. She put the pen aside immediately and went out to greet her.

"How lovely to see you, Mrs Woodrow."

"Oh, do call me Edith, please." Edith Woodrow shook Cecilia's hand warmly and began to remove her hat and coat. "I do hope you've got a warm drink, or should we go over to the Flat Iron Hotel?" She gave Cecilia a conspiratorial wink and stopped removing her hat, but instead replaced the pin. "Come, my dear, we can equally well discuss my business there, and I shall pay for your time just the same. I'll even buy the tea."

Cecilia was smiling broadly. She got the impression she might like working for Edith Woodrow. She took up her own coat, locked the office and followed Mrs Woodrow across the road to the hotel.

Edith Woodrow was a well-built woman, who Cecilia thought must be at least seventy years of age. She'd seen Edith at the women's meetings, but knew little about her except for two things. Edith's husband had left her well provided for, and their only child had moved out west when she married. Since she left, Edith had heard no more of her daughter and both the girl and her husband were feared to have died.

As they arrived at the hotel, and once again Edith began removing her outdoor garments, Cecilia found herself distracted by the sheer length and colouring on the plumes which adorned the older lady's flamboyant hat. The woman's coat was a similar burgundy to one of the feathers and Cecilia thought she might like to wear such bold colours, instead of the more modest ones she normally chose.

"Now, you probably wonder what all this is about," Edith said, once their drinks had been poured and the waiter had moved away from the table. "As you'll be aware, I have a very comfortable living and no descendants to worry about now, as far as I'm aware. I've been thinking about this for some time and I'd like to set up a scholarship fund to support girls from Pierceton who wish to go on to university." She took a large sip from her china cup, then placed it back carefully on the saucer.

Cecilia nodded but had the impression there was more Edith wanted to say, so she waited.

"I did think about working with one or other of the universities to sponsor a place with their institution." She paused, taking a biscuit from a plate that had been placed between them. "It's just that I want it to be specifically for girls from this town and I don't want to limit what they should study or where they should be. Do you see what I mean?"

Realising it was her turn to speak now, Cecilia nodded. "I do indeed see. And you'd like me to draw up the necessary documents?"

"Rather more than that, my dear. I would like you to be

a trustee and administer the scheme. I'm talking about a large sum of money and I don't doubt there could be quite a bit of work involved in its governance. I'm presuming it will need more than one trustee and I had wondered about asking Ellie Cochrane if it was something she would be prepared to assist with."

Cecilia smiled broadly. "It would be my pleasure to work with such a trust fund, Edith. And I would be only too happy to work with Miss Ellie, if she were agreeable."

"Well, that's settled then. Now, why don't you tell me a little more about your husband's political ambitions? I've been talking to Dorothea Pritchard and I'd like to see if there is any way I can help there, too."

Later that day, when Cecilia had the chance to finish the letter to William, she was delighted to be able to fill it with so much positive news. Not only was Edith looking to have her establish the trust fund, but she wanted to provide William with financial support for his campaign. Finally, she set about recounting the visit to the office by Edwin Steinmann, and felt proud as she relayed how happy he now was with their services.

More than anything, Cecilia hoped that somewhere amongst the good news there might be something to cheer William and to help him bring his father out of the malaise into which he'd sunk.

Finally, Cecilia locked the office and set off to the farm to collect Thomas from Miss Ellie.

"Well, aren't I honoured?" Miss Ellie smiled broadly at Cecilia as she went into the farmhouse.

"And why would that be?" Cecilia asked innocently, after kissing her son.

"I had a visit from Edith today and I must say she could not have chosen a better person to set the trust up for her.

It will be my pleasure to work with you on it, although I dare say you won't need a great deal of input from me."

"Did she tell you she plans to assist William in his campaign as well? I can't wait to tell Dr Pritchard." Cecilia picked up Thomas, ready to take him out to the trap for their journey home.

"Something tells me you may find Charles already knows." Miss Ellie raised an eyebrow, making Cecilia think Miss Ellie might herself know more than she was letting on.

William's next letter brought the news Cecilia had been longing for. As it was now Saturday, she was able to sit down to read it as soon as it arrived.

... I will be on the train arriving into Pierceton on Thursday 5th and cannot wait to see you both. I know I had said I would be back a little sooner, but I did not feel it was wise to leave my father. However, I cannot see what good I do by staying. Briggs has assured me he will keep an eye on Pa and will contact me if he thinks my being back here again will help...

She took Thomas out into the garden to the little swing. The blossom was out on the old apple tree, one branch of which was adorned with ropes hanging down to a little plank seat. Thomas was still too young to sit alone on the seat safely, and Cecilia sat with him on her lap, gently moving forward and back in the sunshine.

"It really is time we had a little brother or sister for you to grow up with as a playmate." Cecilia sighed as they continued the motion of the swing. It was hard, watching Molly pregnant again, when she longed to have another child of her own. She knew the others thought it was as much hers and William's choice as nature's way, with the law practice being so important, but they'd been trying to increase the size of their family for a while, without success. Thomas would be two years old in September and, despite being an only child herself, she'd imagined having a large family, all fairly close in age. She tried to tell herself it was best this way, but her heart said otherwise.

She was still rocking gently, although she could tell Thomas had fallen asleep in her arms, when she heard men's voices close by. She held Thomas tightly and stopped swinging, straining her ears to hear.

These were not the voices of her usual visitors, but rough voices she didn't recognise. Their housekeeper had the day off and there was no one else around. She suddenly felt quite vulnerable. She tried to make out the words.

Cecilia heard the sound of glass breaking and gasped, drawing Thomas closer to her. Her breathing was heavy as she waited for what was going to happen next. She wanted to confront the intruders, but she was frozen to the swing, straining to listen but hearing nothing further. The silence was almost more eerie than the sound of voices had been. She'd no idea if the men had gone or were now somewhere inside the Red House, having gained admission.

A thought played through Cecilia's head, and at another time she might have laughed aloud. It never occurred to her to lock the door. If they'd broken a window to gain entrance they could have saved themselves the trouble. Her thoughts moved on rapidly, to what she should do next.

Where was Cady? Why hadn't she barked? Cecilia's eyes began to dart around in search of the little dog. There was no sign of her.

She took deep breaths and tried to regain control of her legs. She needed to get help from somewhere and, though it was further than going to a neighbouring property, she knew she'd find more support at Cochrane's Farm. Shakily, she began to stumble across the field, still carrying Thomas.

When she eventually reached the cabins, tired and out of breath, James was tending his little patch of garden in front of his porch. He took one look at Cecilia and came rushing over to her with a stool.

"Here, let me." James reached and took Thomas from her arms. He put the boy onto his hip and held him with his right arm, then used his left hand to offer support to Cecilia as she, still shaking, collapsed onto the seat.

"Now, what's caused this?" he asked. "Should I go up to the house and get Molly for you?"

Cecilia simply nodded.

The next thing she knew, Miss Ellie was beside her.

"Here, drink this." Miss Ellie held out a small glass of brown liquid.

Cecilia recognised the smell of the whiskey, but drank it down without argument. She looked up at Miss Ellie. "Thank you."

"I'll make tea in case that's a better reviver, but in my experience something stronger is usually the best starting point. Now, child, what's happened to cause this?"

Cecilia shook herself. "I heard men's voices, followed by breaking glass, when I was outside with Thomas. I don't know who it was or whether they're still there, but I couldn't go to find out on my own."

She'd barely finished speaking when Miss Ellie replied, "You can forget the hot drink. You just wait there, my girl. I'll be back in two minutes. I'd be prepared to gamble on who's behind this." She marched back across to her own cabin, and before James had so much as reappeared, Miss Ellie was heading back, loading her shotgun as she walked.

Cecilia gasped.

"We'll have none of that, my girl, now come with me. Maybe we'll deal with those Reese boys once and for all."

"Ellie, wait up." James was puffing as he came back from the house with both Molly and Daniel behind him. "If anyone's going after those boys it'll be me and not you."

"Don't you think I'll do them enough damage, cousin?"

"I fear you might shoot all too straight and fill them with shot. I'll not see you hanged ahead of them."

"They won't get anything more than they deserve. Leave the boy there and come with me, then. But you'll have to hurry if you're going to stop me being the one who fires first."

James passed Thomas back to Cecilia, who sat dumbstruck at the behaviour of these two people she thought she knew so well. James was just going into his cabin when Molly caught up and saw Miss Ellie.

"Oh, sweet Jesus, no." She turned back to Daniel. "What should we do?"

James came back out of the cabin with his own gun. "None of you be a-worrying. You all stay back here. I've kept that girl out of trouble so far, all these years, and I'm not about to stop now." He hurried after his cousin, who was still striding across the field.

119

CHAPTER 15

"Am I ever happy to see you?" Cecilia threw her arms around William, the moment he stepped down onto the platform.

"And I you, my darling, but why the look of concern on your part? Your letters gave no hint you were missing me quite that much." He held his wife's hands and looked closely into her face. "I'm guessing something's happened since your last letter, which has left you anxious. Is Thomas quite all right?"

Cecilia nodded. "Yes, he's fine, but there really is a lot to tell. I think it best we go to the farm and then everyone can tell it together. How was the journey and how is your father?"

William held tight to Cecilia's hand as they walked out of the station to the waiting carriage. The porter brought his bags and William thanked him before climbing up to join his wife. "Do we need to go home first, or should we go straight to the farm to collect Thomas?"

"Oh, we most definitely need to go to the farm first." Cecilia grimaced and William really began to wonder what had gone on.

It was a surprising mix of people ready to greet them at the farmhouse. Unusually, there was no sign of Miss Ellie, although Mrs Hawksworth, Molly and Daniel were all there, together with the children and the dogs.

Having first greeted his son, William turned to the

others, who were all looking grave. Then he noticed Cady was limping and bent down to pet the little dog. "I can wait no longer; will someone tell me what's going on?" He turned to his sister, who nodded slowly.

"You'd best sit down. I've prepared lunch so you'll have food inside you before you go down to the courthouse."

"Courthouse? But..." He looked around the room at each of them. "Miss Ellie? Again?"

Molly nodded. "Cecilia hasn't told you any of it yet, then? I think we should let her tell the story, but both Miss Ellie and James will be needing your assistance as soon as you've eaten."

William slumped into a chair, though he didn't feel at all hungry anymore. Cecilia sat next to him and took his hand as she began the story.

"At least you've seen that both Thomas and I are all right, and even Cady is recovering from her ordeal, so please don't let that red hair of yours dictate your reaction. If it does, it will be you in the cells, alongside Miss Ellie and James."

William ran his hand through his hair. He could feel his tension level increasing and the instinct to fight rising to the surface. He tried to stay calm but wanted to get up and pace the room to allow at least some vent for the feeling.

Molly intervened, speaking to him sternly. "Brother of mine, Miss Ellie and James are depending on you, so don't you go losing that temper of yours. We need you to be the best lawyer you can be now, and not the street urchin you once were."

William nodded and held his hands up in supplication. "All right, but please tell me exactly what's happened, or I can't do anything, never mind be an effective lawyer. If

James is involved, this isn't about a women's rights demonstration."

Cecilia told the story up to the point of her seeking help at the farm, then Daniel took over, as he'd been the one to follow Miss Ellie and James back to the Red House.

"I was the only one who didn't have a gun," he said ruefully. "I did pick up a shovel, so I wasn't empty handed. I started checking the area around the house, but Miss Ellie went marching straight in and James was close behind her. It was only a couple of minutes, I'd guess, before I heard the shot fired."

William nodded. He was starting to get the picture and was about to ask questions when Molly took over.

"So here are the things you probably want to know. Both of the Reese boys are still alive. The first shot…"

"First! You mean Miss Ellie fired more than once?" William was incredulous.

"Er, no," Daniel said, "the second seems to have been fired by James."

William nodded again but remained quiet.

"As I was saying, the first shot struck Jacob Reese's hip, side on. I'm not sure where Miss Ellie was aiming — she's an excellent shot so I don't suppose she was far from her target. Then apparently James shouted, 'This one's for Ben,' and promptly shot Reuben Reese in his right shoulder. Thankfully most of the pellets missed him. James said he wanted to stop the man drinking rather than kill him." Molly paused at that point, looking intently at her brother.

"What were they actually doing in our house and what happened to Cady?" William's tension had eased a little and he reached for some bread and cheese.

"As you might have guessed, those boys had been

drinking again. They've not done a great deal of damage to the house, but they were in our dining room, drinking what there was of the bourbon on the sideboard." Cecilia also seemed to have relaxed a little now the story had largely been told.

William leaned over and kissed her. "And Cady?"

Cecilia's face clouded again. "We don't exactly know. We think she'd been kicked and then they'd tied her up with some wire they found in the yard. Daniel heard her whimper and found her in an empty water barrel. She was shaking, but seems to be recovering well." Cady looked up at them with big soulful eyes. "I may have been spoiling her a little since it all happened. It turns out she rather likes sleeping on our bed."

William smiled broadly. Something else he was going to have to get used to. "And how much damage have they done to the Red House?"

"Well, of course there was the rock. That broke the window by the kitchen door. The door wasn't locked but they clearly hadn't tried it first." Cecilia sighed.

"I think you'll find that door sticks slightly. Maybe it didn't give immediately when they tried it, or am I being too generous?"

Cecilia nodded. "The latter, I suspect. Anyway, there's the window. They drank the bourbon and spilt some on the carpet. The main damage, though, is from the shot pellets, which are now lodged in the sideboard. I think that's everything. The Reese brothers' wounds weren't deep and the doctor cleaned them up pretty well."

"Well it sounds like Miss Ellie and James were quite rightly defending our property. They may have gone a little too far, but I doubt the sheriff would make any charges stick against them. What has he said?" William left his half-eaten bread and got up from the table. "I suppose I'd better get down there."

"He hasn't said much. I rather think he was using waiting for you coming back as an excuse to keep them both locked up for a day or two. He could have dealt with me, but he wouldn't hear of it. I suspect Miss Ellie would be furious if she knew, so perhaps we ought to keep that gun of hers locked up."

Cecilia looked so much happier now the story was told. She picked Thomas up and sat him on the chair his father had vacated.

"I'll leave the carriage here and walk to town. It will give me time to think." William kissed Cecilia, waved to the others and set off to find the sheriff. In truth, it felt good to be back working after his time away in Dowagiac, although he'd rather have been dealing with someone else's case than bailing out Miss Ellie and James.

"Hello again, Sheriff. I believe you've been waiting for me before releasing the dear persons who defended our property in my absence." William raised an eyebrow as he looked intently at the sheriff.

"Well now, sir, you know I have to gather all the evidence and see if there are charges to be brought."

"And are there?"

The sheriff sucked his teeth. "It seems there were no other witnesses than Jacob and Reuben Reese, and I'm kind of supposing they didn't have no one's permission to be on the premises. They say as they don't need no permission, seeing as it's rightly their house, so if you can produce the documents that prove it's now in your ownership, I think we can decide there'll be no charges brought."

"And if I want to bring a case against them for

trespass?"

"Well, now…" The sheriff sighed. "Most of the damage was caused by those there guns, and those boys didn't fire them, so I'm guessing you'll need to bring the case against James and Ellie Cochrane. You sure are welcome to do that, sir."

"Sheriff, you know I'm the rightful owner. Just release Miss Ellie and her cousin. You've made your point that those Reese boys can even pull your strings. Let these good people get out of here, now you've done the Reese family's bidding."

"Now, you look here, Mr Dixon, sir, I'm only doing my job same as any other. I held those Reese boys when they'd trespassed up at the farm and I'm holding —"

William wheeled around. "Trespass! You know damn well it was arson and near enough murder. They killed Ben, for God's sake, and burnt my sister's farm down. Now are you going to release them or do I need to go back and get Miss Ellie's gun and help them shoot their way out?"

The sheriff held up his hands. "I'm going, Mr Dixon, sir. I'm going."

William paced up and down the room, waiting for the sheriff to return with his friends.

When Miss Ellie walked in, her head held high, she looked a little dishevelled but none the worse for her ordeal. "Good day to you, Sheriff. I do have to say, your hospitality is not of the same standard as I received in Washington, but probably comparable with Dowagiac. You really do need to find someone to cook for you." Then, leaving the sheriff open mouthed and without a word of reply, she marched out into the street with James and William trailing behind.

By the time William got outside the building, Miss Ellie was already some distance up the road, on her way, he presumed, home. He shook his head. James had, at least, stayed a moment to shake his hand before following on behind his cousin. William stood and looked along the length of the road in both directions. The street was relatively quiet for a Thursday afternoon. Cecilia would be taking Thomas home and would not be coming back to town. He could go and join them, or go to the office for an hour or two first. He was still deliberating when Dr Pritchard's carriage came along and stopped beside him.

"If you've managed to spring those jailbirds, we've got a campaign to get started on. Jump up."

William grinned. "An excellent suggestion, sir. An excellent suggestion."

Dr Pritchard was heading back to his own home, and took William with him so they could talk before the doctor had to go out on his next house call.

"Now, I've taken the liberty to offer your name as speaker for a number of meetings around the area. We need to get you known as widely as possible. You're not going to get far if you stick within the boundaries of Pierceton. I know it's a while before you'll need to be winning your nomination, but we don't have any time to lose." Dr Pritchard pushed a sheet of paper across his desk to William. On it were listed a number of dates, times and places for him to speak in the coming weeks.

William took a deep breath and looked up at Dr Pritchard. "Do you really think I'm ready for this, sir?"

Dr Pritchard waved his question away. "You've no time to be having doubts. You need to be working on your speeches. You'll need a different one at each location, in case you find some of the same people attending. For the most part, the audiences will be different, but you can't take the risk. Keep the messages largely the same but tailor them for the people likely to be present. But more of that later."

William looked down the schedule. He was going to be very busy. "How on earth am I going to fit all these in and still keep my law practice going?"

"Don't worry about that now. I've got a few ideas. Cecilia has done an excellent job in your absence and I'm sure she's up to the challenge this little opportunity may present."

William nodded. His first appointment was the following week and he knew he'd need to get off on the right foot.

"Now…" Dr Pritchard tapped the rich mahogany desk with the end of his pen. "This is what I want you to do."

By the time they'd finished running through the length and nature of the speech William would be giving, as well as the type of people Dr Pritchard expected to be attending, the afternoon was drawing to a close.

Dr Pritchard drew his watch from his pocket. "Well now, where's the afternoon gone? I've got a patient with gout who's grumpy at the best of times. It will never do to keep him waiting. I could drop you at your home on the way, if that helps?"

"Indeed it would, thank you. Cecilia's going to be wondering where I've disappeared to."

"Get that young lady working on your speeches with you. She'll give you wise counsel, I'll be bound. Dorothea! Dorothea!" Dr Pritchard was shouting to his wife from the doorway to his office. "Ah, there you are. I'm off to sympathise with the old curmudgeon about his feet." Then, turning to William he said, "I can do little more than sympathise, if he won't do the things I tell him. Right, we're off." He picked up his dispensing bag and scurried out to the carriage, leaving William trailing in his wake.

CHAPTER 16

"Is Sarah around?" Molly asked in as light a tone as she could, when she'd finished with the deliveries to the general store.

"She's out." Joe's reply was curt and in contrast to his conversation when they had been dealing with business matters earlier.

"Could I trouble you to tell her I called and that Miss Ellie is now home and quite well?"

Joe snorted. "I'll thank you not to involve my wife in matters relating to that old witch."

"Joe!" The reprimand was from his mother, who was working quietly in the back of the shop. "That is no way to speak of Miss Cochrane."

"Mother, mind your tongue in front of customers and don't you be contradicting me. Good day, Mrs Flynn."

Molly was stunned by how Joe had spoken to his mother and by his sudden formality. He'd known her as 'Molly' since they were children. How could she contact Sarah without having to go through Joe and the store? She wondered if writing to her might be an option, but felt certain Joe would scrutinise any post that came for his wife.

"I will bid you both good day." Molly went out of the store, clenching her fists with anger and the injustice of the situation. Once she'd climbed aboard the cart, she sat for a few minutes, thinking over what had occurred before setting off. She was about to gee the horse along when she saw Sarah at the corner of the building, with her finger to her lips. Sarah pointed a few yards along the road and Molly immediately understood her intent and walked the horse slowly for a few paces until they were out of view of the store's windows. Then she stopped and waited.

Sarah climbed up beside her a few minutes later and Molly immediately set off.

"I found the key to the back door. If we can stop further along, we can talk and I can be back before they find I've gone." Sarah's eyes were darting around to make sure no one could see her.

"Sarah, be honest with me, how bad are things?" Molly wished she could look her friend in the eye as she answered, but she needed to keep her own eyes on the road ahead.

"I'm fine, really I am, and he does love me. It's just his way. All men are like that sometimes, aren't they?"

As Molly glanced across, she saw the jut of Sarah's jaw and realised she was trying to convince herself as much as anyone else. Being away from prying eyes, Molly pulled the cart to a halt. "Sarah, no, not all men are like that. Why don't you leave him?"

Sarah gasped. "I couldn't possibly. He needs me. He loves me. I love him. What about the children?" Sarah had begun shaking and Molly slipped an arm around her friend.

Knowing Sarah had to go back to the store, Molly didn't want to risk her being in such a state that her actions would be obvious. She adopted a matter-of-fact tone and changed the subject. "Miss Ellie and James have been released. There are no charges being brought against them. The Reese brothers will recover... unfortunately!"

"That's good, then," Sarah's voice was quiet and she picked at the sleeve of her drab brown dress. "I'd best be going. Give Miss Ellie my love." Then she glanced around them, climbed down from the cart and scurried back toward the store.

As Molly watched, Sarah stayed close to the buildings and then, looking over her shoulder, slipped around the side of the general store, presumably to let herself in at the back. Molly shook her head. How awful to have to live that way. She couldn't imagine what it must be like. She waited a little longer, almost expecting Sarah to reappear, and then turned back to encourage the horse toward home.

When she got to the farm, Molly threw her bonnet down onto a chair and marched over to the kitchen. She made a lot of noise bashing the kettle onto the stove and pulling a saucepan down from the shelf. "I cannot stand by and do nothing to help Sarah." She started to prepare dinner for them all, venting her anger on the vegetables that she was slicing. "No woman should be treated that way. Marriage doesn't give a man the right to do as he pleases."

"I regret to say, for the most part it does!" Miss Ellie took the knife out of Molly's hand and took over the chopping.

Molly went to get water to fill the pan, slopping it over onto the floor as she returned.

"You're right to be concerned, Molly." Liza Hawksworth sighed heavily. She fetched a cloth for the floor. "I haven't got a good feeling about what's going on in that house, from the time I've spent with Clara, Mrs Spencer. I don't think young Joe's behaviour is what you'd hope for Sarah — or toward his mother, for that matter."

"What do we do?" The pan made an almighty clang as

Molly put it over the heat.

Thomas began to wail. Molly's shoulders dropped. "Now look what I've done." Her anger dissipated as she saw the alarm she'd caused in the children. "I'm sorry, Thomas — was Aunt Molly making too much noise?" She picked him up and blew bubbles at him to make him laugh. She wished that other problems could be so easily fixed, and gave him a big hug, before putting him back down to play with Cady, who still showed signs of a slight limp when she walked, but was otherwise all right. For good measure she gave Mary a hug as well, and then went back to the kitchen where Mrs Hawksworth and Miss Ellie were still busily working.

"Now, where were we?" Molly took the knife back from Miss Ellie. "I'm perfectly safe again."

Before she had time to return to the subject of Sarah, William came into the kitchen.

"Ladies, sorry, I was looking for Cecilia. I went down to the cabin but James said you were all up here."

"Dada." Thomas waddled over to his father and William picked him up.

"We haven't seen Cecilia yet. I think she had a meeting to go to in town. She said something about drumming up support for your forthcoming speech." Miss Ellie wiped her hands on her apron and went over to him.

William groaned. "That was why I was looking for her. I wanted to rehearse my speech."

"William…" Miss Ellie's voice was serious. "I hear things when I go into town. Some of it's nonsense, but well, I have heard there might be some sort of a protest planned, so you should probably be prepared."

"That's all I need. Still, I suppose it will give the newspaper something to write about and I do want them to cover it. Thanks for the warning. Now then, little man, let's go and see if we can find your mother." He waved to them all as he took Thomas out into the yard.

"What type of protest?" Molly asked, stirring the stew.

"Well…" Miss Ellie gave a long pause. "They say the Klan are involved."

Molly stopped what she was doing and stared at Miss Ellie. "But I thought they only existed in the south of the country."

"It's hard to say. There are men without an original thought in their heads who will copy anything that takes their fancy."

Mrs Hawksworth nodded. "That's what Franklin said." She gasped and covered her mouth.

Molly and Miss Ellie both turned their attention to Mrs Hawksworth, who had gone a deep shade of red.

"Liza?" Miss Ellie said. "What did you just say?"

"Oh, it's nothing." Liza Hawksworth waved her hand, as she might do for any triviality.

"Liza!" Miss Ellie's voice was stern now. "Did you just say what I think you said?"

Still covering her mouth and blushing, Liza Hawksworth nodded.

Miss Ellie led her across to the table and pulled a chair out for her friend to sit in. Molly gave the stew a quick stir, then put a lid on the pan and quietly followed.

"Now," Miss Ellie said, in a tone that brooked no argument, "I presume you're talking about Franklin Marsh — and whether it's that Franklin or some other Franklin who I don't know, I'd rather like to know what's going on." She was smiling broadly at Mrs Hawksworth now and Liza responded with a giggle, which rather took Molly by surprise, coming from someone of her age.

"Well, I guess you'd find out at some time or another, so I may as well tell you now." Liza looked from Miss Ellie to Molly and back again. "I've been walking out with Franklin Marsh these last few weeks."

"But... but..."

Molly had never seen Miss Ellie lost for words before. The reaction certainly seemed appropriate now.

"And before you ask, yes, he knows I'm a married woman, with precious little I can do about it. It's just... well, it's been nice to be paid a little attention. I'm not used to flattery and I've found I rather like it." She touched her hair as she spoke, looking very much younger than the late-middle-aged woman she was.

Molly smiled. Then to spare Mrs Hawksworth's blushes she said, "Well, I can honestly say I was not expecting that. You've made me completely forget what it was we were talking about."

Miss Ellie was not as ready to leave the subject behind. "And there was me quite certain he was as wedded to that bar as some of his regulars. Come to that, I didn't think there was much hope for either of us, at our ages." She sighed. "Well, I'm happy for you. If I've never managed to find the right man for me, it doesn't mean I begrudge it for others." Miss Ellie moved her head back, as though to get a better view of her friend. "You aren't just doing this to help us get information on those Reese boys, are you?"

From Mrs Hawksworth's girlish embarrassment, Molly was certain she knew the answer to that question. She went back over to the kitchen to finish the dinner preparations, but moved around as quietly as she could, so she'd be able to continue to hear the conversation. Molly smiled, watching the two women.

"By the look on your face, Liza Hawksworth, I'd say

you were rather sweet on him. Is it serious?" Miss Ellie was still wide-eyed, looking at her friend.

"Is what serious?" Daniel came in through the back door and stamped his boots on the mat before starting to unlace them.

With the exception of Molly stirring the pot on the stove, the kitchen went quiet.

Daniel looked up, bewildered. "Did I say the wrong thing?"

The moment was lost and all the women burst out laughing.

"No, my darling," Molly said. "We'd just been talking about the meeting William is going to be speaking at.

Daniel frowned and looked around at each of them in turn. Molly tried hard to keep a straight face, as it was clear he'd not been convinced by what she'd said. She'd move things on to a different subject now and explain to him later, when the others had left.

As they sat down to eat, Molly was quiet. Her head was spinning from all that had gone on in one day. Between Sarah's problems, the Ku Klux Klan and Mrs Hawksworth's revelations, she didn't know where she was. She felt exhausted. Considering she was only six months pregnant she was already huge and seemed to need to eat considerably more than normal. She presumed her size was because her muscles weren't as tight as they used to be, but how much bigger would she become in the next three months?

She was glad when, shortly after dinner, James made his excuses to head back to his cabin and Miss Ellie said she would walk with him, whilst Liza swiftly cleared the table and cleaned up in the kitchen before going up to her room. Molly sank into a chair, ready to tell Daniel all that had gone on, but before she could even begin, she felt her eyelids drooping and gave in to her fatigue.

CHAPTER 17

"Franklin, I couldn't possibly." Liza's heart was beating fast at his suggestion. It was years since she'd been as happy as this, if she ever had been. Underneath the rough exterior, Franklin Marsh was a tender soul, at least where she was concerned.

"Who here knows you're married, except those who care about you? C'mon, Liza, I never thought I'd be wedded to anything other than that bar until you came along." Franklin took her hand in his as they sat on a bench, looking out across an orchard.

Liza noticed the blossom coming out on the trees. The gentle tint of pink would be a perfect colour for wedding flowers. She sighed. "I can't stand in the eyes of God, knowing I've already got a husband. You can't ask that of me, even if the pastor doesn't know."

"Then live with me as my wife and to hell with the pastor."

"Franklin Marsh, you can't go saying things like that. Whatever will people think of you?" Liza snatched her hand away from his.

Franklin laughed a gentle teasing laugh. "The bit about the pastor or the bit about you living as my wife?"

Liza got up from the bench. "What kind of a woman do you think I am, Franklin?"

He got up and went across to her. His strong, rough hands took hers tenderly. "A mighty fine one, Liza, but I don't just want to sit on a bench with you, even if it is a sunny afternoon."

"Maybe that's all I'm good for," she said, looking down, suddenly filled once again with self-doubt. Then it was Sarah who flashed through her mind, and she recalled that her own doubts came not through any deficiency in her own character but because of the treatment she'd received at the hands of Ned, her husband. "It's too soon," she said quietly. "I know so little about you. How do I know you'd treat me well?"

Franklin Marsh nodded. "I can see that's a fair question, after all you've been through. Just give me the chance to prove myself, Liza. You'll see."

"But you didn't stand up against those Reese boys, did you?" The words were out before she could stop herself. If she was honest, though, it was that which was really troubling her. How could a man be good enough, if he'd supported those brothers in their crime?

She expected Franklin to pull away. She even thought he might shout at her, but that was all based on her past experience of men. Instead he stood in front of her, still holding her hands tenderly and nodding.

"If you'll give me the chance to prove myself, Liza, I promise I won't leave you disappointed."

She nodded. He couldn't know that she was frightened she'd be disappointed if she set her hopes any higher than they were right now. In her heart, she didn't see herself as worthy of any good man coming into her life. Maybe that was what attracted her to Franklin.

It was time for Franklin Marsh to make his way back to the bar. Their precious couple of hours was at an end, and Liza sighed.

"I will think about it," she said earnestly as they

walked. In truth, she doubted she'd think about much else.

Whilst it would be a big step to move here completely from Iowa, the reality was she had little of her own to go back to. Living under her sister's roof had never been a chore, but she could make no corner of it truly hers, and good as her sister and husband had been to her, they needed space of their own, even now their children had flown. What few belongings she'd left behind when she'd packed for this trip would be easy enough for them to send on to her. None of that was sufficient reason for Liza to return there. She watched Franklin's retreating back as she left him at the corner nearest his saloon. Could he give her the love and, more importantly, the respect she'd never received from Ned?

She looked in the milliner's window as she passed. She didn't want for much, but a new hat now and again would be a treat. She sighed, knowing that wasn't a good reason to take on a man, even in her position.

"The one with the brown feather."

Liza jumped.

"Oh, I'm sorry," said Ellie, "I didn't mean to startle you. I just think the one with the brown feather would suit you well. Liza, whatever's the matter?"

Liza shook her head and kept her eyes downcast. What was the matter with her, indeed? Surely she should be happy, after the things Franklin had said, but she had no idea what she should do. How could Ellie advise her? She hadn't been married once, let alone been asked to commit bigamy. For all that, Ellie was her friend and a true one.

She linked her arm through Ellie's and turned away from the hat shop. "If you've got the time, let's walk as we talk."

Liza could see Ellie smiling as she told her all that had

gone on, but she said nothing until they got to the end of the story. "And that's why I have no idea what to do."

Ellie stopped and turned to face her friend.

Liza stood stiffly. What advice could Ellie possibly have to give?

"You and I," began Ellie, "are very different people. You weren't born to make your own way in the world and you aren't content in your own company."

Liza looked up a little. Her friend was not going to simply condemn her actions.

"If Franklin Marsh can make you happy, I will help you in any way I can. But…"

Liza's shoulders slumped. She'd known there'd be a 'but'.

"Oh, now don't look like that." Ellie put her arm back through Liza's and continued to walk.

Whilst it was easier to be honest when she wasn't staring Ellie in the eye, what could her friend have to say that would be better taken without Ellie looking at Liza?

"But…" Ellie was taking time before continuing. "There are a couple of questions it would be wise to ask yourself before doing anything too rash. The most important, after all you've been through, is — will he be kind to you? If you think he can make you happy, then don't let anything else stand in your way." Ellie looked around at her friend, grinning broadly.

Liza found herself blinking in surprise.

"Oh, don't get me wrong…" Ellie raised an eyebrow in her distinctive way. "There are other questions and I'll get on to those, but that's by far the most important. We'll find a way to deal with the others." She waved a hand, as though dismissing them before she'd even started.

"Maybe I don't know him awfully well, but I do think

he'd be a good man and take care of me," Liza replied quietly.

"Good," said Ellie. "Now, on to the other points. Is there any way that Ned would give you a divorce?"

Liza gasped. "He'd no more do that than ever he'd keep quiet if he found out I'd remarried without one. After what I did to him, he would take any opportunity he had to see me suffer."

Ellie nodded and sighed. "Yes, I can see that, but you did no more than was fair and right."

"Ned's not a man to see either fair or right. He's only interested in what's good for him."

"Indeed. Which brings me to my final and somewhat delicate point. Can you really give yourself to a man who may be shielding Ben's killers?"

Liza said nothing. That was the question she didn't want to ask herself. There were questions she wanted to ask Franklin, but she was too afraid of the answers. Instead, she was trying to convince herself it could only mean that he had no knowledge of what had gone on, and could add nothing to the investigation. Did she really believe that, though? They continued to walk in silence.

Hadn't telling herself what she wanted to believe been at the heart of her staying in an abusive marriage for as long as she had? How could she hold her head up now, if she went into another relationship doing that self-same thing? Or perhaps Ellie was saying those things because she was jealous and didn't want Liza to be happy? Liza stopped. She was doing the same thing again, trying to find a way to make reality palatable, when the truth was staring her in the face in a way she didn't like.

"I have to ask him, don't I?"

Ellie nodded. "Oh, Liza, I'm sorry that I can't just be

happy for you and leave the difficulties aside. I just don't want to see you hurt again, either in body or in mind."

There was nothing Liza could do until she saw Franklin the following day, so when they returned to the farm she took herself off to her room to think about what it was she would say to him.

After a sleepless night, Liza was reluctantly prepared to face her fears. She knew doing so was essential and yet she would still far rather avoid the confrontation. She met Franklin by the orchard bench once again, as had become their habit. Ominously, the sky was dark, and in the dullness of the day even the blossom looked reluctant to show itself.

"What ails my dear lady?" Franklin asked as soon as he saw her. "Are you about to rebuff my advances?"

"Oh, Franklin, I don't know what I should do. There are things I must ask you before I decide."

"Yes?"

He had taken her hand in his and, pleasant as it was, it was making Liza lose her nerve.

"That night, last year..."

Franklin Marsh sighed heavily and sat down. "Go on."

"The night when..."

"I know which night you mean." His voice was tender, and Liza felt her hopes rising.

"Well, how much do you know about what really happened?" There, she'd said it. There was no taking the question back.

"That's just it, Liza, I don't exactly know anything. Oh, I can guess what must have been afoot; there ain't a man in the town as can't and one of those old boys has even confessed to it. But the truth is, none of us exactly witnessed what went on or could swear to it in court."

"Isn't there anything they said that you could swear to?"

"That'd just be hearsay, wouldn't it?" Franklin wasn't looking at her now.

"Not if it was what the Reese boys themselves were saying. Franklin, are you afraid of those brothers, same as everyone else around here seems to be? And are you still running up that slate of theirs, knowing what you know?" Liza was starting to feel anger and indignation, rather than self-pity for what she was facing.

"But, Liza, if one of them confessing to the sheriff ain't going to make any difference, how would me telling what I know change things?"

"That's not the point though, is it? You're turning a blind eye, same as most everyone else is doing, even though a good man was killed and a house burned down. Good day, Franklin. Thank you for your kind offer, but I don't think it would be right for me to accept."

Liza's legs didn't feel as though they belonged to her as she got up from the bench and walked away. She desperately wanted him to call to her, to give her some reason to turn about and go back. Instead, she looked straight ahead and kept on walking, forcing herself to keep her chin up and her face forward.

CHAPTER 18

"Yes, I've got it." William reached into his inside jacket pocket once again to make sure he did have a copy of his speech. He'd practised it so often he could probably give it word for word even if he lost the papers, but it gave him comfort to know they were there.

"Right then." Dr Pritchard was bouncing slightly from foot to foot with apparent excitement. "I've got one other little surprise for you before we set off."

Cecilia grinned broadly and William realised that, whatever it was, she clearly already knew. He heard a door open on the landing, and Dr Pritchard moved aside so William could see who was coming down the stairs.

"Pa!" William was delighted to see his father joining them. "But why didn't you say you were coming? I would have picked you up at the station."

"This fine gentleman..." Mr Dixon turned to Dr Pritchard. "... Has persuaded me it might be in the interests of my health to take a few weeks away from Dowagiac, and has offered me his hospitality."

Whilst William stood dumbstruck, Cecilia moved forward to greet her father-in-law.

"We're delighted to see you, sir. I'm only sorry you can't see Thomas tonight."

"All in good time. I'm here for a little while, so I can spend plenty of time with my grandson. Now, I do believe you have a speech to give and our carriage awaits."

Dr Pritchard ushered them all toward the door and the waiting horses. Cecilia was not attending the meeting, but would stay with Mrs Pritchard, awaiting their return.

"Wish me luck," William said to her as she waved to them from the doorway.

"Be bold and confident — it's not luck you need," she called to him.

"If I'd known you were here, Pa, I could have practised my speech with you."

His father laughed. "Then perhaps it's better you didn't know. I shall enjoy hearing it for the first time this evening."

That night's venue was on the edge of Pierceton, although others that were booked were farther afield. As they approached, William could see men with lanterns outside the hall and presumed they were there in greeting, until the carriage got a little closer.

"It looks like we've got company," Dr Pritchard said. "Are you all right, William?"

William gulped and nodded. He was determined that no man wearing bizarre white robes was going to put him off his stride. "Ben was a good man," he said quietly.

"Do you know who they are?" Mr Dixon was asking Dr Pritchard.

"I could take a guess at some of them. If they'd stand still long enough, I could probably tell by their height and stance." He laughed without humour. "I've no doubt examined most of them, at one time or another, or made the mistake of bringing them into the world." He sighed. "But I can't name any of them with great certainty."

"I won't be put off by them," William said defiantly, and began to get down from the carriage.

"It's not your being put off that's going to be the

problem," said Dr Pritchard, following close behind. "I doubt you're going to have much of an audience."

William pursed his lips, and turned to them and smiled. "If that's the case, I'll save this fine speech for another occasion and find other words to say this evening."

"A wise approach, son." His father clapped him on the shoulder and the three of them headed through the circling Klan members and into the hall.

William wanted to take the time for a good look at the protesting men, to see if there were any he recognised, but he thought it better to do that after the meeting, rather than be too unnerved beforehand.

He might as well have stayed outside, however. At least, there he would have had an audience, even if an unwilling one. Inside, there was just the man who had organised the meeting, and no other.

"I'm sorry, Mr Dixon. I hoped those boys would change their minds."

William remembered the wisdom Dr Pritchard had imparted to him — that every single person he met might make the difference to whether he was ever elected — so he reassured his host that he need not worry. "We'll give it another ten minutes and then maybe step outside to address the protesters."

The man sucked air through his teeth and shook his head. "I'm not sure you'll be wanting to do that."

If he could survive the streets of New York, how hard could this be? He simply smiled at the man.

When it was clear no one else was going to attend, William stepped outside, bracing himself to raise his voice to be heard. He found only the empty night and not a trace of what had gone on before.

With no speech given, the journey back to Pierceton was subdued, despite Dr Pritchard's attempts to be cheerful.

"Well, I dare say if that had been your fourth meeting or even your third, it might not have been so hard to take as your first. It can only get better from here."

"Can it? Or will this happen at every one? I assume the Reese family is behind this, whipping up feeling against Ben. How far does the influence of that family stretch?" William had visions of hooded men preventing any audience from hearing what he had to say.

Dr Pritchard gave a hearty laugh. "They might have parts of Pierceton in their grip, but I doubt anyone in Warsaw has ever heard of them before... except maybe Justice Warren, and I don't suppose he's much of a devotee."

Mr Dixon sat a little straighter. "I can see this campaign is going to take a lot of work. Perhaps I'll come into the office tomorrow to see how I can lend a hand. Whilst I'm here I may as well make myself useful."

Dr Pritchard gave William a knowing smile and William frowned. He began to get the impression this last development had been the good doctor's intention.

William's first speech in Warsaw would be the following Saturday. He was grateful it was a daytime meeting and the journey could be done by train. It would give William plenty of time to go over his speech once again in his mind. If he needed to make a strong impression anywhere, then it was there. He wasn't yet at the point where he'd be invited to speak from the balcony of the Kirtley Hotel, but, if he could get this right, he would be one step closer to doing so.

When Saturday arrived and they approached the hall, William breathed a sigh of relief. There were no protesters outside. He took a few deep breaths. A tall man came out to greet them, formally dressed and with a fine ebony walking cane. Despite his own best suit, William feared he might be underdressed for the occasion. However, the greeting was warm and he relaxed a little; clearly Dr Pritchard already knew the gentleman.

The meeting was still an hour away, which gave ample time for refreshment after their journey and for William to learn a little more of his audience.

When they came back into the entrance porch from the side room, William was gratified to find a number of men already milling around. He went through to the main hall to prepare his notes and ensure everything was in place and saw that a further twenty men were already seated. How had he been described, in order to attract such a crowd? He let the thought pass before he felt too unworthy of the occasion.

He laid his pocket watch on the lectern in order to ensure he didn't speak too long. The hands showed precisely eleven o'clock when his host rose to bring the now full meeting to order and introduce him.

William's heart was beating fast as he rose to take his place. He took two calming breaths, looked around the faces of those present, dipped his head slightly in acknowledgement to them all and began.

"Fellow citizens of Kosciusko County, it is an honour and privilege to attend your meeting today and I appreciate your invitation. Many of you will ask why I am not beginning my political career with town matters, or perhaps looking to serve at a state level? Those are good questions. I am young; I have time on my side. However, I want to use that time and the energy I have due to my age, to work for the improvement of our whole great nation.

"There can be no other nation on God's earth where a man, any man, can achieve all that is possible here. We have seen great change since the end of the Civil War and we must not lose the opportunity we have been given. Already, we are seeing some of the rights that Lincoln's men fought for being eroded, and I say we must hold fast to those rights to ensure we move forwards and not back..."

Once he got into his stride, William paid little attention to the notes in front of him, but spoke from the heart and with a passion that could not fail to move the audience in front of him.

"... And so I ask you to give me your support, young and inexperienced in politics as I am, and in return I will give you the certainty that no man could work harder to move our nation forward." William took a step back from the lectern.

"Bravo," called a man toward the back of the hall, as others broke into applause.

William looked around, realising that some of the applause was polite, but most was genuinely enthusiastic. He'd made a start. Now he waited to see if there would be questions from the floor.

A gentleman stood up on the end of a row near the entrance doors. "Mr Dixon, thank you for..." He paused as though swilling his choice of words around his palate before spitting them out. "... An enlightening speech." He gave a slight derisory chuckle and William's heart sank. "But might I ask you, what are your views of the death penalty?"

That was not something which William had seen

coming, at least not as the first question. He thought quickly, well aware he could be about to fall into a trap. If the Reese boys came to trial, that could be exactly what they would face, and for all he knew the questioner was well aware of the case. "I believe, sir, that punishment should be proportionate to the crime committed. There are times when it is right to consider an offender to be an ongoing danger to society, and in those situations the action taken by the law must protect the community from any such threat, by whatever means necessary."

He paused. Was that sufficient answer or should he go on to say he didn't believe in death as a means of retribution? He was relieved of the need to go further by another member of the audience, clearly satisfied with his answer, standing to ask his own question.

"What are your views on slavery?"

This was one he had rehearsed, but he still knew he needed to word his answer with care.

"It was the founding fathers of this nation who laid down that 'All men are born equal', and they made no distinction between rich or poor, black or white. A man may give himself to his labours by his own choice, but his life should never belong to another man, whichever state of this great country he lives in."

Some men shuffled their feet awkwardly, while others chimed their agreement, and William waited for the next question.

From the far corner of the room, one of the audience, sitting slightly apart from the others and wearing an ill-fitting suit, got up and coughed before starting to ask his question. "And what's your opinion on the rights of women?" The voice was husky, almost as though the speaker were nursing some slight ailment.

"Sir," William said, "I hope it is clear from the fact that my own wife works as an attorney within our own law practice that I not only say that I believe in equality for women, but I am living embodiment of that belief. There is no good reason why women should not vote alongside their menfolk and work if they choose to do so. Education should be open to them in the same way it is to me, and they should be able to play their full part in the furtherance of our nation."

Again, there was a mixture of reactions from around the room. As William looked about for where the next question would come from, he was as surprised as others in the audience when the last questioner removed her hat and allowed a tumble of blonde curls to fall to her shoulders.

"Thank you, Mr Dixon. I hope I am therefore correct to presume you have no objection to my remaining in the meeting?" The woman smiled up at him.

William grinned and spoke over the gasps from some corners of the room. "None whatsoever, madam." He was pleased to see the room soon settled. He had no idea who the woman was, but he would have been prepared to put money on the fact that Miss Ellie would know.

CHAPTER 19

It had been a few weeks since Molly had seen Sarah. Both she and Miss Ellie had tried to call to see her at the store, but each time they were told she was out. On one of those occasions, Molly had clearly heard the children and, as Mrs Spencer was in the store with Joe, she had to conclude Sarah was in the back and not being allowed to come forward. Molly had even tried using the postal service to send a letter, doing her best to disguise her writing, but she had received no reply.

Little by little, she'd become more angry on behalf of her friend. No woman should be treated the way Sarah was being, and certainly not if there was anything Molly could do about it. Although she was now well into her sixth month of pregnancy, Molly decided she had to take action. She wanted to see her friend and she was certain Sarah would want to see her.

How dare Joe instruct his wife not to speak with either her or Miss Ellie? This had gone far enough — too far, when Molly thought of his physical mistreatment of Sarah. She left Mary in Miss Ellie's care, not saying that she planned anything more than the usual delivery round, and prepared the cart to go to town.

As the horse trotted rhythmically along the road, Molly rehearsed some of the lines she wanted to say to Joe. Despite everything, she still believed Joe was essentially a reasonable man and would see at least some of the sense in what she said. She tethered the horse outside the general store and decided unloading must be the first priority, in case she was asked to leave. Joe came out to help take the boxes inside and Molly had to take a deep breath to steady her nerve. She needed to control herself, not to rush into words. She bit her lower lip as she worked to pass the goods down to Joe, then climbed down off the cart and followed him into the store. Mrs Spencer was behind the counter, but unsurprisingly, Sarah was nowhere in sight.

"Joe," she said, being able to contain herself no longer, "Sarah has been my best friend for more years than she has been your wife. It isn't right you prevent her from even speaking with me." She could feel her hands trembling and held them tightly by her sides.

Joe wheeled around, a flash of anger in his eyes, but Molly hadn't finished and she wasn't ready to be put off her stride.

"Miss Ellie is her guardian and whilst, of course, now Sarah's married, much of that role passes to you, Miss Ellie still cares about her deeply. She has acted as a mother to her and has a right to be able to see both Sarah and the children." Molly took a deep breath; there was more to say and she knew the next part would be difficult. "I know you think it wrong that we are working women and that we believe women should be equals of their menfolk, but look at your own mother." She paused, turning to look at Mrs Spencer and draw her into the conversation. "She has run Spencer's General Store since your father died. She is just as much a working woman as Miss Ellie and me."

"That's different," Joe snapped.

Molly frowned and tried to keep her voice steady. "How exactly?"

"Ma only ran the store until we... I was old enough to

take over. Now I run it."

Molly nodded. "Whoever runs it now, your mother is still working here. How old were you when your father died?"

"I was eight, but I don't see what that has to do with anything." Joe's face was quite red by now, but Molly needed to carry on. He wouldn't give her much longer.

"So your mother, quite capably, ran the store for nigh on ten years before you could take over from her. I've known you a long time, Joe, and you weren't running the store when you and Sarah were courting and when Henry went off to war." Molly hesitated. "How did your father die? You say he died when you were eight, but was he ill a while before that?" She wanted to show him just how long his ma had been an independent woman and how good that had been.

"Not that it's any of your business how he died, but no, he hadn't been ill. It was very sudden. He fell down the stairs. Ma found him some time later."

Molly froze. Words she'd heard from Miss Ellie went galloping through her head. 'Abusers so often were once abused themselves or witnessed abuse.' The thought that occurred to her was impossible. Had Mrs Spencer pushed her husband in self-defence? She looked across to Mrs Spencer, who looked away suddenly, her face colouring in the same instant as Molly caught her eye, and Molly knew she was right. She gasped and looked back to Joe and then again to Mrs Spencer. She had no idea what to say next.

Hastily, she began to pick up her things and made to leave. Did Joe know what his mother had done? If not, she hoped the same thought had not just occurred to him.

She turned back and stammered, "Good day, to you both."

Molly was torn. She wanted to get as far away from the store as she possibly could, but, if Joe had realised, she didn't know if she dared leave Mrs Spencer alone with him. All she could think to do was get back to the farm, find Miss Ellie and Mrs Hawksworth and ask for their counsel. Maybe this was something they should involve Cecilia in, too? Surely, Joe wouldn't hurt his own mother? But if he was prepared to hurt his own wife, then his boundaries of what was right were already blurred and there was no telling what he would do.

Molly's heart was pounding as she left the general store and stumbled back onto the cart. She hadn't untied the horse and had to climb down again to do so. She flicked the reins to indicate the horse should move, but no voice came when she tried to shout. As the cart jolted over the track back to the farm, all that kept playing through Molly's mind was 'Mrs Spencer killed her husband. Mrs Spencer killed her husband'.

Molly went straight down to the cabins in search of Miss Ellie when she got back. "Miss Ellie, Miss Ellie," she called as she approached.

"I think she's up at the house." James was sitting on his own porch, puffing on his pipe. "Are you all right, missy?"

She stopped, registering what he'd said. Why hadn't she tried there first? She knew that was where Miss Ellie had been with the children when she went out. "I'm fine, thank you James, but I really need to speak to her urgently." A thought struck her. "James, did you know Mr Spencer, Joe's father?"

He took a long puff of his pipe before answering. "That was a bad business, that was."

Molly nodded. He wasn't about to say any more, so she turned in the direction of the house to look for her guardian.

Seeing James had brought more calm to Molly, and by the time she reached the house she was less flustered. Miss Ellie was at the table, writing a letter.

"Molly, is everything all right?" she asked, getting up and removing her half-moon reading glasses and laying them aside.

"I need to speak with you in private."

"Whatever's happened?" Miss Ellie looked across the room to where the children both appeared to be asleep. "Here, sit down and tell me."

"Did you know Joe's father, Mr Spencer?"

"Ah!" was all Miss Ellie said in reply.

"What do you mean, 'ah'?" Molly wasn't sure if she should wade in with her account of the afternoon or wait to hear more from Miss Ellie.

"Are you about to tell me 'like father, like son'?" Miss Ellie asked.

Molly squinted at the older lady. "Did you know that? Did you let Sarah see Joe, and me see Henry, knowing their mother had been abused by their father?"

"No, child. I most certainly did not. That is something I would not have encouraged, if I'd thought there might be a risk to the two of you."

Molly felt her shoulders relax. "What, then?"

"Back in those days, I thought they were a nice respectable family. I knew Joe's father had died when he was a child. We all did. It was a shocking tragedy. One day he was in the shop and the next he was dead. He was still so young. I never thought a thing about it until I was speaking with Dorothea Pritchard a few weeks ago. I was asking her advice on how I could best help Sarah. She's a great deal of experience, you know. She often helps

Charles, where patients need someone to talk to."

Molly nodded. She knew that was so often the case with a doctor's wife, from things Cecilia had said about her own parents.

"Anyway, it was she who came out with the line 'like father, like son'. It explains a great deal, but I had no idea before that. Clara is one of Dr Pritchard's patients. I think she's walked into as many cupboards as Sarah, from what Dorothea said."

Molly sighed. "Then perhaps we should be going to Dr Pritchard now, as I may have put her in some danger. You see, I might have just revealed to Joe that his mother pushed his father downstairs."

Miss Ellie gasped.

"Oh, I could still be wrong, but the look on Mrs Spencer's face…" Molly shuddered.

"Right, we need to take action. Charles is definitely the best person, as he can call on Clara without suspicion. I'll walk into town now."

Their exchange was interrupted by a sharp rap at the door. Molly marched over and opened it, to find Franklin Marsh standing there with his cap in his hand.

"Excuse me, Mrs Flynn, but is Mrs Hawksworth home, please?"

Molly was astounded to see this brusque saloon owner behaving in such a meek fashion. "You'd best come in." She turned to Miss Ellie. "Have you seen Mrs Hawksworth this afternoon?"

Miss Ellie nodded. "I believe she's in her room. I'll go up and ask her to come down. Then I shall be away."

Several minutes passed, in which Franklin Marsh stood awkwardly, moving from foot to foot, while Molly began to sort out the supper. Eventually, Miss Ellie came downstairs.

"I'm afraid she doesn't wish to see you."

Franklin Marsh's face fell.

"I believe she's told you that unless you'll do the right thing, she has no desire to spend time in your company. You've had a wasted journey, Franklin."

"Thank you," he said quietly, and walked back out of the farmhouse kitchen.

Molly and Miss Ellie looked at each other and shrugged at the changed demeanour of the man. "What love can do," Miss Ellie said, and shook her head. "Now I really need to go to see Charles."

CHAPTER 20

Cecilia was sitting at her desk opening the morning's post when her father-in-law came in. He stood before her, looking stern and serious, and her heart missed a beat.

"Whatever's wrong?" She called through to William's office. "William, your father is here."

Still looking at Cecilia, Mr Dixon senior. said, "What would you think about me lending you a hand in the office?"

"Are we not doing well enough, sir?" William looked stricken.

"Far from it, son, I would say you were doing exceedingly well. I'm asking because I would not wish to presume a welcome and would not want to get in the way." He turned back to Cecilia. "And I'm asking you, dear lady, as I suspect it might affect you rather more than it would my son."

"Pa, why don't you explain a little more fully? Do you mean for a short time, or are you thinking of moving to Pierceton?"

Cecilia saw the twinkle in Mr Dixon's eyes and smiled broadly. She came around the desk and took his arm in hers. "We would be delighted if you joined us, wouldn't we, William? I'm not sure how we could fit another desk in here, but we have space upstairs that we hardly use, but for storage. Something could certainly be arranged there."

"Oh, do say you'll stay, sir. It would give us the greatest

pleasure in the world to have you near at hand. But what of your own practice?" William was almost bouncing with excitement.

"It may have escaped your notice, William, but I have not attended to my own practice in Dowagiac for some weeks. When your mother fell ill, I didn't know how long it would be, but I asked one of my fellow lawyers in Dowagiac to take over most of my files. I have an agreement in principle with him that he will buy the remainder of my practice if I choose to pack up. I'm not really ready to retire, but these last few weeks here in Pierceton have made me realise I can still be useful, especially if you are successful in a political career. That's why I'm asking Cecilia's permission. If you are elected, it would be Cecilia who would have to see me on a regular basis, rather than yourself."

"Oh, sir," Cecilia said, clapping her hands together. "I should be delighted if you were to join us. I'll be honest, if William wins this election, I shall be left with far more work than one person can do. Then, with the state not recognising women as attorneys, I would have endless trouble where court work is concerned." She looked down. "Besides, I'm sensible enough to understand that having a man here will bring the practice more credibility than if I were to try to run it on my own."

"More fool any man who underestimates you, young lady. You're a fine lawyer. Better than my son, but don't let him hear I said that." George Dixon turned to his son and smiled broadly. "You chose exceedingly well when you decided to marry. Your mother and I were both delighted with your choice."

"Thank you, sir."

Cecilia smiled to see William blushing at his father's

words.

William turned back to Cecilia, shaking his head. "Do you really think that? About people not taking you seriously?"

"Oh, it's not everyone, but certainly there are those who would be only too happy to see me fail." She laughed. "Some of those people would quite like to see you fail too, so I won't take it personally. Of course, there is one other reason that having another attorney in the practice would be good. I do rather hope we'll have a brother or sister for Thomas at some point, although nothing seems to be happening on that front at present." She sighed.

"All in good time, my dear." George Dixon patted her hand. "Well, I suppose before I start getting myself too settled, I should make sure they will register me here. There's little I can do if the State won't say I can." With that, he raised his hat to them both and walked briskly out into the street.

Any further discussion was brought to a close by the bell ringing and a woman Cecilia recognised from the women's meetings coming in. "Good morning, Mrs Saunders, how may we help you?"

As she shook Cecilia's hand she said, "Good morning, but please call me Catherine."

"Very well, Catherine, how may we help?"

"I understand in some other parts of the country women have been presenting themselves to vote in elections and taking legal action against the State if they are refused. I want to be prepared. Would you be willing to represent me, if I need you to?"

"Why, of course, we would be delighted to do that." Cecilia felt a thrill of excitement. This was exactly the sort of case she wanted to take on.

"That's good, as there may be a number of us. We don't want to come to you just because you're a woman. Eddie speaks very highly of you." Catherine sat very straight in her chair, holding her bag neatly in her gloved hands.

"Eddie?" The name didn't sound familiar to Cecilia.

"Edwin Steinmann. He's a hard task master, but a fair one. If you impress Eddie then you'll soon find others follow in his footsteps. Thank you for your time, Mrs Dixon. I shall look forward to working with you." Catherine got up from the chair and was on her way before Cecilia could even open the door for her.

Cecilia had barely got back to the post before the bell rang again and Dr Pritchard bounced in. "Dorothea and I were wondering if you'd like to come to dinner this evening. I suspect there'll be one or two practicalities you want to discuss with George."

From his broad grin, Cecilia couldn't help but think this wonderful man might have played a large part in the decision Mr Dixon had taken. "Thank you, and not just for dinner. Yes, of course, we'd be delighted to join you, but thank you too for all you've done for William's father."

"Not at all, young lady. I just had a bit of an inkling of what he might be going through and made sure I was there in case he needed someone. See you around seven o'clock. Patients to see, places to be." And he too was gone.

The rest of the day was quieter, and both she and William left the office on time, collected Thomas from Miss Ellie and headed back to Dr Pritchard's.

"Where do you think Pa will live?" William said as the carriage made its way back into Pierceton.

"We've plenty of space at the Red House. I won't mind if he'd like to join us there." Cecilia had been thinking about that very thing earlier. Mr Dixon was fit enough to look after himself and, she guessed, would make his own friends in the town, so he was unlikely to be around all the time. She thought, too, of her own parents and what she would hope William might say if it were one of them rather than his own father.

William said nothing in reply, but simply took her hand. It was enough for Cecilia to realise how touched he was that she found the thought acceptable.

George Dixon looked brighter and happier than Cecilia had seen him since he'd arrived in Pierceton. He looked younger and had far more colour in his face, too.

"I've already booked to go back to Dowagiac by train, leaving here tomorrow. There will be a few things to do while I'm away, so I expect to be gone a couple of weeks. I thought it might take me a while to sell the house, but I sent word that I was considering it a week or so ago and have heard there is a buyer interested by return."

"Sir, I haven't discussed this with Cecilia, but I'd like to see the house one more time before it's sold. And, for that matter, visit Ma's grave."

As William said the words, a cloud passed across his father's face and in a faltering voice he said, "Briggs has said he'll keep Ma's grave tidy for me. It will be hard to leave it."

"I'm sorry, sir." William looked to Cecilia and she rested her hand on his arm. "I didn't mean to upset you."

"No, son. That's the hardest part of deciding to leave. I feel more concern for that than I do the house, even though we lived there together all those years. Once Ma was no longer there it could have been any building to me." He sighed, and Dr Pritchard passed him a small glass of bourbon.

"I can't come immediately," William continued.

"Perhaps I could join you there in a week or so?"

"That would be a pleasure for me, thank you, son. There is one other thing." George Dixon's eyes were shining, and Cecilia wondered what else he had in store.

"With the help of Charles, I've already found a house to move into here."

"Really, sir? But we thought you might come to us." William looked as much disappointed as surprised.

George chuckled. "Well, that is very kind of you both." He looked across to Cecilia and nodded. "But I'm sure it wouldn't take long before I'd outstayed my welcome. You youngsters need your space and, in any event, I'll be a lot nearer than I was in Dowagiac." He went on to describe a small house close to the centre of town, within an easy walk of most places. "The former owner was a patient of George's, but they've decided to strike out west to see if they can make their fortune. They're braver men than I am, that much is certain. There is one thing you may be able to help me with."

"Anything we can." William's eagerness made Cecilia smile.

"The house doesn't come with any land. I'd already planned to leave Bounty in Dowagiac. She's too old now to want the upheaval and I've made arrangements with Briggs for her care. However, I would like to bring Brandy, and wondered if you might have enough grazing for her to come to the Red House?"

William's face was alive with excitement. "Really, sir? And would you like me to ride her sometimes to keep her fit for you?"

"More than that, William. I would like to give her to you as a gift. My riding days are a little behind me now. I'm happier in a carriage than on horseback, but I know how much you enjoy it and I just thought…"

"Oh, yes please, sir." He turned to Cecilia. "Brandy is the finest horse. You'll love her. Maybe one day Thomas can learn to ride her too. Oh, Father, thank you."

"Well, that's all settled then. If you can spare my son, I should be very glad of his company for a few days to say our goodbyes to Dowagiac. I've lived there all my life, so it's going to be strange to leave it behind. But if my parents hadn't made the move they made, I would never have had the opportunities I've had, so moving must be seen in a positive light. This is a new chapter for me, and thanks to Charles I'm a little more ready to face what it brings."

The rest of the evening passed as much with George's excitement at what lay ahead as with the poignancy of what he'd leave behind. Cecilia couldn't help but admire his positive spirit and wondered what the fine doctor had done to help her father-in-law through his immediate grief and the malaise he had fallen into as a result. As soon as his new house was in his name, she would help to prepare it ready for him to move in. She thought the project might be rather fun, especially as Dorothea had offered to work on it with her.

CHAPTER 21

This time it was Pa who met William off the train when he arrived in Dowagiac. Although tired from the journey, William was longing to update his father on his campaign progress.

"You're looking mighty pleased with yourself," Pa said as he shook William's hand.

"Is it that obvious?" William grinned. "Before I tell you my news, how are things here?"

Pa shrugged. "They'll be much better for your arrival. I'm rattling around from room to room like a billiard ball bouncing off the cushions. Now, why don't you tell me what's making you so happy?"

"Well, sir, I've given four speeches now and they've gone exceedingly well. I haven't had any more protests to face and Dr Pritchard thinks we're starting to have an impact."

"That is good news. Just remember, this is a long race and not a sprint, and you won't go far wrong."

William thought about his father's words over the next days as he said his goodbyes to the places he'd known in the latter part of growing up. It felt strange to think it might be his last trip to somewhere which had had such a major influence on his life. He'd lived there longer than he'd lived in any place so far and it still had the easy feeling of home. As he walked around the town and noticed the changes, even in the last year, he began to understand why some politicians fought so hard to maintain the status quo. Change was discomfiting.

William had no packing of his own to do at the house. He'd moved out when he married Cecilia, some time before their Pierceton move, but as he helped his father, occasional memories from his youth came to the fore and they would stop for a while and reminisce.

When he got back to the house after a walk, a letter from Cecilia was waiting for him. Seeing her handwriting made him smile and he took the letter to the sitting room, which was still partially furnished.

He made himself comfortable on the settee by the window and slit the envelope open. He missed Cecilia and Thomas a great deal, and the few minutes reading their news was always something he savoured.

My darling William,
I am sorry to be the bearer of bad news.

William uncrossed his legs and sat up straighter.

Yesterday while at the office, I received a visit from the sheriff, looking for you. It seems that on the matter of Hewlett's Farm there have been accusations of impropriety and a suggestion that a large sum of money has gone missing.

In the light of the information he has been given, the sheriff says he has no option but to open an investigation, and wishes to speak with you at his office immediately upon your return.

William felt himself sweating. He had never done anything even vaguely suspect, at least in his adult life. How could there be anyone who would say otherwise? He read on.

Although the sheriff asked if I could give him the file in question, I took the opportunity to say that I did not have knowledge of where it was located and suggested you take it to him on your return. I have since taken the liberty to go through the file and have found not the least thing of which you should be concerned.

"But of course there isn't. I haven't done anything."

I think it might be prudent for us to have a copy of the documents before the file is given to the sheriff, and am now in the process of making such a copy. We can ask for them to be notarised before you hand over the file.

Thomas and I are both well and look forward to your return.
Yours with all my love
Cecilia

William got up and began to pace the room. He knew there was nothing wrong with the work he'd done on that matter. Admittedly, it had been a large and complex transaction, but his profit from the work had been his own fee. How could anyone say otherwise?

William went in search of his father, who was packing books in the library. "Pa, read this." He handed the letter to his father and stood awkwardly, waiting.

George Dixon read right to the end of the letter before looking up at William. "And so it begins."

"What do you mean, sir?"

"When a man puts himself forward for public life, there will always be some who don't agree with the views he holds. You found that when the so-called Ku Klux Klan stopped you speaking in Pierceton — or, more to the point stopped you having an audience. Anyway, there are others who will behave in a devious and in some cases outright dishonest manner in order to stop you. I'm guessing that's what's motivating this action. Do you have any idea who it might be?"

William scratched his head, then refolded the letter. "No, sir, I don't believe I do, unless they have some link to the Reese brothers."

"That would not surprise me from all I've heard. Now, lend me a hand in here. If we're returning to Pierceton by tomorrow's train we need to get a move on." George Dixon turned to survey the unpacked books.

"But, sir, you have a great deal still to do and I thought you wanted to be here for all of it." William knelt down to add some of the volumes to the open crate.

"Some things are more important than whether I do my own packing. I can make arrangements for everything I want to be sent on. You're going to need all the help you can get in Pierceton, and if I ever doubted it when Charles said that to me, then I certainly don't now."

William sat back on his haunches. "Sir, what exactly did Dr Pritchard say to you?"

George Dixon was grinning at his son. "Never you mind, but I'm glad I'm moving to be there to help."

With the new impetus their decision gave, William and his father achieved a remarkable amount of the packing in the remaining hours of the day, and Briggs was left with full instructions to oversee the rest.

"Take care of your father, sir," Briggs said to William when they were ready to leave. "He's a good man and has been very generous to my family."

"And to me too, Briggs…" William paused, feeling slightly awkward about what he wanted to say next. "And Briggs, if there's anything you need, anything at all, I hope you know you can call on my support now as well as my father's."

"That's very kind of you to say, sir."

Despite the formality, it looked to William as though the corner of Briggs' mouth was twitching slightly, and given how much his own behaviour had changed since childhood, he could see that Briggs might be amused.

William gave a sheepish grin and added, "I've learned a great deal from my father and a fair amount from you too. Thank you."

Briggs nodded and William turned to join his father boarding the train.

"And now our real work begins." Pa sighed as he took out a legal pad and began to make some notes. "Cecilia was quite right to think of getting a notarised copy of those documents before you hand them over. You wouldn't be the first person who's been set up in this way. Most are not so well prepared."

By the time the two of them stepped off the train back in Pierceton they had a clear plan of what needed to be done. George would act as his son's lawyer and attend the sheriff's office with him. Their main objectives were to find out who had originated the accusation, and what money had been hidden and where. It was going to be no easy job, but William's reputation depended on it, and if they failed he could forget any chance of a career in either law or politics.

William and Cecilia met George Dixon in the office early the following day.

"Are we going to tell the sheriff we have a notarised copy of the file, or only produce it if we have to?" William was rushing around making sure he had all the papers he needed before going to see the sheriff.

"That depends how long you want this mess to continue. Have you seen this?" George handed the latest newspaper to his son. The headline read 'Candidate Under Investigation'.

William slumped into a chair. "How did they get hold of the story?"

"I'm guessing from the same source as set the whole thing up." Pa took the notarised copy of the file that Cecilia was offering to him. "Now, listen to me. You can fail to mention this copy and make a clever point later, humiliating the sheriff and making yourself unwelcome in those parts of Pierceton which still hold you in esteem, or you can be upfront and put this whole thing to bed quickly, without any further loss of face."

Driven by the nervous energy he was feeling, William roared with laughter. "You're right, of course. I do rather like scoring points against the other side, but I guess that's not always the best thing to do." He got up with new determination. "Thank goodness I have such good advisors around me." He kissed Cecilia on the cheek. "Wish me luck, and if my father comes back without me, assume I've been locked up."

George Dixon raised an eyebrow to Cecilia and held the door open for William to leave the office.

"Have we got everything?" William made to turn around and go back in, but his father put a hand on his arm.

"We have everything we need for today. Cecilia has made sure of it." He moved the hand to William's back and propelled him forwards toward the sheriff's office.

William turned one last time and looked back at the window. As he saw Cecilia standing there, watching them go, his heart missed a beat. For her and for Thomas, he had to sort this out quickly. He wasn't a street-fighter now, and point scoring would win him no friends, however satisfying it might seem.

"Sheriff, I believe you know my father, Mr George Dixon."

"I sure do. Pleased to see you, sir."

The formalities out of the way, the three of them sat down.

"Now, this ain't rightly an interview." The sheriff looked uncomfortable as he sat behind his desk with the two of them in front of him. William couldn't help but notice the man had put on some weight and didn't appear to have found any new clothes to contain his girth.

"Sheriff, what exactly is William being accused of?"

The sheriff rocked on his chair and William wondered if it would cope with the strain.

"It has been reported to me" — the sheriff was suddenly using a formal and precise voice — "that when Mr William Dixon, undertook the transaction for the large tract of land out west from Pierceton, just south of Wooster, formerly known as Kosciusko, there was a difference in the amount charged to his" — the sheriff coughed — "client, and that paid over to the other side. That difference amounting to the grand sum of $5,000."

"That's a large sum for someone to be claiming, Sheriff. And you've asked my son to bring our copy of the paperwork in, so you can check the veracity of the claim?"

"Yes, sir."

"And how long will you need the file for, Sheriff?"

The sheriff rocked some more and then said, "I don't rightly know, sir. I'm not the fastest reader and may need to get me some help on the matter."

George Dixon nodded sympathetically, and William

admired the way his father was trying to build a rapport with the man.

"Am I right in assuming you have in your possession copies of documents from the parties to the transaction?" George asked.

"They may not actually be in my possession right now, but that's pretty much the long and the short of it." The Sheriff was nodding and, to avoid his own anxious fidgeting, William focused on the movement of the man's second chin.

"Would it help you if I were to pinpoint the corresponding documents in our file, to save you having to go through everything else?"

"It would help me if you were to point to the actual words." The sheriff gave out a loud laugh. "No, sir, I need to get the whole file looked at. I shall need it for a few days."

George Dixon nodded. "Take as long as you need, Sheriff. We took the opportunity to have a notarised copy of the file made, in case we were to need to refer to it while the original was with you."

The sheriff ran his finger around his collar. William admired how his father had made sure the sheriff knew they could prove if anything was altered in their copy of the file, without actually having said it to him.

"Now, there was no need to go doing something like that, Mr Dixon, sir. I ain't going to be holding on to your file awful long." The sheriff was sitting up straighter now.

George Dixon smiled. "It was no trouble, Sheriff. It's always best if all parties are looking at exactly the same documents." George pushed the original file across the table to the sheriff and then put his own copy on the table and opened it, showing the first of the notarised documents on the top of the pile. Pa was leaving the sheriff in no doubt that they really did have an official copy and that if changes were made now it would be obvious.

"Is there anything else today, Sheriff?" George smiled broadly. "If not, my son and I will be getting back to the office, where we have other clients to keep happy."

"No, sir. That is indeed all. I'll call by when I want to talk about this further."

George and William got up. George replaced his hat and nodded to the sheriff and William quickly followed suit.

"Then we'll bid you good day."

Leaving the sheriff still rocking on his chair and frowning now, they headed back toward Dixon's Attorneys.

"William," his father said as they walked, "would you mind if I took this file home with me to Dr Pritchard's house? I think we should ensure it's kept safe."

"Of course, sir, but that seems a little unnecessary."

"I don't think so, son. We've seen what those boys are capable of. We can't be too careful."

After that they walked in silence, and William wondered what else might not be safe.

CHAPTER 22

"I'm quite sure it was Mr Spencer," Liza Hawksworth said to Ellie, as she removed her bonnet in the kitchen of the farmhouse.

"You're sure what was Joe?" Molly was still wiping her hands on her apron as she came in from the dairy.

"The man I saw coming out of that house." Liza placed significant emphasis on the word 'that'.

"Now come, Liza, you can't go jumping to conclusions. Perhaps he was undertaking a delivery." Ellie shook her head and smiled at Molly. "Maybe you're letting your imagination run away with you."

"Well…" Liza put her gloves and hat on the chair. "Whether it's my imagination or not, Franklin told me a while ago the things that go on in that house, and it's not a place for a respectable gentleman. Besides, you didn't see him. The way he was looking around to check no one saw him — that was no delivery round, at least not of the sort the store would need him to make."

"Liza!"

"Oh, don't be such a prude, Ellie. You were a farmer, for goodness sake. You may not have been married but you know enough about the animal world to know what men are like. I just wonder about poor Sarah, if she knows the sort of place her husband's been frequenting." Liza picked her outer garments up and headed upstairs.

Ellie sat down heavily in a chair. Perhaps Liza was right and she was becoming the sort of person she'd always hoped she wouldn't. As she pondered how, in a small town like Pierceton, she could broaden her horizons, she picked up the basket she had been weaving and continued working on it. Was it too late in life for her to undertake further studies? As she got lost in thinking about what she would like to study, she pulled the willow harder than she intended and then looked down to see her basket was going out of shape. She cursed and tried to concentrate.

Molly came to sit close by.

"Don't you go telling me I'm a silly old thing as well." Ellie checked herself. "I'm sorry, I think Liza might have touched a raw spot. Her seeing Franklin has left me feeling a bit out of sorts. Oh, it's silly at my age to feel jealousy of such things, but I suppose a girl never quite gives up hope."

Molly looked confused. "And were you interested in Franklin Marsh?"

Ellie snorted with laughter. "Oh dear, no. It isn't the person I'm jealous about, it's the situation. Now, we'll have less of this." She finished off her piece of willow and began to weave a new one in. "If it wasn't that, what was it you were going to say, child?"

"I was going to ask if you thought I should be telling Sarah about Joe?"

Ellie paused what she was doing and looked into the distance. "No, child. That girl's already got enough problems. Dr Pritchard has been keeping an eye on her the best he can, but it's a bad situation and no mistake. I don't think our adding to things is going to benefit anyone. I've a good mind to go in search of Joe myself, though. He might think he's master in his own home, but he married one of my wards, and any parent would likely have something to say about his behaviour. I wonder if Cecilia would accompany me."

Since it was a Saturday, Thomas was not at the farm, so there was less likelihood of Cecilia calling in. Feeling in need of fresh air, Ellie laid aside her lopsided basket, smiled at the result of her annoyance and prepared herself to go out. It was a warm, sunny day. What on earth had she been doing sitting inside in the first place? The sun on her face as she went across the yard immediately lifted her spirits. Why, at her time of life, she should start having a hankering to have a man in her life, she had no idea. However, she did feel some attention would be nice. It was all too easy to start living her life for the younger ones around her and forget she still needed a life of her own. The loss of William's mother had hit her hard. She'd enjoyed her times in Dowagiac, working with Margaret Dixon in the women's movement there.

The fields were dry at this time of year, so the path to the Red House alongside the crops was a relatively easy one. It took little time before she could see Brandy's paddock, and she made her way over to the fence. Brandy came across to her immediately and was more than happy to receive some attention.

"Well, girl, what do you make of Pierceton? It's not such a bad place for a single girl to live. I don't think I really expected to spend all my life on my own, but I'm not good at compromise. When I look at what Liza Hawksworth has been through, and now Sarah, I should count my blessings." All the time she was talking, Ellie gently stroked Brandy's nose and the horse nuzzled her in return.

Ellie became aware of a shadow falling over the horse's flank and turned to see George Dixon joining them.

"Am I interrupting?"

Ellie smiled. "Not really. I'm on my way to see Cecilia, as it happens, and stopped off to spend a little time with this beautiful girl."

"I may not ride these days, but I do like coming to talk to her. I find she's a very good listener when I want to talk about my late wife." George took an apple out of his pocket and held it out to the mare.

"You'd be welcome to talk to me about Margaret. I was only thinking earlier today how much I miss her friendship." Ellie stood back a little and smiled, watching Brandy happily munching at the apple.

"I wouldn't want to put you to the trouble. I can be pretty bleak company when I start thinking about how much I miss her. Moving to Pierceton has been a bigger step than I could have imagined. Charles and Dorothea have been very kind, but they are busy people and the youngsters need to have their own lives."

George was talking as much to Brandy as to Ellie, and she wondered if he'd remembered she was there. He fell quiet and the only sound was Brandy finishing the final part of the apple. Once she'd swallowed, she nuzzled first George and then Ellie, to see if there was anything further on offer.

"That's all for now, Brandy. I'll bring you something else later." George turned to Ellie. "Shall I walk with you up to the Red House to see if we can find Cecilia?" He offered her his arm and they walked in companionable silence, enjoying the sunshine.

Cady came running across the garden to meet them. Cecilia and Thomas were sitting on the swing and Cecilia broke into a broad smile as they approached.

Thomas stumbled over to his grandfather, who immediately lifted him up.

"This is a lovely surprise. I'll bring some cold drinks out, shall I?" Cecilia indicated a table and chairs on the patio outside the main dining room windows.

"That would be most pleasant, thank you." Ellie sat at the table and watched George taking Thomas back across to the swing.

George was still with Thomas when Cecilia returned with a tray. She was about to call her father-in-law when Ellie stayed her arm. "Can I speak with you for a moment, before the others join us?"

Cecilia put the tray on the table and sat next to Ellie.

"It's about Sarah. Liza saw that husband of hers coming out of a house of ill-repute in Pierceton. As Sarah's guardian, I felt I should perhaps speak to him about the unacceptable nature of his behaviour toward Sarah."

"And where do I come in, exactly?" Cecilia poured out the lemonade into the glasses.

George and Thomas were already coming back across

the garden to them, but Ellie had already covered the difficult part of the conversation and so felt comfortable to continue.

"I wanted to ask if you might come with me when I go to speak to Joe?"

Cecilia nodded, looking thoughtful. She looked up at George. "Pa, in your opinion, as Sarah is my client, would I be compromised by going with Miss Ellie when she speaks to Joe about a personal matter appertaining to his and Sarah's marriage?"

George was taking a pipe from his pocket and filling it with tobacco. He looked to each of them. "Do you ladies mind? It's a bad habit I've started since I lost Margaret."

Ellie waved a hand to show it was of no consequence to her, and he turned his attention back to his daughter-in-law.

"It would be better, as much for Sarah's trust in being able to confide in you, for you not to accompany Ellie. Might I suggest as an alternative — that I go with you instead?" He sat back and inhaled deeply through the pipe, a contented look settling on his face.

Ellie blinked. Would she be comfortable, addressing Joe on the subject in hand in front of another man? Then Liza's accusations of her being a prude ran through her mind and she felt determined to demonstrate that was not the case. "Thank you. If Cecilia has no objections, I would be happy to accept your generous offer."

Thomas pulled himself up onto Ellie's knee and the subject moved on, except as far as agreeing they would go on Monday afternoon, when the store was likely to be quieter.

As they sat relaxing in the sunshine, Ellie could hear approaching hooves coming along the lane at some speed.

Cecilia frowned and got up from her chair. "William? But why the hurry?"

It was indeed William, and as he jumped down from the horse he was a little out of breath. "There's been a break-in at the office," he panted as both he and the horse tried to recover. "The sheriff's not around. I'm glad to find you here, Pa, can you come? And you too, Cecilia? We need to find out what's missing."

"I can guess what they were looking for, and thankfully they won't have found it." George got up and finished his drink before following his son.

"Oh, now what am I to do? I can't very well take Thomas with me; he'll only make things worse."

Ellie laid her hand on the girl's arm. "I'll take Thomas back to the farm. Don't you worry about us. We can go to see Brandy again on the way. What do you say, Thomas?"

The little boy nodded solemnly and the matter was settled.

CHAPTER 23

William surveyed the offices of Dixon's Attorneys. The door had been forced, so at least the windows were intact, but inside was a different matter and there was paperwork all around the place.

"I'd like to see that newspaper reporting on this! Some real news would make a change." He picked his way through to the back to find no space had been left untouched. "Where's the sheriff when there's serious work to do?"

"William…" George spoke in his fatherly, commanding voice. "You aren't going to make things any the better by stomping through the crime scene. Now, please don't touch anything for the time being. I will go in search of the sheriff again, and when he's seen all there is, we'll start sorting everything out. It won't take so long for the three of us. And you're right, I will also see if I can get the newspaper to cover what has gone on. We might just be able to turn this to your advantage."

William slumped down into his desk chair and scowled. "I don't see how this can be to our advantage in any way."

"Trust me, son. It can."

George gave a reassuring smile to his son, but William was in no mood to return the gesture. As George went in search of both the sheriff and the newspaper, he sat with his head in his hands.

"I think your father's right." Cecilia spoke softly and her voice calmed William a little.

William was frustrated by having to sit and wait. He wanted to be doing something. Ideally, he wanted to be out in search of the reprobates who'd done it, but the chance of getting to the bottom of this was probably no greater than getting the Reese boys tried for arson. When would it all end?

It was a good half hour before George returned, but when he did he was accompanied by both the sheriff and a man who William knew to work at the newspaper, but had not been formally introduced to.

"This ain't pretty." The sheriff was looking around the office. "When did you find it like this?"

William's instinct was to respond with a cutting remark, but he held his tongue. It was Cecilia who spoke, but the whole time she did so, the sheriff continued to look at William and his father and address his questions to them.

When the sheriff began to ask if they had any idea what the thieves might have been looking for, it was George who answered. "Sheriff, I think you probably know that as well as I do. If this doesn't relate to the little matter we saw you about yesterday then I'm President Ulysses S. Grant!"

William smiled for the first time and had the confidence to speak without giving in to his temper. "Sheriff, you and I both know the value of the file copy we've retained. Nothing else has gone missing, and thankfully we had the foresight to ensure the file was not here." He turned to the newspaperman, who was taking in every word of what was being said. "And, sir, given I have irrefutable proof that I am entirely innocent of the case that some are trying to bring against me, I suggest you think carefully about what your paper might write, in order to prevent you libelling me. Perhaps it would be more effective to cover my political campaign impartially, and not listen to the tittle-tattle of every prejudiced naysayer in the town." William had a thought and smiled his most winning smile. "I would be more than happy for you to do a full interview with me, so I can answer any of your questions in person."

The newspaperman, Zac Harrison, peered at William through his spectacles and stopped trying to take notes. He was hesitant as he said, "I'll speak with my editor, sir."

William wanted to roll his eyes. He suspected, as with all things in this town, there'd be family connections somewhere which would make it unlikely he'd be fairly reported. He forced a smile. "Thank you, Mr Harrison, I can't ask for more than that."

The sheriff turned to Zac and gave a genial shrug. "Will you excuse us here now, Zac? There's some other questions I need to ask these fine people before I'm done."

Zac moved toward the door, but William could see he wasn't keen to leave. He made a point of ensuring the sheriff was aware Zac was still in range, before turning back to the lawman. The last thing they wanted was the newspaper having any more ammunition to use.

"Well, now." The sheriff ambled his girth further into the office. "Who was the last person who can vouch for these premises being in good order, other than your good selves?"

William opened his mouth to answer, but his father got in ahead of him.

"Sheriff, are you trying to suggest one of us would have done this?"

William was balling his fists, finding it increasingly difficult to control his temper.

"Well, sir, I'm bound to think that it's a possibility."

William looked to his father, but it was Cecilia who responded. "Sheriff, of course I wouldn't presume to tell you how to go about your job…"

"No, you most certainly wouldn't, ma'am. I don't think we need detain you further. I was speaking with the Misters Dixon."

William was quite ready to wade in. How dare the sheriff speak to Cecilia in that way? But it was Cecilia who answered for herself.

"Sheriff, might I remind you — I too am an attorney with this practice. Now, as I was saying…"

The sheriff looked dumbstruck, and for a moment William felt like cheering.

"… There is no logical reason for any one of us to do this to our office. As my colleagues have made clear, we have a fully notarised copy of the file that was handed to you. That file will prove beyond doubt that William is innocent of any wrong-doing, and if you allow the matter to go anywhere near a court of law, it will only serve to demonstrate to the judge how easily fooled you can be. In the interests of your own career, might I suggest you think very carefully before deciding what to do next, or I might just provide all the information that's needed to Mr Zac Harrison, and leave him to draw his own conclusions."

The sheriff was opening and closing his mouth but saying nothing.

"Now, if you will excuse us, Sheriff, I believe you have some potential suspects to go and talk to, and we have an office to tidy up ready for business on Monday." With that, Cecilia got up from where she was sitting, walked to the furthest end of the office and made a point of beginning to carefully sort through each paper she picked up, in order that it could be returned to the correct file.

The sheriff was still standing mute and William wanted to punch the air. Time and time again he was reminded why he was so happy to be married to this amazing woman.

William managed to politely say, "Good day, Sheriff," without smiling, before turning his back and going to help Cecilia. He looked back to see his father had taken the sheriff's arm and was manoeuvring him toward the door and out into the street.

A few moments later, George returned without the sheriff.

"I am most sincerely glad you are on our side and not working for any of the other firms in town." George laughed heartily. "You've certainly sent the sheriff away with a few things to think about. My son is a very lucky man."

"And don't I know it? That's certainly brightened the day." William felt positively happy as he organised the files.

Cecilia simply smiled and continued to sort out all the papers around the floor.

Early in the afternoon, she got up and headed toward the door. "If you would excuse me for a short while, I have a couple of errands to run which really can't wait."

William got up, kissed his wife on the cheek and then carried on working while she went on her way.

After Cecilia returned, it took them another couple of hours before most things were straight and the door lock repaired. William stood back and surveyed the office with satisfaction.

"I don't suppose they'll try to break in here again, but I suppose that doesn't mean other places aren't at risk." He sighed.

"Well, let's hope the sheriff does his work quickly." George Dixon took up his coat and hat and went with William and Cecilia into the street.

William laughed. "The sheriff's put on so much weight, I don't suppose he's going to be doing anything very quickly."

Once outside, George made to walk in the direction of Dr Pritchard's and the Red House.

"We have to collect Thomas from the farm before we go home," Cecilia said, taking William's arm.

George hesitated. "Then, if you don't mind, perhaps I'll join you." He looked uncertain.

"Of course not — you can join us for supper afterwards if you'd like to." William would be delighted for his father to eat with them, as he really wanted to talk about how to get his campaign back on track. Somehow, he had to win the newspaper over, and he had no idea where to start. The election was only a matter of four months away, and as yet he had convinced few people in his own area, let alone in the wider district. He could wait for the next opportunity, in a couple of years' time, but patience had never been one of his stronger qualities.

Once they arrived at the farm, as was so often the case in the summer months, everyone was sitting outside the cabins. Thomas and Mary were happily pottering about, with doting adults all around ensuring they kept out of mischief. John was playing with Cady and Junior, throwing sticks for the little dogs to chase.

"It looks as though your day has been a little less fraught than ours." William happily accepted the beer that Daniel offered.

"It's not a bad life, as long as you don't mind working

dawn till dusk pretty much every day of the year. Not that I'd swap. Nothing would have me being indoors all day." Daniel sat down again and closed his eyes.

"Give us a song, Daniel," Molly called to her husband.

"Must I?" Daniel said, but William knew he wouldn't really mind.

John stopped throwing the stick. "I'll sing, Pa."

They all turned to John, who wiped his hands on his trousers and took a deep breath.

And come tell me Sean O'Farrell tell me why you hurry so
Husha buachaill hush and listen and his cheeks were all a glow

Even Mary and Thomas fell silent, spellbound by the haunting song. No one moved as John's beautiful voice rang out into the evening. He sang through all the verses to the end.

Death to every foe and traitor! Whistle out the marching tune
And hurrah, me boys, for freedom, 'tis the rising of the moon.

"'Tis the rising of the moon, indeed." George looked up into the sky. He got up from his seat on the bench and moved away to the neighbouring field. Miss Ellie quietly got up and followed.

Cecilia gently nudged William, who frowned. He looked past his father and Miss Ellie to see what it was Cecilia was looking at, but he could see nothing and shook his head.

CHAPTER 24

"Have you seen the headline?" George Dixon came into the office, brandishing the morning's newspaper in the direction of his son.

William had been in the office for a couple of hours already and had not seen the newspaper. He had no wish to do so. After the last few days, he couldn't see it would be anything other than further bad news.

"Good morning, Pa. You seem overly cheerful, considering how things seem to be going."

George grinned. "I rather think you might change your mind when you've seen this." He turned the paper around and held it in front of William.

Malicious Actions Leave House of Representatives Candidate Undaunted.

As much as the headline, it was the opening paragraph which caught his attention.

William Dixon, one of Pierceton's strongest ever candidates for a seat in the House of Representatives, is determined that the malicious campaign being waged against him by his opponents will not deter his candidacy. In the latest of a long line of actions, thieves broke into Dixon's Attorneys, searching for the copy of a file which unequivocally proves Dixon's innocence in the recent accusations which have been manufactured against him.

This newspaper does not believe that the town should be represented by men who would support such behaviour against an innocent man, and, having researched the policies for which Mr William Dixon stands, we are throwing our weight behind his candidacy. We believe he will be an excellent Representative for this District…

William's jaw dropped as he'd read what was there. "But who? What?" He went back to the beginning of the article and was about to reread what Zac Harrison had written when his father spoke.

"I suspect Cecilia might be able to enlighten us as to some of what's there." He raised an eyebrow toward his daughter-in-law and William followed his gaze.

Cecilia was feigning innocence and pretending to focus on the file in front of her.

William began, "When you went out for an hour or two on Saturday…"

"I just had a couple of errands to run, as I told you." She smiled up at them both and looked quickly back to the file.

George Dixon adopted the expression William knew only too well from seeing his father in the courtroom. "And where exactly did you go, in order to fulfil those errands?"

William waited eagerly for an answer, until it dawned on him that, for the first time, his father had met his match. He roared with laughter, got up from his own desk and went across to his wife. He took her hands, pulled her gently to a standing position and began to jig around the office, with Cecilia protesting somewhat unconvincingly.

"Have I ever told you, my darling girl, that marrying you was the best thing I ever did?"

"You might have mentioned it once or twice," she said, laughing and a little out of breath.

"How did you manage it?" He held her at arm's length and grinned. He was quite possibly the most fortunate man in the world.

"I told Mr Harrison the whole story, from your life on the streets of New York to your being adopted by Mr Dixon and then risking everything to save Daniel. I told him how it was you who went in search of Ben and brought him back to live out his days here, and then about the arson and our not being able to do anything to bring justice for that poor, dear man. Then I told him about the things that have happened during your campaign — the Ku Klux Klan, the false charges and, of course, the break-in. Nothing more than that."

"I hope you didn't tell him 'all' about my life on the streets." William stopped suddenly and frowned. He knew there were things in his past that it would be better not to make public.

Cecilia rested a hand on his arm and smiled. "I'm not sure even I know all there is to know, but you can rest assured that Mr Zac Harrison is now firmly on your side. I may have taken the liberty to tell him you would be addressing a meeting on Wednesday evening, if he would be free to attend."

"You, my darling wife, are simply wonderful. Now, what do we do about the sheriff?"

Cecilia broke into a broad smile.

"I rather think my daughter-in-law might have addressed that too. That wouldn't have been the other of the errands you ran on Saturday, would it?" George shook his head but was smiling broadly. "If you managed to make the sheriff see sense, I have a lot to learn from you, young lady. After the way he ignored you when he was here, I dread to think how you got him to take notice."

Cecilia simply smiled. William realised she had no plans to elaborate. He hoped the sheriff would have the good sense to drop the whole matter, though the man could not afford to lose face, so William suspected they needed to be wary.

"Well, I must be off." George checked his pocket watch. "I don't want to keep a lady waiting."

William watched him go. "Which lady?" he asked Cecilia.

"Oh, he's going with Miss Ellie to talk to Joe, I believe. She asked me to go with her, but as Sarah's attorney I was concerned there might be a conflict. Your father very kindly offered to go instead."

William noticed Cecilia's mouth was twitching as she answered. "Is there something more you're not telling me?" he asked.

"Nothing specific. He was very ready to volunteer, which surprised me a little."

William frowned, not really seeing what Cecilia meant. He too would have happily accompanied Miss Ellie, if she'd asked.

There was no sign of the sheriff over the next couple of days and William focused on making his speech for that evening as strong as it could be. He wasn't going to offer unattainable dreams to those who heard him, as some of his opponents seemed to do. If he was going to win in the primary election, he had to do so based on policies the voters could trust. He really had little time to waste, if his name was to appear on the main ballot a few months from now. Both Zac Harrison and the sheriff had the power to make or break any hope he had of a political career.

One thing which saddened him as he prepared to go out that evening was that Cecilia would not be present to hear him. After all she'd achieved with the newspaper, he felt keenly the sense of injustice at her needing to wait at home. He resolved to harbour that feeling and turn it into a passionate call in his speech.

As William took to the platform, he had only two thoughts in mind. How could a country ever be great which denied a voice to half the population, and what would be the next day's headline?

"Gentlemen, under President Lincoln this country made great strides toward equality. The Civil War ended slavery in the South, and the 15th Amendment to our Constitution said men would not be denied the right to vote based on 'race, colour, or previous condition of servitude'. The northern states of this land fought to bring about that freedom and equality. I ask you tonight, do you believe in equality?"

There were murmurs of assent from around the room and William knew the reaction to his next comments would be vital to everything that happened from thereon.

"I'm pleased to hear you do. Now, gentleman, I ask you to look around this room. What do you see? If, like me, you see a room full of gentlemen, all of whom are white-skinned, you will realise we are a long way from that equality being a reality. Already, the reforms which were put in place are being undermined in the South. We cannot allow that to happen. We must lead the way. We must work to bring about genuine equality, not just for those the 15th Amendment sought to include, but our womenfolk too. They must be given the chance to play their part in this nation and they have a right to do so…"

When he finished, William received a standing ovation.

He raised a hand and acknowledged the small crowd. He felt the first thrill of hope that he wasn't beaten yet. As he came down from the platform, one after another of the men who had listened greeted him and shook his hand. He did notice one or two who left quietly, but not many. His father slapped him on the back.

"A fine performance, but before you get too carried away, don't forget, the better you start to do, the more your opponents will try to stop you."

William nodded. He knew his father's words were wise ones, but for now he just wanted to enjoy the moments of success.

The following morning, William was awake at first light. He kissed Cecilia and Thomas and was out of the door in the direction of the office by seven o'clock.

"It's a fine thing, when the newspaper is more important than breakfast with your wife and son." Cecilia's face was arranged in a pout, but her twinkling eyes and twitching mouth gave away her good humour.

"And you wouldn't have it any other way." He waved to them as he left, and hurried on into town.

As soon as he could find the newspaper, he searched through for the story. The main local story related to problems at one of the sawmills, but given a good position and headed 'Reform Must Continue', Zac Harrison had been as good as his word. Not only had he fairly reported the meeting William had addressed, and given a good account of William's speech, but he was urging the paper's readers to take William seriously as their candidate and to give him their support.

William sat down heavily in his chair, smiling and feeling a little dazed. He was still sitting there, if truth be known, dreaming, when his father came in.

"Well good morning." His father removed his hat. "It seems you're the talk of the town this morning. Let's hope that's the case after election day, too."

Coming back to reality for the first time in a good hour, William said, "I guess the hard work has only just begun. It's no good me getting too carried away."

"On that subject, I have half an idea." George was sitting on the edge of William's desk. "What about challenging your opponents to a debate? Making it a public meeting and inviting all to attend, and I really do mean all."

William sat up a little straighter. "How would we go about it?"

"Well..." His father paused and stroked his chin. "I hoped Cecilia's friend Zac Harrison might get the newspaper to set something up."

Before William had time to reply, the sheriff came into the office and both William and his father stood to greet him.

"Sheriff," George said, nodding to the arrival.

William cleared his throat and forced a smile. "How can we help you, Sheriff?"

"Well." The sheriff scratched his stomach. "I thought I'd drop by and bring you gentlemen some good news."

"Oh?" George spoke cautiously.

William felt like getting hold of the sheriff and shaking him, but maintained his restraint and followed his father's lead.

"Well," the sheriff continued, "it turns out the gentlemen" — he put heavy emphasis on the word 'gentlemen' — "who informed me of their loss at your hands, don't want to press charges."

"Sheriff…" William's fury made his voice wobble slightly as he addressed the man. "Do you mean…?"

Before William was able to get any further with his tirade, George Dixon moved forward and stepped in. "That's very kind of you to let us know, Sheriff." George took the sheriff's arm and escorted him back toward the door. "We wouldn't want to take up any more of your precious time. Thank you kindly for dropping by."

Once the sheriff had left the office George turned to face his son. "If you make an enemy of the sheriff now, William, he'll remain an enemy and you will be looking over your shoulder all your days. However, if you allow him to leave with his dignity intact, you just might find you have a friend when you need one. He may not be able to say so, but he knows you're innocent and that those who accused you have led him a merry dance. He doesn't need you to spell that out to him."

William's earlier triumphant mood was shattered. He felt like a recalcitrant child who had received a dressing down, and even though he could see his father was right, he didn't want to give Pa the satisfaction of knowing it. He got up from his chair and went out into the street for some air.

CHAPTER 25

The summer months were always the most pleasant to work outside on the farm. Whilst the hours were long, Daniel didn't mind the hard work and had little difficulty getting up in a morning. The cows were as happy to see him bright and early as they were later in the day, and getting them milked was a good way to work up an appetite for breakfast.

Molly had planned the farm carefully when they'd expanded into the old Reese land. Daniel had thought it would be easiest simply to increase their planting of corn but Molly had argued for trying other crops. As he examined a field of corn and noted the paucity of strong healthy plants, Daniel couldn't help but be glad for the wheat she'd settled on.

As he went about his labours during the heat of the day, his thoughts turned, as they so often did, to Ben. Even now, he missed the companionship of them working together with Duke, Ben's former dog, at their heels. Now, he had much the same relationship with John and enjoyed their times together with Duke's son, Junior, running about. He still enjoyed singing as he worked, though he was equally happy to hear John's voice.

As he mused, it occurred to Daniel he hadn't seen either John or Junior that morning. Whilst he didn't expect John to work all hours, the boy was never happier than out here in the fields. Daniel presumed Molly had given him some chore in the dairy or that he was looking after Mary for an hour or two.

Daniel smiled. It wouldn't be long before Molly gave birth again. Would it be a boy or a girl? He'd be delighted either way, as long as mother and baby were both safe and well.

By the time he'd finished checking over the fields, he decided there was time to call up to the farmhouse for lunch. The hunk of bread and cheese he'd brought out with him earlier would still suffice, but at least he could eat it in pleasant company.

Daniel strode across the farmyard, looking around for John and Junior. He was surprised the little dog had not come barking toward him as he usually did.

"John! John." Daniel felt a prickle of unease at the lack of response and wondered if he might be down at the cabins.

The back door to the kitchen was open and Molly came out as he called.

"Is John with you in the house?"

Molly, who was clearly enjoying a mouthful of whatever she'd been baking, simply shook her head. Once she'd swallowed and licked her fingers, she said, "I thought he must be with you. The last I saw of him, he went to see if he could find any ripe berries down by the copse, but that wouldn't have taken him all morning. I was going to put them in the pie if he'd brought any back, but I've used apples instead."

Daniel frowned. John rarely stayed away from the farm for long. "I only talked to him last night, to make sure his troubles were behind him. Miss Ellie and Mrs Hawksworth are doing a far better job of his education than ever the school was. At least he feels safe here. I'll check the cabins and then head down to the copse. It's odd that Junior hasn't come back. I suppose he will, when he's hungry."

"If you aren't coming in for lunch, at least take some pie with you." Molly went back inside to bring a slice out to him. "I'd come myself, but with this bump..." She looked down at her massive girth. "I shall be glad when I've given birth. It feels as though I'm carrying an army already, and there are still weeks to go."

"I'll be home long before you go into labour, this time." Daniel grinned, remembering finding Molly giving birth to Mary on the kitchen floor.

The smell of the pie overwhelmed him, and he took his first mouthful before he was even back across the yard. He could save the bread and cheese until a little later.

When he got down to the cabins, James was sitting in the sunshine, quietly puffing on his pipe. Except for the smoke curling up and away as he breathed, nothing was moving. He opened an eye as he heard Daniel approach, and took his pipe out of his mouth.

"And to what do I owe this pleasure?" James stood up and stretched.

"I was looking for John. We've not seen him all morning, which isn't normal. I don't suppose he's here?"

"I might have been napping, but I'm sure he's not been down this way. Ellie went out mid-morning and I've not seen hide nor hair since then."

"Molly said he may have gone looking for berries, so I'll head on down the field to the copse to see if he's there."

"Mind if I join you? I could do with stretching my legs. I don't want these old bones giving up just yet."

James fell into step with Daniel and they went along the edge of a field of wheat which was close to being ready for harvesting. Daniel hoped the baby might wait until harvesting was done, but he suspected that wouldn't be the case.

Daniel strained his eyes to see all around the copse as they approached. There was no sign of movement. The best berrying was on the far edge, so he planned to work his way around the side of the trees, rather than going through the middle. The cool dark in between the trees presented some great places for a child to play, if he didn't mind the creatures he might find there, but if John was on a mission to collect berries, he was likely to have been focused on his task. Daniel thought he heard something and put an arm out to stop James so he could listen. Nothing.

He was grateful the ground was dry, as it made the uneven mud easier to cross, although the stream ran close up on the far side, so that might be harder. He stopped again. "John! John! Junior!" Then listened intently. Nothing.

James shook his head. "Perhaps he's gone on someplace else. Would we be better to split up? I'll go through the trees to the other side and work around toward meeting you at the far end?"

Daniel sighed. "We might need to get up a search party. It's going to be hard for two of us to cover all this ground."

"I can go back, if it helps?"

"Let's try what you suggested first. Maybe we'll be in luck. As long as that little dog's not injured, he'll let us know where we can find John, as soon as he hears us." Daniel was surprised that Junior hadn't yet come out to greet them and wondered what might be preventing him doing so.

A further half hour passed as Daniel worked his way

along the edge of the copse. He was progressing slowly, trying to check all of the surroundings rather than just what lay ahead. Once or twice he heard a twig break; maybe an animal or even James moving about. There were still no answers to his shouts.

Ten minutes further on, Daniel thought he should turn back to get a larger search party, but then he heard something. He stopped, straining his ears to pick up any sound. It might have been a whimper, but it was very muffled. It was coming from somewhere inside the wood, not on the edge.

"John! Junior!" Daniel listened again. He could hear a faint noise.

"James! If you can hear me, I think they're in the wood." Daniel thought it might be best for the two of them to go in together, rather than separately. He looked around for a large stick to beat back the undergrowth, then listened again. He was getting near to the end of the trees; James couldn't be far away. He shouted again and tried a whistle. This time there was an answering whistle. Was it James, or could it have been John?

Daniel decided to make his way into the wood, slowly and carefully, moving branches and bushes aside as he went. Every couple of yards he stopped and listened, then gave a lone whistle and waited for the response. Whichever of them was replying, they were getting closer.

Next time he stopped, he could definitely hear a whimper. He was sure it was Junior, but why wasn't John responding, if Junior was hurt? Then he heard other noises — something thrashing through the undergrowth away to his right. "John!"

"No, it's me, James."

"Be careful." Daniel wondered why he'd wasted his

breath on something so obvious. He moved a little further forward. He could hear James more clearly now. He listened again for the whimpering. He was sure that had come from straight ahead, but among the trees it was easy to become disorientated. Yes, there it was. "James, bear slightly to your right and keep going forward. I'm heading that way too. I think I've heard something."

"Will do."

Even in the dim light of the thick of the trees he could start to make out James's movement.

As Daniel beat back more undergrowth he heard James cry out, "God help us!"

Daniel changed course and tried to move quickly in the direction James had called from.

"Be careful, Daniel. John's breathing but unconscious. He's been caught in a trap."

Daniel beat harder at the undergrowth to work his way through safely. "And Junior?"

"I haven't seen Junior. John's bleeding badly from his leg. We need something to tie around it."

Before Daniel had even reached the spot where John lay, he'd removed his shirt to act as a tourniquet. He dropped down on the ground beside John and felt the boy's pulse. It was weak but regular. He and James heaved open the jaws of the trap and laid it aside where it could harm neither man nor beast. Daniel tore his shirt in two and tied one half tightly around the leg above the wound.

James suddenly got up. "Did you hear that?"

Daniel tried to listen as he tied the bandage off.

"There it is again. Either it's Junior or there's another animal nearby." He brushed more undergrowth aside and moved a little further into the trees. "Dear God!"

Daniel was trying to lift John, ready to carry him back.

"I've found Junior. He's in another trap. And if you ask me, these traps look pretty new. There's no rust."

"Can you bring him? I need to get John back as quickly as I can." Daniel had the boy in his arms now.

"Wait, Daniel. If there are traps this close together there may well be more. Let me bring Junior; his leg seems broken, but he's not bleeding much. Fortunately, it's only clipped him rather than getting proper hold. I can get him out on my own. I can carry him and use my other arm to clear our path back out of the wood."

Whilst progress would be slower, Daniel could see the sense in what James was saying and, holding his son close to share the warmth of his own body, he waited for James to release Junior and pick up the stick.

Daniel didn't have the energy to talk on the return journey. His heart was pounding, as much from anxiety as exertion, and he wanted to get the boy safely back to the farm. However, what he really wanted to know was who had been laying traps on his and Molly's land. They didn't belong to the farm, that much was certain. If there was no rust then they didn't predate Molly's ownership of the land — but he'd need to worry about that later. For now, only two things were important — saving the lives of his son and his dog.

CHAPTER 26

Miss Ellie was coming across the yard as Daniel returned with John. "Oh dear, Lord, whatever happened? Molly," she shouted. "Molly!" She stripped off her bonnet. "You take him inside. I'll fetch Dr Pritchard."

Daniel had no time to answer as Miss Ellie laid aside her basket and headed straight for the stable. He took John indoors and settled him along the window seat. The boy was still unconscious, but Daniel thought his pulse was slightly stronger.

Molly came over with iodine for the wound. "It's going to need more than this. I do hope Dr Pritchard can come, although I've no idea how we're going to pay him. We're already struggling to pay the bank this month."

"We'd rather lose the farm than lose John," Daniel said, as he brushed the boy's hair away from his face. "How's Junior?" He looked across to where James had laid the little dog in his basket by the stove.

"He'll be as right as rain by the time I've finished with him. I'm going to make a splint for that leg, and once he's had that fitted and had something to eat he'll be back by John's side before you know it. I need to persuade him to stay put while I get things together." The little dog looked up mournfully as James spoke.

"Bring his basket to my side here. I can work around him. If he knows he's close by, he won't try to go anywhere." Molly moved slightly to make way for James to position the basket, with its patient ensconced within.

As Molly continued to clean up John's wound, James hurried out of the kitchen.

It was hard to tell whether John was still unconscious or sleeping. He looked so peaceful and his breathing now seemed even and regular.

"There's little more I can do now, until Dr Pritchard gets here," Molly said, sitting back a little. "Wrap the blanket around him, but keep it off his leg. I'll get a hot sweet drink for when he wakes up. I think he's going to need something. Children are stronger than you think. I'm sure he'll be fine."

Daniel wasn't sure if she was trying to convince herself or him. John looked anything but fine.

It wasn't long until James was back, with some wood and muslin. He knelt down beside Junior. "This may hurt, little fellow. You're going to need to trust me." He looked up and across to the hearth. "Molly, could you pass his bone over here? It might be good for him to have something to bite on, other than me."

Molly passed the bone and James enticed the dog to take it in his jaw before he took hold of the offending leg. "Just remember, young chap, if you could run through fire to save Molly and Mary, this should be nothing to you."

Daniel was amazed as James quickly and expertly manipulated the dog's leg, with barely more than a small yelp from Junior. Before the dog had time to wriggle, James had attached the splint and neatly bound it to the leg.

Laying the little dog carefully on the bed, James got up. "Now, what can we find him to eat?"

Before anyone had the chance to go elsewhere to look, Daniel took some cheese out of his pocket and unwrapped it. "This should get him started."

James brought the dog's water bowl over so it was close enough for him to reach without having to stand, and then offered him a little of the cheese. Junior sniffed the cheese, but didn't eat it. Instead he looked up at John, who still lay along the seat with his eyes closed.

"Well, I'll be." James shook his head. "He won't take anything until he knows that boy's going to be all right."

"Then let's hope he is." Miss Ellie came into the kitchen, perspiration beading on her forehead. "I'm sorry it's taken so long. Charles was out on a visit and I had to track him down. He'll be with us shortly."

Daniel watched Miss Ellie take a moment to wipe her face and neck and wash the cloth out in the sink.

"I see James has been showing off his true vocation. It's a shame he never had the chance to work with animals. He's always had a knack. He spent our childhood rescuing every injured wild beast he could lay his hands on." She shook her head. "Now, how can I help?"

"I don't think there's much else we can do until the good doctor arrives," James said to his cousin.

"Except to keep an eye on Mary for me, please. She's reached that age where trouble comes looking for her." Molly indicated the far corner, where Mary was building a little house out of the logs Molly had brought in earlier.

Miss Ellie smiled. "In my experience it will be many long years before she stops finding trouble, looking for it or not." She went over and sat close to Mary.

Liza Hawksworth came downstairs and, after checking there was nothing she could do to help, quietly joined Miss Ellie.

Daniel took John's much smaller hand in his and spoke quietly to the boy. "I hope you can hear me, wherever you are right now. We love you, son. I don't know who set those traps, but I sure do plan to find out. Our family should be safe on our own land. We'll get you strong, and Junior. He's a tough little fighter. He got over the fire and he can get over this. You need to come through, too."

"Why don't you sing to him?" Molly was stroking John's hair, the two of them side by side by their son.

Daniel looked at Molly in surprise. He didn't feel much like singing. It didn't seem the time, but maybe that was what John needed. He racked his brains for a song that was a ballad rather than a reel, and settled on one that had been a favourite for years.

As I was a walking one morning in May,
I saw a sweet couple together at play
O, the one was a fair maid so sweet and so fair,
And the other was a soldier and a brave grenadier

He had no chance to get further into the song, as they heard hooves out in the yard. Molly got up and went to the kitchen door to welcome the doctor.

When he came in, Daniel was surprised to see Mr Dixon follow immediately behind.

Dr Pritchard came straight over to where John was lying. Daniel moved the blanket aside so the doctor could more easily see the wound in the lower part of John's right leg.

John must have come at it sideways and the trap had sprung on his lower leg, from his ankle to just above the knee. It was a large wound and the doctor pulled a face when he saw it.

"I'm going to do what I can to treat it before we see if we can bring him round. I suspect this is going to hurt." He looked closely at the wound. "It appears Molly has done a good job of cleaning it up, but it goes quite deep and I can't be sure there's nothing left in the wound." He frowned as he inspected the injury, section by section. "Now that's odd," he said, peering even more intently. "Where did you say this happened?"

Daniel described where the wooded area was — on the far part of the land they'd bought from the Reese family, but still with a field beyond it on each side, so that it was completely within their own land and did not border that of another.

It was George Dixon that Dr Pritchard addressed when he next spoke. "If I were a betting man, I'd say this was a new trap, not one that's been outside for very long. Unlikely to have been there many weeks, never mind months or years."

"That's exactly what I said, looking at the traps." James was on his feet in an instant.

George narrowed his eyes. "What makes you say that?"

Dr Pritchard looked up at George. "The absence of the sorts of dirt and debris that I'd normally see with a wound of this type. It's far cleaner than I'd expect."

"There was no rust on them at all," James added.

George Dixon nodded slowly.

Molly, who was now standing behind the doctor, her hands firmly on her hips said, "Are you saying what I think you're saying?"

"The trap that caused this has been set recently." Dr Pritchard pursed his lips and turned back to attending to John. "On the plus side, it does mean there is far less chance of infection."

Molly turned to Mr Dixon. "Now what can we do?"

George Dixon shook his head. "The first thing to do is call on the sheriff, and that's something either I or William will happily do for you. Unless we can demonstrate those traps are new and find who they belong to, we're going to have some difficulty proving the responsibility for this."

Molly clenched her fists. "Again!"

It wasn't like her to raise her voice and it made Daniel start. However, he noticed John's eyes flicker in reaction, and smiled.

"Doctor, did you see that?"

Dr Pritchard was smiling too. "All in good time, Daniel. All his signs seem good and there's no more I can do now to dress these wounds. At least there's no bones broken."

"Which is more than can be said for young Junior here." James was still sitting by the little dog and gently stroking his head.

"It looks as though you've done a fine job of that, James. He's clearly in good hands." Dr Pritchard returned his attention to his own patient. "Now, I want you to give him a few drops of this every few hours. It will ease the pain, but he needs to rest. There's to be no moving about until the healing is done." He handed the bottle to Molly. "I'm going to see if we can bring him round now, and he needs something hot and sweet to drink. He may want to eat something; a growing boy like this. As long as this wound doesn't become infected John has had a very lucky escape."

Dr Pritchard took the smelling salts from his bag and removed the lid.

As soon as the bottle top was off, Daniel could smell the salts. They would be very strong, placed so close to John's nose. He wasn't surprised when the boy stirred slightly. It took a little while longer before John's eyes flickered open.

"You're going to be fine," Daniel said, with a confidence he didn't completely feel.

John moved his eyes to his father and Daniel smiled. Then he began to sing *The Nightingale* to his son once again.

Soon after, Molly held a cup to John's lips, as Daniel raised him to a more seated position and the boy took a sip of the warm honey drink.

Seeing the boy, Junior let out a little woof of satisfaction, but thankfully stayed where he was. James held out the piece of cheese to the dog, and this time he took it hungrily.

There was another knock at the door and Mr Dixon went over to answer it. Daniel bristled when he looked over to see him lead Franklin Marsh into the farmhouse.

"What's he doing here?" Daniel's last encounter with Marsh had not ended happily.

"Excuse me, sir."

Daniel blinked. Was Marsh really addressing him as 'sir'?

"What is it?" He couldn't stop his own voice being harsh.

"I heard about the accident. How is the boy? You folks have had so many troubles. Is there anything I can do to help?"

Molly answered quickly, "Both John and Junior should recover if we're lucky, thank you."

Daniel couldn't stop himself from adding, "As you can see, we're all quite busy, if you'll excuse us."

"Yes, of course, it's just, well… if you don't need help here, I'm going to the sheriff with all that I know."

Daniel looked at Marsh properly for the first time and paid him some attention. "And what would that be?"

Marsh moved his hat from hand to hand and looked uncomfortable. "This may be the end of my business. It's not going to be easy."

Daniel wasn't interested in Marsh's sob story. They'd lost a house, a dear friend and a baby as a result of those Reese brothers, quite apart from the latest problems, which he also presumed were down to them. He tried to keep his voice level. "And what exactly will you be telling the sheriff?"

"Those boys weren't drunk, the night they set fire to your house."

Now everyone turned to Marsh. Silence fell in the kitchen.

"Oh, they came into the bar bragging what they were going to do, but they didn't touch a drop that night. There's no way they were lost when they were on your land."

Daniel gently rested John's head on a cushion and got up from the seat. "Say that again."

"The Reese boys knew exactly what they were doing and I'm going to see the sheriff to tell him. I'll even stand up in a court of law if I have to."

Liza Hawksworth, who had been standing in the shadows at the far end of the room, came forward. "Do you want me to go with you, Franklin?"

"No, Liza, this is something I have to do on my own. I just wanted you all to know. Good day to you." Without saying anything further, he nodded and went back out of the farmhouse.

Daniel's heart was racing. Could this finally be the breakthrough they'd been waiting for? He went back to sitting with John.

After a few moments of quiet, everyone began to resume the things they'd been doing when Franklin Marsh arrived.

Molly looked uncomfortable as Dr Pritchard began to

pack his bag.

"The thing is, sir…" She looked awkward as she tried to find words. "We can't afford to pay you at the moment. We lost the corn in the end field and we're struggling to pay our bills this month. If you can wait a few weeks until the crops are sold, it should be different."

Dr Pritchard smiled warmly and laid a hand on her arm. "Please, don't trouble yourself, young lady, my account has already been covered." He turned and looked meaningfully at Mr Dixon. "You have nothing to find, now or at any time in the future. And whilst we're on the subject, that goes for your confinement as well. I shall be ready and waiting, just as soon as you need me."

"Thank you," Molly and Daniel said at the same time. Daniel didn't know whether to laugh or cry. He turned to where George was standing quietly, waiting for Dr Pritchard. "Thank you, sir. We cannot tell you how grateful we are."

George Dixon waved the thanks away. "It's my pleasure." He took up his hat and followed Dr Pritchard outside.

CHAPTER 27

"How much notice do you need?" Zac Harrison had been making notes on his pad as George Dixon outlined his idea.

"What do you say, William? I can't see it being much different to any other speech." Pa got up and went over to the window looking out to the street. "Your schedule would allow for it as soon as next week."

"I'd do it tomorrow, if the other candidates agreed." William couldn't see there would be much to gain by waiting, except to give the others he was against more time to prepare. He was fairly clear on his own views and quick on his feet when he needed to be.

George Dixon laughed heartily. "Tomorrow would be just fine, if you wanted to debate without an audience or a roof over your head." He turned to Zac. "I guess the practicalities need to come first, and if this is to be a newspaper venture it might be better if we didn't get involved in those choices. Of course, we're indeed happy to have you in our corner, but it's better for all concerned if you can appear to support us by independent choice rather than being in our pockets."

"Wise words, sir." Zac got up. "I guess I'd best make myself scarce and go to ask the other candidates if they're willing to participate. "I'll come back to you as soon as I know where and when it's going to take place. I've a mind to speak with the newspapers in Warsaw and Columbia City and see if we can set up a series of events."

"Maybe even out as far as Fort Wayne," William mused out loud. He was going to have to win votes from all of them if he was ever going to get as far as Washington.

Zac nodded. "I'll see what I can do." Then he headed off back in the direction of his own office.

"Even if you're beating the associates of those Reese boys in the political field, we still need to bring the brothers themselves to justice. Those traps were a nasty business, but all the sheriff can do is shrug. He even came out with me and agrees they're newly set, but that proves nothing." For a moment, George grinned. "Getting the sheriff down to the wood was no small matter, I can tell you. I suspect that's the furthest the man has walked in a long time."

William stopped and thought about what more they could do. "Were the traps bought or made?"

"I'm no trapper, but I'd reckon it would take a professional to make the ones we found. There were six of them in total. I didn't look to see if they had any tradesman's mark. Why?"

"Well…" William pondered as he spoke. "What if we could track down the store from which they'd been bought, and that store were to have a record of who purchased them?"

George sat a little straighter. "I do believe you should

be doing the sheriff's job. That's exactly what he needs to be doing. I wonder if it's even crossed his mind." George took out his pocket watch. "I've got enough time. I might pay the sheriff a visit. I can at the very least ask him a question or two which may allow him to have that thought for himself."

"If he even wants to." William had little confidence the sheriff would want to find evidence that linked the crime to anyone in particular, let alone the Reese boys.

William went back to reading a copy of the New York Daily Times from the previous week. So much for the hard-won reforms of only a few years earlier. Reconstruction in the South following the Civil War was doing anything but move the country forward, as far as William could see.

He was still reading when his father returned.

"Cecilia's being one step ahead of the sheriff in getting that file notarised, might just be helping us in the trapping issue."

William put the paper down. "How on earth could that be the case?"

His father was grinning. "It seems now, when a line of enquiry is suggested to him, the sheriff thinks we might already know something and, if he doesn't look into it, he's worried we might be about to make a fool out of him."

"That's probably easier to do than the man would like to think. Where is Cecilia, anyway?" William hadn't seen her since breakfast, which was most unusual.

"I suspect we might afford her a day off once in a

while, although in reality I don't suppose that's the case. I believe she had an arrangement to meet Sarah Spencer and was doing so away from prying eyes."

"And where in this town could she possibly bring that about?" William felt frustrated that his father wouldn't simply tell him what he knew.

"I believe," said George, "the younger Mrs Spencer may have had an appointment today at the surgery of the good Dr Pritchard."

William laughed. "Let me guess... where my dear wife happens to be visiting Mrs Pritchard, probably on some important matter on my behalf."

"Quite so," said George. "Now, if you'll excuse me, I too have an appointment, and in my case I am taking the afternoon off."

William had no opportunity to ask his father where he was going, as George slipped out of the office before his son had time to say anything further. William instead set about making a record of the types of questions he thought he might be asked in the debate, as well as ones he would like asked of the other candidates and which he had reason to believe might show him in a favourable light.

He went back to the newspaper and looked through all the national news to see what else he might need to be informed upon. If these debates went ahead, he had to come out of them looking like the strongest candidate, in order to justify the newspaper's backing and secure his place on the ballot.

He was still deep in concentration when Cecilia came

in.

She greeted him with, "I've just seen your father walking arm in arm with Miss Ellie."

"Is that remarkable in some way?" He was really only half listening to what Cecilia was saying.

"William!" Cecilia's tone was exasperated, and he looked up. This time she enunciated each word slowly and carefully, but said exactly the same words.

William, now looking up from what he had been doing, copied her style of speech and said, "And... I... said... is that remarkable in some way?"

Cecilia laughed. "Oh, William, darling, at times you can be very slow."

William harrumphed and was about to go back to what he was doing when Cecilia gave him a winsome smile and sat on the edge of his desk.

"What I am trying to tell you is that I think your father might be walking out with Miss Ellie."

William frowned. "You mean...?"

Cecilia nodded to him solemnly.

Running his hand through his hair, William got up from his desk and started pacing across the room. "But Ma's only been dead these past few months — how can he?"

Cecilia looked at him seriously. "And would you rather he was sad and lonely? You do know Miss Ellie lost a dear friend in your mother too, don't you? I would think they could find a good deal of comfort in each other's company."

William tore a small piece off the edge of his newspaper and started tearing it into even smaller pieces and piling them up. "But Pa loved Ma. He adored her."

Cecilia came over to him and rested her hand on his. "And none of that changes. They don't have a limited amount of love they can only bestow on one person. Why don't you think about it like this... does your father love you any the less because you married me?"

William looked up startled. "No, of course not."

"And do you think your father loves me now, too?"

"Well, yes, of course. He loves you as he'd love a daughter." William frowned.

"Then can't you see, if he doesn't love you less because he loves me as well, then the love he has to give is not limited? Just supposing he began to have feelings of love for Miss Ellie, or for any other woman. That would never take away from the love he had and still has for your mother."

William looked down and began tearing another piece of newspaper. Logically, he could see what Cecilia was saying, but this was Pa, his pa.

Cecilia left him to his thoughts and went to her own desk.

He'd not asked her how it had gone, seeing Sarah, but he didn't feel much like it now. He sat for a while, staring at nothing in particular and letting his mind fret over what Cecilia had told him. How could he be so stupid? He now understood some of the things Cecilia had been trying to get him to see in recent days, but he'd been too blind. He'd never thought his father would consider a woman other than his mother. If he were honest, he really didn't like the thought at all.

The rest of the day passed slowly, but William couldn't have said exactly what he had to show for it. He'd certainly looked at the files he was meant to be working on, but he wasn't sure if he'd read any of them. He'd spent an awful lot of time staring into the distance, he did know that.

"I'm going to collect Thomas. Are you coming with me or going straight home?" Cecilia was putting her bonnet on in front of his desk.

"Excuse me?" William blinked a couple of times, as though just waking up.

Cecilia smiled at him gently. "I'm going to collect Thomas; shall I see you at home?"

William nodded, but said nothing in reply. He didn't feel much like seeing Miss Ellie or the rest of the family right now.

The next few days passed unhappily for William. Pa had been his rock since he was first taken into their home. There was no one William looked up to more. His birth father had walked out on Molly and him when he was a child, and he'd lost both his birth and adoptive mothers. William was terrified of losing Pa. Although he went into the office and saw his father there, he found it hard to talk about anything other than the work they needed to do or the upcoming speeches he would give. He'd avoided going to the farm and had invited no one back to the Red House. Cecilia said nothing about it, although at times he could see in her eyes she was disappointed.

He was in the office on his own when he heard the bell. He'd deliberately avoided looking up when people came in, so as not to have to greet his father or meet his eyes. It was not until there was someone standing in front of his desk, coughing to attract his attention that William took any notice. He raised his eyes slowly and was surprised to be greeted by the sight of heavy farm overalls, rather than someone in a suit. It took him a moment to register it was Daniel standing there, looking uncomfortable.

William got up quickly. "What are you doing here?"

"I might ask you much the same thing. We haven't seen you in days. I'm sure Cecilia will have told you that both John and Junior are making good progress, but we all miss you."

"Aren't you in the middle of harvesting? How can you spare the time to come into town? Is something wrong?" William was thinking of all the scenarios that might be important enough to take Daniel from his work, especially with John not being able to help.

"You're right, I can't spare the time. But some things are more important than work, don't you know?"

William smiled, hearing one of the old Irish expressions that both of them had almost completely left behind these days. "So why are you here?"

Daniel sighed, a look of despair on his face. "You really don't know?"

William shook his head.

"Do you remember when I first met you in New York? Your red hair would get the better of you then, too, although you did have rather more of it." Daniel grinned awkwardly. "There were times when you and me saw things differently. When we fought, we'd normally end up rolling around in the dirt until we were exhausted, then we'd slap each other on the back and move on. We'd ruin that precious suit of yours if we were to roll around in the dirt now, though we'd hardly notice on my clothing, as I spend half my life in dirt." He laughed, but William didn't join in. "Anyway, I guess what I'm trying to say is, you're an adult now and you need to find the adult version of rolling around in the dirt, so you can stop sulking and move on. Your pa is a good man and you're hurting him. You're hurting all of us by cutting yourself off. Just think about it."

Daniel said no more, but turned around and left the office. If anything, William felt more annoyed now than he had earlier. He took up his hat, locked the office and headed back to the Red House. What he needed to do, more than anything else, was to go for a ride on Brandy and blow some cobwebs away.

CHAPTER 28

William didn't take much time off from work these days. If he wasn't in the office, he was busy working on his campaign. As he saddled Brandy, he reflected that he couldn't actually remember the last time he'd been out for a ride, just for the pleasure of doing so. Then it came to him — it had been in Dowagiac, when his mother died. He hugged Brandy's neck to his face.

"Why do we lose the ones we love, Brandy? My natural father left. My mother took other men to her bed just to put food in our mouths. She died, now Ma has died, and Pa…" William could feel the tears coursing down his cheeks as he turned around from the horse. Balling his fists, he raised them up to the sky, and shouted "Why? Why, God, why?"

He sank down beside the horse, which hadn't flinched as he'd shouted. Curling up with his fists to his eyes and thinking no one could see, William wept. As much as for anyone, he wept for Ma Dixon. Until now, the tears hadn't come, but suddenly he needed the release only this could bring. Brandy reached her head down and nuzzled his cheek and neck, and he could feel her nose against his skin. It was the feeling of finest velvet. The feel of Ma's blue dress — and he reached a hand up to touch the horse's nose in return.

"May I join you?" George Dixon, still fully suited, sat down on the ground next to William. "I miss Ma too. I miss the touch of her hand. I miss her scent wafting into the room. I miss her beauty and being able to just look at her. I miss watching her sleep; her chest rising and falling so softly with each breath. I miss the sound of her voice, and yet she's still the voice in my head. If she were here now, she'd be mightily upset to see any rift between us. She'd be right, too. You are my son and there is no one in the world dearer to me than you are. If, by seeing Ellie, I were to lose you, it wouldn't be a price worth paying and I'll tell Ellie that I can see her no more, except in company. But I'm lonely, William."

For the first time in days, William was looking at his father.

"I'm too young to be on my own the rest of my days." George shook his head sadly.

"But you've got us." William frowned.

"Yes, son, I know I have and that in itself is a blessing, but you and Cecilia have each other. I still need someone by my side. Please think about it."

William nodded, but was too choked to find words.

His father got up, brushed the loose dirt from his trousers, patted Brandy and walked back up to the house.

William wiped his tears on his sleeve and took a few deep breaths. He got up and swung himself into the saddle on Brandy's back. They set off, slowly at first, but as they got into a gentle, even, harmonious rhythm, they began to pick up speed and despite the stillness of the day, William enjoyed the feeling of the air rushing past his cheeks.

Conscious of Brandy's needs in the sunshine, he made sure not to go too far, and when he brought her back to the house and dismounted he brought her fresh water before paying any attention to his own needs. How times had changed since he was a child. "Thank you," he whispered to Brandy as he led her back out to her paddock after washing her down. He kissed her velvet nose and headed back to change.

It was still relatively early, and as Cecilia would go first to the farm to collect Thomas, William decided to go back past the office before going on to the farm. Daniel had been right, he'd been away too long. He felt a new peace as he walked through the town, something he hadn't felt for a long time. He was thinking about nothing in particular, but enjoying the warmth of the day and the occasional sound of a cardinal singing; its bright plumage a contrast to the hedgerows he passed.

He was walking past the newspaper office when Zac Harrison came rushing out to him. "I was looking for you earlier. It's all set up."

For a moment William was slow to catch his meaning. He felt a jolt and his eyes widened. "They've accepted? All of them?"

"All the ones in easy travelling distance of Pierceton. I've got two still to persuade." Zac was looking rather pleased with himself. "Next Tuesday."

"Yes!" William punched the air.

"I thought you'd be pleased." Grinning, Zac slapped William on the back and returned to the newspaper office.

William's thoughts were no longer empty as he walked. Instead, ideas were zooming around his mind like coyotes fighting over meat. He needed to speak with his father. He stopped and smiled. He really needed to speak with his father — and not just about the debate.

William was whistling as he walked across the farmyard toward the house.

"And what are you so happy about all of a sudden, brother of mine?" Molly was carrying a pail of water and William took it from her.

"Because I'm a very lucky man. Do you know if Miss Ellie is around?"

"I think she's got the children down at the cabin so John can get some rest in peace."

"Thank you," he replied, leaving the pail in the kitchen, waving to John and going back out of the kitchen door before Molly had the chance to ask anything further.

He could see Miss Ellie sitting on the porch before he arrived, and was pleased to see there were no other adults around. He knew Mary and Thomas would not be far away, but he hoped they might be asleep or busy playing, so as to give him time to say what needed to be said.

He took a deep breath as he approached and was pleased Miss Ellie did not look up and see him too soon. When she did, she smiled.

"Miss Ellie," he said, taking another deep breath. He could feel his hands shaking. "I owe you something by way of an apology."

Miss Ellie raised both her eyebrows and blinked in apparent surprise. She said nothing, but indicated William should sit on the porch near where she was seated.

"I think," William continued, "I may have rather lost sight of what's important in the last few days. I'm sorry."

Miss Ellie waited a moment, possibly to make sure he'd finished what he wanted to say. Then she said, "William, you don't need to apologise. I rather think your father may be very relieved that you've felt able to, but you've done me no wrong requiring an apology. We're all grieving and sometimes we don't know how best to express it."

William was about to reply but Thomas came carefully up the steps from where he and Mary had been playing in front of the cabin. He ran straight to William, who picked him up and sat him on his knee.

"Good heavens," said Miss Ellie. "He's filthy; you'll get it all over your suit."

William thought back to his father, sitting by him earlier in the day. "Some things are more important than a little bit of mud." He kissed his son's forehead and Thomas began earnestly to tell his father what he'd been doing. Not all of his noises were coherent yet, but William did his best to pretend to understand.

He was still sitting there with Thomas on his knee when Cecilia arrived. She stopped abruptly when she saw him. He turned Thomas toward his mother and waved the boy's hand, while himself breaking into a broad grin. Thomas clambered down from his knee, arms outstretched to his mother. William got up and followed.

"I thought I might just come along and see how he was doing."

Cecilia tilted her head to one side and nodded slowly. "And how is he doing?"

William grinned again. By the way she'd asked the question, she wasn't referring to their son.

"Very well indeed, thank you. Although I do need to go in search of my father. We have a date for the debate."

She raised an eyebrow to him. "And is that the only reason you wish to speak with him?"

"I may need to offer him an apology, as well as Miss Ellie." He turned to where Miss Ellie was pretending she couldn't hear. "Do you know if my father is coming to the farm this evening? It would be awfully nice to join you all for dinner."

Miss Ellie blushed, something William didn't think he'd ever seen her do before.

"I do believe he is."

"Good," said William. "Would you excuse me,

darling?" He kissed Cecilia. "I really wanted to have a word with Daniel as well."

William bounced off toward the farmhouse, but at this time of year it was as likely that Daniel would still be working out in the fields. He felt humbled that his friend had taken time out of his busy day to come up to town to talk some sense to him. When he got to the kitchen Molly was there, but there was no sign of Daniel.

"He's still harvesting," she said, and looked at the clock. "It could be a while before he's in."

"Do you have any spare overalls? And which field is he in?"

Molly smiled, but said nothing about William's odd request. She led him over to the barn and found some overalls and boots, and William made his way awkwardly toward the field. He'd never worn overalls of any sort and they felt cumbersome and coarse. The boots were heavy and made his feet feel like stone.

He was sweating by the time he got to the field and found where the men were working.

Daniel removed his hat and wiped his brow. He looked wide-eyed at William. "I never thought I'd see the day."

"No, I don't think I did, either. I reckoned if you could take the time out of your day to set me straight, when you've so much else to do, then the least I could do was try to repay the favour. Where do I start?"

A farmhand was chewing on a stem of wheat as he worked. "I reckon you'll be needing one of these, Master William," he called, passing William the tool he'd been working with. "It's called a cradle. All you need to do..."

Daniel laughed and took the cradle out of William's hands. "Ed's joking. It takes far longer to learn how to use than you'll be working in the fields." He passed the cradle back to Ed. "William will work with me, gathering up and tying. Now let's get moving or this field won't be done till midnight."

As everyone fell back to their roles in the team, William marvelled at how they all knew the part they had to play. He'd never had to learn teamwork, not in this sort of way, and he felt almost envious of the companionship it seemed to bring. He watched closely to see how Daniel used a stem of the wheat to tie each bundle, ready for bringing together in the field. He tried to copy, but his first few attempts looked nothing like Daniel's ones. After that he began to get better and concentrated hard as he worked.

When they got to the end of the field a while later, it was Ed who slapped him on the back. "We'll make a farmhand out of you yet."

William stood up, rubbing his back and grinning broadly. He'd enjoyed himself far more than he could ever have expected, and wondered if Daniel might mind him helping again in future.

As they went back to the farmhouse for supper, William felt as though he'd earned his food in a way he was really not used to.

He felt a jolt as he saw his father there. Much as he was ready to apologise and to acknowledge he'd been wrong, seeing him alongside Miss Ellie still felt mighty uncomfortable. He nodded to his father, but struggled to find words.

He was glad the conversation quickly turned to other things. He'd thought the main news of the evening would be about the debate, and he'd looked forward to the attention that would bring, but it was his father who brought the more important news.

"The sheriff's been conducting an investigation."

"Well, that's a pleasant change." Even William gave his father his full attention.

"Those traps were all bought from the same store by none other than Jacob Reese. The problem he has is that whilst it's one thing proving who they belong to it's quite another proving that's who set them on your land. We do know they must have been set after you bought the land. At the moment it looks as though we have another situation where we can prove everything except what the court needs to know in order to bring about a conviction."

Daniel thumped his fist on the table, making William jump. He wasn't used to seeing his friend showing such uncontrolled anger. Molly stayed her husband's arm.

"Thank God John is recovering and wasn't killed," she said quietly.

Daniel got up from the table and without another word he took his hat from the peg and walked out into the evening. Molly turned and looked at William and he nodded. In a reversal of their childhood days, when he was the hot-headed one and Daniel would come after him to calm him down, now it was his turn to do that for his friend. He excused himself and went out into the yard.

CHAPTER 29

The rest of the gathering sat in silence for a while. Although Molly knew Daniel was not normally hot-headed, when he did become angry he was capable of as much as the next man. Eventually, Molly got up to clear the plates and serve the apple pie that was waiting on the side.

She dropped the dirty dishes she was taking to the sink, as a wave of pain ran through her. "Oh mercy, me. Not now."

Miss Ellie was beside her in an instant. "Let's get you upstairs, my girl. George, you fetch Charles Pritchard. Liza, you clear up this mess and keep an eye on the children. Cecilia, you help me get Molly up to bed. James, you drew the short straw. Please go and find that husband of hers."

Molly, who was becoming aware of more regular contractions, was grateful that this time she wouldn't have to do everything on her own. Miss Ellie and Cecilia were supporting her on the way upstairs when another contraction swept through her body and she groaned loudly.

"You're doing fine, my girl."

The strength and certainty in Miss Ellie's voice was more comforting to Molly than anything had been when she'd been in labour in the past, and she was grateful that at last her guardian would be present for the birth of her child.

Cecilia went about preparations in the bedroom, stripping the bed back and making it comfortable in a manner only an experienced mother or a doctor's daughter could do. Molly found it surprising that Cecilia and William had not yet had another child. Even given Cecilia's wish to focus on her career, it was unlikely Mother Nature would allow Cecilia complete control. A thought began to niggle away at Molly, but she didn't have the energy to pursue it. The contractions were closing in on her. This baby would not be as long in coming as either Mary or their first child, Michael, even though he had been born prematurely.

As Miss Ellie held Molly's hand, Cecilia continued bringing pails of water and towels ready for the imminent arrival.

"Squeeze my hand that hard and it'll be me needing Dr Pritchard when he arrives, rather than you."

Miss Ellie's matter-of-fact calmness made Molly smile. She imagined her dear guardian being just the same if their positions were reversed and it was she, rather than Molly, giving birth.

"Breathe deeply and steadily, that's my girl."

"Daniel!" She so wanted him to be there, quite apart from being worried where he'd gone.

"I'll go and find out." Cecilia was waiting patiently at the side of the bed, ready to fulfil any need that came up.

Molly screamed. "Oh, dear Mother of Jesus, this one isn't hanging around." She panted in and out, giving in to the overwhelming desire to push. When the contraction passed, she fell back onto the pillows. Miss Ellie mopped Molly's brow and had hardly finished when the next wave overwhelmed Molly.

None of her surroundings had much meaning to Molly after that. She was lost in a world of breathing, pushing, screaming. She focused on nothing except this new life. After another prolonged and painful push, Molly fell back on the pillows. This time, as she heard a cry, a smile spread across her face. She opened her eyes to see Miss Ellie lifting her newborn infant, but as Molly looked, another contraction swept through her body and she screamed.

"Dear God, I think it might be twins." Miss Ellie was carefully cleaning the firstborn child as she spoke.

There was a knock at the door and Dr Pritchard came in. He washed his hands in the basin and came straight over.

"Well, Charles, it looks as though you're in time, after all." Miss Ellie moved aside for the doctor.

Molly heard Miss Ellie's voice but felt confused. How could this be going on, when her baby was born? The next wave of contractions hit her and this time the pain was overwhelming.

"This one's the wrong way around. We need to see if we can turn him." Dr Pritchard was quite calm. "This isn't going to be pleasant. Molly, try not to push for the moment."

Molly thought of the times she'd had to help one of the cows when things didn't go right. She tried to be calm, as panicking wasn't going to make hers or Dr Pritchard's job easier. In her head this was happening to someone else. This wasn't her body; it was just a farm animal. Everything was going to be fine.

She hadn't realised Daniel had followed the doctor in, until he gripped her hand. She briefly looked up into his worried face. "You made it," she said, but then another contraction overwhelmed her and she screamed with the pain.

This time Dr Pritchard's voice was more authoritative. "I need you to hold on, Molly. We're not quite ready for this one to come out."

But she couldn't hold on. Her body wanted to push, more than anything in the world. She heard Miss Ellie encouraging her to control her breathing, and Daniel whispering he loved her. She wanted everything to go away, to be free of the pain, to feel she could just lie there in peace with her newborn baby. She felt as though she were drifting away; somewhere, a long way away…

"Molly, stay with me." The sharpness of Daniel's words pulled her back, but the pain was too much to bear. She wanted to drift, so very much, she wanted to drift…

"I think we're ready. I want you to push now, Molly, as hard as you can." She thought it was Miss Ellie speaking but it looked like Dr Pritchard.

The room was swimming as the next wave of contractions overtook her. With all she had left, Molly screamed. Then she fell back against the pillows, no longer conscious of anything going on around her in the room.

As Molly's eyelids fluttered and the room began to come into focus, for a moment she was confused as to where she was. "What…?"

"Sh, sh. You're all right. Everything will be all right." Daniel was by her side, tears running down his cheeks. "I thought I was going to lose you. Oh, Molly, nothing matters except that you and the babies are all right."

"We have twins? Where are they?" She began to try to prop herself up, but Daniel gently stopped her.

"You need to lie still a while. I'll bring them to you. They're right here." He took first one baby and laid it against Molly's right breast, and then the other against the left.

"Are they boys or girls?" Even in her exhaustion Molly was comforted to know they were both well. "I knew I was large, but I never thought for a minute there was more than one."

"They're both boys. I'd say they're pretty much identical, but then most babies are, to me." He laughed.

"What shall we call them? I hadn't even begun to think of names this time."

"There's no hurry, although I'd dearly like to call the first one Ben. I'm not altogether sure whether I know which one that is now."

Molly tried to look down at the tiny bundles happily suckling at her breasts. "Ben. Ben. Yes, one of you is Ben. And the other?"

"What about Charles, after Dr Pritchard? Without his quick intervention, I rather think I might have lost the both of you."

"Yes, Charles. I like that. Benjamin and Charles. Ben and Charlie. I think you should bring Mary and John to meet their brothers." She reached over and touched his arm.

Daniel's face was positively radiant as he looked down at them all. He nodded to her and swallowed, but said nothing. He quietly went out of the room in search of the other children.

Molly rested her eyes a moment and must have dozed. When she opened them, Daniel had carried John into the room and Miss Ellie was holding Mary. Miss Ellie put Mary down and the girl stood transfixed.

"You can come closer, both of you," Molly said, checking that Ben and Charlie were comfortable.

Mary took small tentative steps across the room. She had her thumb in her mouth and looked utterly fascinated by the sight of her mother holding her brothers. John, having been lowered to the ground, hobbled forward, taking his sister's hand as he went.

Daniel put a chair for John to sit close to the bed and Mary peered up over the side from where she was standing. Then John kissed his fingers and gently touched them to the head of each of the twins. Quietly he said, "I promise to be the best big brother you could ever have. I'll be there for you whenever you need me."

Molly looked across to Daniel and saw his eyes were glistening as much as hers felt damp. How lucky they were to have adopted John into the family, and thank God his injury hadn't been any worse. His healing was slow, but in time he should be back to normal. She sighed.

The twins were starting to drift off to sleep. Miss Ellie, who was missing nothing of what was happening, stepped forward. "They'll have to share the crib until we can get another one sorted out. I dare say making a second will keep James out of mischief for a few days. Come now, children, your mother needs to get some rest while the twins are sleeping." She took Mary's hand. "I rather think Dr Pritchard would like to look in before he leaves, too. Shall I send him up?"

Molly nodded, but was struggling to keep her eyes open. Even the discomfort she was feeling would do little to prevent her sleeping tonight.

It took Molly longer to be back on her feet from the birth of the twins, than it had when Mary was born. Feeding them was exhausting. She was grateful that Miss Ellie simply moved back into the main farmhouse and took over all the household duties without needing to be asked. Daniel was still busy harvesting, but came back to the house at every opportunity to see them. When he did, he couldn't stop smiling. Miss Ellie made sure to bring Mary and John up regularly, both to see their mother and their brothers. Despite a little frustration that she was falling behind with her work, Molly could never remember being happier.

"How are you managing the dairy?" Molly asked Miss Ellie, when she came in with some lunch.

"We have a secret weapon there." Miss Ellie raised an eyebrow and grinned.

"Which is? Surely you aren't doing all of that, as well as looking after the children and the house?"

Miss Ellie laughed. "No, Cecilia volunteered to do some. She's leaving town an hour or so earlier and coming back and spending two or three hours in the dairy each day. I think she's rather enjoying herself. William's so busy preparing for tomorrow night's debate. I think she's glad to have something to do."

"That really is kind of her. Can you ask her to look in to see me when she's next here?"

Miss Ellie nodded, then fussed over both of the twins before going back downstairs.

It was later that day when Cecilia came in. Molly patted the bed so she would come and sit close. Molly took her sister-in-law's hand in her own.

"You haven't been in to see me since the boys were born and yet you're being so kind."

"It's nothing," said Cecilia, waving her other hand in a dismissive gesture.

"Actually," Molly continued, "I don't think it's nothing, at all. I think you may be finding it all rather difficult. I've seen the wistful look in your eye. I don't mean to pry, and you can tell me to mind my own business if you'd like to, but would I be right in thinking you'd like a bigger family of your own and are struggling to conceive?"

Cecilia bit her lip and nodded slowly.

"You don't have to talk to me about it, but sometimes talking can help."

"We've been trying since not long after Thomas was born." Cecilia took her hand away from Molly and held it with her other hand in her lap, looking down as she spoke. "It isn't helping that William's so busy."

"Have you talked to him about it?"

Cecilia's eyes widened. "Good heavens, no. What would I say?"

"Does he even know how unhappy you are?"

Cecilia bit her lip once again and shook her head. "I do love working as an attorney. It's what I've always wanted, but I never realised that I'd want to be a mother as much as this, and whilst I was an only child, I don't want that for Thomas. I really am very happy for you and Daniel." She looked across to the crib where the boys lay sleeping. "But every time I see your growing family, I feel a pang because I want another one of my own."

Molly nodded. "May I talk to William? He is my brother, after all. One of us needs to tell him how you're feeling."

Cecilia looked up at Molly through her long lashes. "Would you?"

Molly smiled and took her hand once again. "Of course I will. It's the least I can do, when you've been so very kind to me."

"I think you'll get more sense out of him after

tomorrow's debate, but I'd be very grateful."

Molly squeezed her hand. "Consider it done."

CHAPTER 30

Of the twelve candidates taking part in the Primary election, to determine who would appear on the final ballot, the newspaper had persuaded seven to take part in that evening's debate. The ones who would not be present were those who lived further afield. William was determined he would travel to any location he was asked to, even if it meant staying overnight. He supposed some might not be able to be leave work or family behind, but, looking down the list, he suspected it was more about those who felt secure in their support. He knew he was coming from the back of the race, and if any debate could bring him a few more supporters, that could only increase his chances of appearing on the final voting paper.

He looked along the platform at his opponents. Some were rather more hirsute than he was, and he paused. Would things like that play well with the voters? He was gratified to see at least one candidate who looked more like a mouse wishing to hide from the gaze of the audience than like a prospective politician. What they had in common was that they were all white and obviously all men. William smiled to himself wondering if any of the audience would be women on this occasion.

The chairman of the meeting, a dour figure of around sixty or seventy years of age, looked intently at each candidate and back to his list. William presumed he was contenting himself with the identity of each. He had hoped the chairman might be someone he knew, but that wasn't the case. The man looked over his half-glasses at those assembled to listen, nodded and brought a gavel down on the table to call the meeting to order.

"Gentlemen, I won't waste time on many words myself, as I know it's the candidates you've come to hear. We're fortunate to be the first staging-post for these hustings. I believe there are three more fixed for the coming week, before the voting for who goes forward to the main ballot. We will open questions to the floor in a moment, but I'll ask each candidate to give us a few words of introduction first."

William listened intently to his opponents. He wanted to know every strength and every weakness, every pitfall and every opportunity that sparring with them might present. Of the other six, he gauged his main adversary to be a fellow attorney from Warsaw. The man was perhaps twenty years older than he was and had vast experience, not only in law but in politics as well. It was clear he would argue well, but William needed to understand what he stood for, to know how best to fight against him.

What William had, which he was willing to bet none of the others possessed, was streetwise cunning. He didn't plan to resort to dirty tricks, but he wasn't afraid of a fight, though this one would be with words rather than fists. More than that, his background gave him an understanding of parts of society of which he suspected his colleagues on the platform had no experience.

The audience, like most of the candidates, looked to be well-to-do, white, and middle-aged or older. He remembered his first speech in Dowagiac and how, more than anything those gentlemen had wanted to elect men just like themselves, who would do little to rock the boat.

He wouldn't pretend he was something he wasn't — his days for that had passed — now, however, he knew more about how to carry his audience, rather than confront them.

Following their brief introductions, the audience had many questions, and with seven of them to answer, the chairman had to keep their answers short. William worked hard not to waste a single word.

"What do you think the approach should be to Reconstruction in the South?"

Some candidates wanted to take a hard stance, bringing the southern states into line. William's main rival, as he saw him, was, on the whole, avoiding giving direct answers to any of the questions. William wanted to stand out as being different.

"Sir," he said to the questioner, "I see it as no different to any business deal which you might enter into. To be successful in a deal, however hard you negotiate, both parties must come away believing there is some benefit in it for them. Otherwise the solution will lack commitment from one side or the other." There were satisfied murmurings and loud applause.

He moved comfortably through questions on slavery, women's suffrage and the economy, and was starting to feel confident until a man he didn't recognise stood and asked, "What's your view on the death penalty?"

William sensed a trap. Here was that question again. He still wanted to bring about a prosecution for the Reese brothers, and if they were found guilty, death was the likely sentence. He didn't want to sound like a hard-liner who'd hang a man for the least of offences, but he didn't want to give licence for anyone to brand him a hypocrite. Maybe it was time to give the sort of answers the Warsaw lawyer had been giving.

"As an attorney, it remains my duty to work to see justice is done and prosecutions are brought correctly under the laws of this land. The rights of all parties must be taken into account, both the victim and the offender. However, it is the judge who must decide what punishment is appropriate. I do not stand as either judge or jury, but as an advocate for whomever I represent."

He thought he'd covered the point sufficiently and the chairman would move on, but the questioner came back with a further point. "Sir, and what would you argue as an elected politician who had a say in making or unmaking those laws?"

It was not that William didn't know. He was against the death penalty in principle. Taking a deep breath, he prepared to answer. He was about to open his mouth when the mouse-like candidate, having had less of the platform time than his adversaries, could contain himself no longer and stepped in.

"If I might be so bold as to answer on this one, as I've had little chance to speak on other matters…"

William did his level best to look serious and turn his attention to the man, when he really wanted to break into a broad grin.

"… Whilst the Old Testament teaches us an eye for an eye and a tooth for a tooth, you will find our good Lord is recorded in the New Testament as having taken an entirely different view. We are all sinners, and the taking of life should be in God's own hands and not ours." He gave a self-satisfied nod and turned to the chairman. "I'll be happy to go into more detail or answer other questions if you have any."

"No, no, I think we'll move on." The chairman turned

to look for the next question.

The moment had passed and William breathed a sigh of relief.

"It was outstanding." William was full of excitement the following day at the farm for supper.

George Dixon grinned at him. "I think what my son is trying to say is, there are some very good candidates he's up against, but he did a pretty fine job of matching any of them. If the report in the newspaper is to be believed, I was not the only one to be impressed."

"There are still the other debates to get through and then the vote. I hope I stand a pretty good chance of going through, if last night is anything to go by."

"That's as maybe, but voters can be funny things and it's a bit different making an impression on your home ground than it is in the bigger places, where you're not known."

William sighed. He knew that, but he was enjoying his moment of glory.

"I'm very pleased indeed for you," Molly said as she moved away from the table to meet the rather loud demands of the twins. "Perhaps you'd like to come and sit with me, so I might discuss another matter with you."

William felt awkward. "Should I wait until you've finished feeding the boys?"

"Oh, for pity's sake, William, how else do you think they're going to eat? It's all perfectly natural and you've nothing to be embarrassed about."

"You're forgetting he didn't grow up on a farm. It's amazing how much difference it makes when you spend your whole life around animals." Miss Ellie was smiling. "Perhaps William would help me clear up first and then he can come to you."

Molly sighed.

"Yes, of course." William was out of his chair and helping to clear the table before anyone could comment further. Once he could see that both the twins had been fed and Molly was cradling them as they slept, he went over to join her. The rest of the family were still sitting talking around the table at the other end of the room.

"Can I join you?"

"Oh, brother of mine, what am I to do with you? Come, sit."

He perched on the edge of a seat, having the impression this was going to be a difficult conversation and not in the same vein as the congratulatory ones he'd been enjoying.

Molly spoke quietly. "Have you noticed how sad Cecilia is?"

William blinked. How could Cecilia be sad? She was happy with how everything was going for his campaign and she loved working in the office. "I think you must be mistaken. Cecilia has never been happier. She has everything she's ever wanted."

Molly gently shook her head and indicated across to the table.

Cecilia was sitting looking down, taking no part in the conversation. William frowned. "Is she ill?"

"In a way, yes. Cecilia would like to have more children than just Thomas. I think she'd like more time to be a mother, but more than that, she'd like a little more time with you. You're neglecting her, William."

"But I see her all day in the office as well as at home. I..."

"William, that's not the same. When did you last spend a day with Cecilia and Thomas — enjoying each other's company, playing together? You won't have a bigger family if you're never at home."

"I didn't know she wanted one. I always thought…"

"Whether she wanted more children or not, you need time for the two of you when you aren't going to fall straight to sleep, or worse, when she's already asleep when you get home. You've got the best wife a man could have. Don't take her for granted. There, I've said too much. Now, be gone with you, brother — I've a husband to attend to."

Junior limped over and nudged Molly's hand.

"By the look of that, I think Junior's feeling neglected too." William grinned at Molly and kissed her on the cheek. "Thank you. I'm a lucky man and no mistake."

"Pa," William said, when he returned to the table. "I know I need to be at the hustings in Fort Wayne on Saturday evening and you had intended to accompany me, but would you be amenable to a change of plan? Would you and Miss Ellie look after Thomas this weekend so that I can take Cecilia with me, please?"

When Cecilia looked at William, it was as though a light had turned back on in her face, and he could have kicked himself for not having noticed that it had at least dimmed, if not gone out altogether.

Miss Ellie gently touched Pa's arm. "It would be our pleasure, wouldn't it, George?"

George Dixon nodded to his daughter-in-law and smiled.

CHAPTER 31

William held Cecilia's hand as they travelled to Fort Wayne. "I've been a bit of a fool, losing sight of the most important person in my life. I'm sorry."

"You know, if you're elected, we're going to have to manage a lot of time being apart, unless we all move down to Washington. It's going to take work by both of us. Do you think, rather than me staying to run the office, Thomas and I should move with you and ask your father to keep things going here?"

William looked across at the shy look on his wife's face. "Is that what you want? I would never ask you to leave your career behind for me."

"It wouldn't be for you, it would be for us. Besides, talking to Molly made me see how much I want time to be a mother too. Thomas may turn out to be our only child, we don't know, but I don't want to look back and find I've missed all of his growing up in order to chase my own dreams."

William nodded. He too was at risk of that. "Will you come to the hall when I speak tonight?"

Cecilia smiled. "Yes, as long as I don't have to dress as a man to come in. If they'll have me as I am, then I'll be by your side."

"If they won't have you there, I'll decline to speak. There's no good my saying I stand for equality, if it doesn't mean anything."

Cecilia squeezed his hand.

When the train pulled into the station, they still had plenty of time to look around the city before the debate.

In comparison to Pierceton it was a grand city, with buildings in Greek and Gothic styles. They both stopped and stared in wonder.

Whilst Cecilia pointed to every detail as she drank in her surroundings, William was suddenly aware that winning a base of support in Pierceton, Warsaw and other surrounding towns would be of no use to him if he couldn't make an impression here. Zac Harrison had shown him one or two newspaper clippings suggesting he'd received some favourable coverage ahead of the debate, but his campaign would be won or lost based on that night and how it was reported.

"It's going to be a big week for all of us," Cecilia said, as they sat on a bench in one of the city's parks. "With both the Primaries and going to see the sheriff about the Reese boys. One way or another, our lives won't still be the same at the end of it."

William was quiet for a moment. "Of the two things, justice for Ben and stopping what the Reese boys are putting my sister through is the most important."

"And I'm the more proud of you for thinking that's so. If you don't get elected this time, you can try again. We won't get another chance in the other matter."

They sat quietly together, enjoying the sunshine. A small part of William wondered if it might be better if he didn't win. A life in politics could be hard for all of them.

The hustings did go well, and although it was made clear that Cecilia being there was highly irregular, she was allowed entrance and sat close to the platform, where William could see her smile. He was now on reasonable terms with most of the other candidates and especially greeted the mouse warmly. His gratitude for the man's unwitting assistance in Pierceton, and the fact that ultimately he saw the man as little threat, made it easy to be generous. There were others with whom he would always remain watchful.

Thankfully, there were no questions from the audience deliberately geared to catch him out, other than would be faced by any candidate, and William made a good attempt to answer them all. Now, he had to wait for the polls to close and the votes to be counted.

The break had done both him and Cecilia good, and when they returned to the farm the following evening to collect Thomas, Molly gave her brother a big smile, but said nothing, for which he was grateful.

Liza Hawksworth was there when they went in.

"Mr Marsh was as good as his word," William said to her. "I'm seeing the sheriff tomorrow."

"That's as maybe," said Liza. "We've a way to go yet, so I'll keep my counsel for the moment."

Miss Ellie laughed. "You're a hard woman, Liza Hawksworth. That poor man is besotted with you."

Liza smiled in apparent satisfaction, but said no more.

What difference he thought it was going to make was unclear even to William, but on Monday morning he made especially sure his shoes were polished and his tie neatly tied. Given the physical appearance of the sheriff, he doubted for a moment the man would be impressed, but William felt the need to try. Cecilia wasn't going to the office until a little later, but she was at the door to wish him luck. He took one last look in the mirror and set off for town. He had time to collect his file from the office before going to see the sheriff, and besides, the sheriff didn't seem to start quite so early in the morning as William.

It was actually Zac Harrison who was the first to greet him. The newspaper man was waiting outside Dixon's Attorneys as William arrived. "I thought you'd want to see this," Zac said, barely able to contain his grin. It was that day's newspaper from Fort Wayne, with the lead story being a report on Saturday's hustings.

William already knew from Zac's face that the report was going to represent good news, but his hand was still shaking as he took the paper and held it close enough to read. Phrases like 'new man in town' and 'the one to watch' jumped out at him. He'd clearly made a good impression; now all he could do was hope.

He gave the paper back to Zac.

"No, keep it. I thought you'd want to show that wife of yours, so I got a spare copy sent."

"Thank you. That's mighty kind." William tucked the newspaper under his arm.

"We're counting on you, William," were the reporter's parting words.

Those words continued to echo through William's head as he prepared to go to the sheriff's office. Molly and Daniel were counting on him and he meant to do them proud.

"Do you want me to come along?" George Dixon was coming into the office as William prepared to go out again.

William hesitated but felt well prepared. "No, you hold the fort here. I'll call you in as reinforcement if I need you."

"Good luck, son."

William nodded and set off.

"Sheriff." William took his hat off as he went into the sheriff's office.

"Mr Dixon, good morning to you."

The sheriff indicated the seat in front of his desk, which, as there were no others in the room except the sheriff's own, caused William to smile.

"I'm guessing you already know that Franklin's been to see me." The sheriff had a good scratch and William moved his chair an inch or two further back.

"I do, sir. Does this mean we can get the case reopened at last?"

The sheriff sucked his teeth. "Well, son…"

Being called 'son' by the sheriff made William feel he was not being given due respect, but he held his tongue.

"… That there all depends on Justice Warren and whether he thinks there's a case to answer."

"How can there not be a case to answer? You've already got a confession from one of them, and now a witness who can disprove the main thrust of their defence." William wanted to take the sheriff by the collar and shake him, but that was more likely to get him put in a cell than secure the result he was after.

"I think you best go speak to Justice Warren yourself, Mr Dixon." The sheriff took a long pause. "That is, if he's willing to give you time."

"Sheriff, how about we both go over to Warsaw to see Justice Warren? That way you can tell him what evidence there is against those boys at the same time."

The sheriff sucked his teeth again. "Well, now…" He stopped mid-sentence, in apparent contemplation.

A thought struck William. "Or might it be better if I were to talk to the newspaper about where we've got to?"

The sheriff sat up a little straighter. "Now, you don't want to be doing a thing like that, son. Maybe we could take a ride on out to Warsaw. I'll send word over to see when Justice Warren would be free to see us. I can't say fairer than that now, can I, son?"

"No, Sheriff. In which case, I'll put off talking to the newspaper for a day or two until we hear back." William knew from the look on the sheriff's face that his threat had been understood. "Good day, Sheriff." He got up and left the office, then took a few deep breaths to try to calm his anger.

There was little time to worry about what Justice Warren was going to say, as the Primaries were the following day. Voters across their District would determine which candidates' names would appear on the final ballot paper. In his heart, William wished this was the end of the whole process. Having to continue the round of campaigning and repeat the debates seemed pointless. It was almost a test of who would stay the course; who had the biggest sources of funding to get through an extended period of campaigning. The whole process inevitably meant a lot of time away from his business, as well as the costs of travelling around the district. It seemed to be an indirect way of ensuring that only the elite could go forward in the first place. However, he couldn't change the world while watching from the sidelines so he had to keep going.

By the middle of Monday afternoon, he was being completely unproductive sitting at his desk.

Cecilia was hard at work, but he decided to interrupt her anyway. "Is it too late in the day to suggest you, me and Thomas take a picnic out for supper, while the weather's still good?"

Cecilia looked back at the file she'd been working on, as though wrestling over the decision. Then she smiled, closed the file and put it in her drawer. "Thank you, Mr

Dixon, I'd be happy to accept."

On the Tuesday, once he and his father had cast their votes, William could settle to nothing.

"William," his father said, "you're in no state to do your work well today. You'd be far better doing something completely different. Why don't you go and borrow some overalls and help Daniel finish the harvesting? Physical labour that leaves you tired is going to be more use than you worrying a pen around a blank sheet of paper."

William grinned. He knew his father was right, although he was uncertain if he'd be any more use to Daniel than he was here, but he was more than happy to find out. He was gratified when one or two people called 'Good luck' to him as he made his way through Pierceton to the farm. He'd need to wait until at least the following day before there was any hope of hearing the result.

Wednesday was as impossible as Tuesday had been, with no news coming through. It took a while for votes from all areas of the District to be counted and then for news of the result to filter back out. William presumed he would learn how to handle these times in future elections, but for now he could concentrate on nothing.

Thursday was an altogether different day. His first visitor was the sheriff. "Justice Warren will see us this afternoon, if we can get on over there."

William frowned. He supposed he could find the result in Warsaw as easily as he could here in Pierceton, but he'd just assumed he would be with family, to celebrate or otherwise. "What time should we go?" He looked at the wall clock and saw it was a little after nine.

"He reckoned three o'clock might be as good a time as any. There's a train about two that would get us there."

William nodded. "Then we'd best be on that train,

Sheriff." The thought of an afternoon in close proximity with the sheriff was not one that filled William with enthusiasm, but he had little choice and the train would be the fastest route. "I'll see you at the station."

The sheriff took his leave and William turned to his father. "Sir, will you join us in going out to see Justice Warren?"

"If I can get word to Ellie that I have a pressing matter to attend to, then I most certainly will. I'll go to the farm now to let her know."

It was an hour or so later when Zac Harrison came into the office. "Well done, sir," he said, holding his hand out to shake William's.

William looked at him, frowning, not wanting to have taken his meaning incorrectly. "Do you have the result?"

"We certainly do. We just received a wire from Fort Wayne. Your name's going forward to the main election."

"Cecilia! Cecilia!" William ran past Zac, looking for his wife. Before she had time to ask what was going on, he caught her up and swung her around, knocking two files to the floor in the process.

When William put Cecilia down her face was glowing. "Does that mean what I think it does?" She looked first to William and then to Zac, still out of breath.

"It most certainly does, ma'am." Zac held his hand out to shake hers.

"And didn't I tell you that he was worth backing?" Cecilia winked at Zac and he grinned back.

"I'd like to do an interview with you for the paper, if you can spare the time," Zac said, turning to William.

"No time like the present, Zac. Thank you."

When William had finished answering Zac's questions, most of the morning had gone and William had left himself less time than he should have done to prepare for his meeting with Justice Warren. He gathered his things together and headed to the station to meet his father and the sheriff.

CHAPTER 32

"My, are you two ever demanding? No sooner does Ben stop crying than you start," Molly said to Charlie, picking him up and rocking him gently. "Thank goodness for Grandma Ellie and Nan-nan, or I'd never get a moment's peace."

"I can help, Ma." John hobbled across the kitchen, using a stick for support.

"Oh, John, would you? When I get Charlie settled I really need to take a nap myself, if you can watch over your sister and Thomas for me? They've been looking for mischief all day."

As she put Charlie down, Molly smiled at Miss Ellie, coming into the kitchen from the dairy, singing to herself. She collected some trays from the side and turned right around, barely missing a beat. Molly's guardian's behaviour was as though she had become twenty years younger. It was wonderful to see, and Molly knew Mr Dixon would treat Miss Ellie as well as any man could; something she deserved after all these years.

Molly settled in the armchair in the corner of the farmhouse kitchen and dozed, amongst the comings and goings of the family. She was awoken by the sound of what seemed like a distraught voice calling her name.

"Shhh, Molly's sleeping. Oh, God preserve us, whatever's the matter?"

Molly forced her eyelids open to see Miss Ellie had

taken Sarah gently by the arms and was looking at her intently. Molly blinked again, in case she was still dreaming. Sarah was indeed in the kitchen with Miss Ellie.

"Sarah?" She was about to ask her friend how on earth she'd found an opportunity to visit, when she looked at the state of her. This was no ordinary call. "Whatever has happened?"

Sarah was shaking. There was clear bruising to the left side of her face, and the area around her eye was starting to colour toward purple.

"Come," said Molly, guiding the rag-doll-like Sarah to a chair.

Sarah simply stared straight ahead, allowing herself to be led but saying nothing. Molly sat with her while Miss Ellie went back to the stove to make a drink. As Sarah began to rock to and fro, Molly spoke to her in a soothing voice.

"Sarah dearest, this has gone too far. He'll kill you, the way this is going. However hard this is to do, you have to leave him. For your own safety. I know I don't know what's been happening, but it looks to me that things are getting worse."

Sarah continued to rock but said nothing.

Miss Ellie came over with the drink and, in her brooking-no-argument voice, that Molly loved so well, took over. "Now, my girl, drink some of this and tell us exactly what the situation is. I won't have you in danger a moment longer."

Eventually and in faltering voice, Sarah began to speak. "I've been talking to Cecilia. It may be that he could stop me taking the children. I can't leave without them." She moved her head for the first time, looking first to Miss Ellie and then to Molly. Then, bursting into racking sobs, she said, "And I'm pregnant again."

"How often is he beating you?" Molly moved to kneel in front of Sarah, so she could see her face.

"I don't know." Sarah seemed far away.

"Sarah, you need to answer me. Is this happening every day?"

Sarah shook her head.

"Every few days?" Molly wished Sarah could tell them clearly.

Sarah shrugged.

"Sarah, I think you should stay here. Somehow, Miss Ellie and I will try to get the children."

For the first time, Sarah looked at her, her eyes wide. "I can't. He'll come after me. I'll lose the children. I can't." Then she broke into heaving sobs.

"Right, my girl, you listen to me." Miss Ellie's voice carried strength and practicality. "If you stay where you are, you'll be losing that baby and probably a lot more besides. We need to get you out of there, with the children, and staying somewhere safe."

"Nowhere would be safe." Sarah shook with sobbing as she spoke.

Miss Ellie took the girl's face in her hands. "Now, you listen to me. I have an idea which will mean you are safe. It's not going to be easy and it will mean you need to go back for a few days. I can only pray you'll be safe in that time. At the end of it, you will be safe and you will have the children with you."

A brief look of hope crossed Sarah's face.

"If I can arrange that, will you do exactly as I tell you and ask no questions?"

Molly held her breath.

Sarah looked at Miss Ellie, open-mouthed.

"Did you understand what I said? You would need to go back now and pretend that everything's all right, until I can get things sorted. It may take me as much as a week or two to get everything arranged."

"I can't leave. He won't let me." Sarah had stopped crying and she seemed to be more aware of what was they were saying. "Where would I go?"

"The fewer people who know the plan the better, and I'm afraid at this stage that includes yourself. If you don't know, then Joe can't beat it out of you, and you can't make any mistakes in what you say to people. When you go back, don't start to pack or do anything which will arouse his curiosity. You will only be able to take with you what you can carry when the time comes, but I'll see to it that you have all you need for you and the children. Do you understand everything I've said?"

"But she won't be safe if she goes back." Molly felt her own panic rising at the danger her friend would be in.

"If Sarah won't leave without the children then there's no alternative." Miss Ellie looked intently at Sarah. "Can you act as though everything is normal for a few days?"

Sarah nodded meekly. "I've been doing it these past years. I can do a few more days."

Molly gasped.

"Dear God, I hope you can. Now, it's best you don't say where you've been when you go home, either. How did you come to be able to get here?" Miss Ellie asked.

Molly passed a handkerchief to Sarah so she could dry her eyes.

"I ran out when he wouldn't stop hitting me. He'll be calm for a while when I get back... sorry for what he's done. It's always the same. For a day or two he'll tell me he loves me and he couldn't live without me. He'll treat me as he should. Then one of the children will scream, or I'll do something wrong, and it all starts again." She looked up at Miss Ellie. "And now I'm so scared for the baby. I didn't want another, but now I'm pregnant I don't want to lose it and the beatings are getting more frequent. Can you really arrange a safe place to go?"

"I do believe I can, child." Miss Ellie's voice was much softer now. "Do exactly as I've said, and I'll get word to you of what needs to be done."

"Will you be all right?" Molly asked as she saw her friend to the door. "You could stay here now if you prefer."

"I'll be fine, at least for a while. I do believe Miss Ellie will help; she always has." Sarah walked out and across the yard, her head down and trying to mask a slight limp.

Molly sighed.

Once Sarah was out of sight, Molly asked, "What exactly do you have in mind for her?"

"Never you mind, my girl. The less you know, the better it will be for Sarah. We're going to have to keep her location unknown to that Spencer family. I only hope helping Sarah doesn't put Clara at more risk. All you need to know at this stage is either I or Liza will be away for a few days fairly soon, so you're going to need to manage without one of us. Maybe we could ask Cecilia if she could lend a hand here instead. A break from that office might do her good too. Now, excuse me, I have preparations to make for Sarah. I don't want to waste a moment."

Molly hugged Miss Ellie.

"We'll have none of that nonsense." But Miss Ellie's mouth twitched slightly as she said it.

Molly couldn't go out to the dairy with four children to look after, so she set about preparing supper in the hope she could spend some time in the dairy later. She'd hardly started when Cecilia came in.

"Have you heard the news?"

Molly assumed she must know how William had got on with seeing Justice Warren, and her heart missed a beat. "What's happened? Will they press charges now?"

"Oh, I'm sorry." Cecilia looked crestfallen. "I meant that William has got through the Primaries. He'll be up for election."

"Oh, but that's wonderful." Molly tried to sound as pleased as Cecilia clearly wanted her to be, but her first thought was that it might mean Cecilia would be too busy to help her at the farm. She reprimanded herself for being so mean-spirited. Given that one of the children was in fact Cecilia's, she felt sure she'd be prepared to help.

"William said they would come straight back here when they return from Warsaw, so they can tell us how they got on there and we can celebrate his first win. Can I help while I'm here?"

Molly burst out laughing.

"What's so funny?"

"Oh, Cecilia, it's just that I feel relieved you've offered. Yes please. I really do need some help. Would you rather do some of the dairy work or look after the children?" She looked at Cecilia's dress. "Hm, I'm not sure you're dressed for either."

"I'll be fine," Cecilia said defiantly. "I'll look after the children for a while if you like. I'm hoping practice with larger numbers might be good for me." She grinned and Molly nodded.

Before she went out to the dairy, Molly had a thought. "Cecilia, what are Sarah's chances legally of keeping the children, if she leaves Joe?"

Cecilia shook her head. "Not great."

"Even though he's been abusing her?" Molly was horrified.

"The law doesn't see her as having rights outside the marriage. I'm afraid it's all based on ownership, and both she and the children are seen essentially as Joe's property."

"Property!" Molly was horrified. "Surely, she's as much right to her own children as anyone has?"

"Sadly, that's not the case. It's the way the English laws were developed. The ones ours are based upon. I know it seems outrageous, if you think about it, but until our politicians see fit to change their views, there's not a great deal we can do."

Molly nodded. "Then we'd best make sure that brother of mine is elected. Does that mean if Sarah left and took the children, Joe would be able to take them back?"

"It does indeed. He would be entitled to do so, and it would be Sarah who'd be in the wrong."

Now Molly understood why Miss Ellie was so adamant she must know nothing of the plans. She had a lot on her mind as she went out to the dairy. She was only half-way across the yard when Miss Ellie came out of the house and called to her.

"I'm away to town, but I'll be back in time for supper."

Molly could see a number of letters in Miss Ellie's hand and presumed they held the key to what she was planning. Molly could only hope the plan was a good one and could be put in place quickly.

Junior hobbled after Molly. It made her smile. He seemed to think having only three working legs should be no obstacle to anything. It was an attitude they could all learn from. He would probably still have a limp when the splint was removed. She suspected it would be matched by the one John would have, so Junior would be in good company.

When she got close to the dairy, she was surprised to hear singing from inside.

Love Divine, all Loves excelling,
Joy of Heaven to Earth come down,
Fix in us thy humble Dwelling,
All thy faithful Mercies crown.

Molly made herself known so she didn't surprise the singer. The singing stopped and Molly found Mrs Hawksworth working hard on a batch of cheese.

Mrs Hawksworth blushed. "Oh, Molly, I don't suppose for a minute I've done it as well as you would, but Ellie said she'd been called away and I knew how tired you were. It's a few years since my butter- and cheese-making days, but you don't forget."

"I'm sure it's just as good as any I could have made today, thank you. I really am very lucky. Is there much more to do?"

"Not a great deal," Mrs Hawksworth said, moving along so they could work side by side to get everything finished.

CHAPTER 33

William followed the sheriff into Justice Warren's room and stopped abruptly. He'd thought they were coming for a private meeting. It hadn't occurred to him there would be others present.

"Gentlemen, are we all here?" Justice Warren looked around.

There were nods from around the table and William felt wrong-footed. He sat up straight when Justice Warren turned to address him.

"As you will no doubt be aware, Mr Dixon, if I determine there is a case to be heard in my court, and I do say 'if', then it will not be down to you to bring that case. That will be a matter for the District Attorney's office, so he is here, in case he has a view on whether he would want to do that." Justice Warren nodded to the man on the other side of the table.

"Most irregular, indeed, most irregular," the sheriff was mumbling quietly, shaking his head.

"Sheriff, if you have something to say, please wait your turn and direct your comments to me." Justice Warren gave him a hard stare. "Now, I have also given the opportunity to Mr Carpenter, who represents the Reese brothers, to be present."

The remaining man on the other side of the room nodded to William and his father. This time William could see the sheriff's mouth move, but no words came out.

"May I remind you all that Jacob and Reuben Reese are not currently on trial, and today is simply to determine if there is a case to answer. Please limit what you have to say to that matter. I do not want to be hearing your legal arguments twice, if a prosecution is brought by the District Attorney."

William was sincerely glad his father had accompanied him. He felt there might be strength in numbers, and the lack of clarity around what was happening bothered him. Most of the law he'd practised was outside the criminal courts, and the way things had progressed so far with this case did not seem to be in line with any textbook he'd come across.

If thinking on his feet had been essential for the hustings, it was going to be even more necessary now, and he needed to be at his sharpest.

"Gentlemen," Justice Warren continued, "I believe new evidence has come to light in the case relating to the fire at Cochrane's Farm. I also understand there is some discussion on whether the case should be considered as murder or arson. Is that correct?"

"Yes, your honour." William cut in quickly, before the other attorney had the opportunity to answer.

The judge peered at the attorney for the Reese brothers, and he nodded in agreement.

"I will allow each of you to speak in turn and will then determine how we will proceed. Are there any questions?"

William could think of an extraordinary number of questions but knew this was not the right time to ask them. "No, your honour."

"Mr Dixon, why do you believe there is a case to answer?"

"Your honour, there is already on record a confession

by Reuben Reese, saying the fire was started deliberately, and we now have a reliable witness who is prepared to swear under oath that the brothers were sober at the time they undertook the action. I believe, your honour, it could reasonably have been expected that there were people sleeping in the farmhouse on the night of the fire, and that a charge of murder is nothing less than should be brought against Jacob and Reuben Reese."

Justice Warren nodded and turned to the attorney who was representing the Reese brothers.

The attorney gave a condescending smile to William, and William had to take a deep breath so as not to respond in some way.

The attorney for the Reese brothers then spoke. "Your honour, my clients were drunk. They got lost and dropped their lamp. You were happy about that when we talked to you previously. Nothing has changed. Given they can't read and write, the sheriff's only got a cross on the bottom of a sheet that someone else has written out. That cannot be regarded as a confession." He looked pointedly at William. "Besides, it was only a black man as was killed, which in my book is no different than a sack of corn. The charge should be nothing more than trespass, and that's a private matter, not one for this court. There is no need for the District Attorney to be bothered by this. I say, if a case is brought against my clients for trespass, then we'll see justice done. What do you say, Dixon?" The attorney sneered.

William could hold his tongue no longer. "Justice be damned."

"Mr Dixon, you will not use language like that in my chamber."

Justice Warren had turned a livid red. William needed

to be more controlled.

"Sir," William said, "even before slavery was abolished, the state of Indiana was a free state, and in my book that gives Ben protection under the law. A protection he has not received. Ben was a free man, even before he moved to live on Cochrane's Farm, and a hero when he did. He died saving a mother and baby from the fire. It could as easily have been they who died. The confession was given to the sheriff here, not to me, and we have a witness who will confirm that Jacob and Reuben Reese were not drunk as they claim. In fact, for once, they had not been served a single drink. For the Reese brothers to be tried for anything less than murder is a scandal that will besmirch the good name of this county for years to come."

Justice Warren brought his gavel down on his desk. "That is quite enough, thank you, gentlemen. Sir…" He turned to the District Attorney, "I wish to hear Jacob and Reuben Reese tried in this court on a charge of arson and nothing more. Gentlemen, you are dismissed."

As they began to leave the courtroom the rival attorney said, in a voice intended for William to hear, "As I said, it ain't possible for the death of a black man to be regarded as murder. It wouldn't be proper."

William's anger left the blood pounding in his ears as he turned away from his place in the courtroom. All his instincts told him simply to punch this man. George Dixon moved swiftly to his side and steered his son in the other direction, out of Justice Warren's court.

"Take some deep breaths, William. He wants to goad you into an action you'll regret. Don't give him the satisfaction. If you do that, you won't be able to serve Molly's needs or bring resolution for Ben."

William's nostrils flared as he looked over his shoulder

to see the other man grinning at him. He knew Pa was right. He'd do his level best to see justice for Ben. The charge might be arson rather than murder, but if they won the case the outcome should be much the same, and right at this moment he'd be happy to see those boys hanged.

They were a quiet party on their way back to Pierceton. William was reluctant to discuss what would happen going forward, in front of the sheriff. At least superficially, the sheriff had supported wanting to see the Reese boys tried, but the case would be out of William's hands. This was now a matter for the District Attorney, and William could only hope to ensure he had everything he needed to make it a success. The rest would be down to the judge and jury, and all William would be able to do was watch. For a moment he mused that, if he failed to be elected to the House of Representatives, he might become a prosecuting attorney, but perhaps a life looking over his shoulder would be less than desirable.

They left the sheriff at the station and began their walk back to town.

"The outcome may be the same, if they're found guilty," his father said.

"I know."

"It might be Justice Warren has made the right decision, when all's said and done. I don't think I believe those boys set out intentionally to kill a man. They thought the house was unoccupied — though, being a house, it was perfectly reasonable to assume that someone would be home."

"I suppose I'm just angry about all that happened."

It was George Dixon's turn to say, "I know." He hesitated before adding, "Those boys aren't so bright. Of course, they should have known this could happen, but I don't suppose they thought it through."

They fell silent for a while, each lost in his own thoughts, until William said, "I need to win that election. There are many laws which need changing. It's only a very small number of the population who are adequately protected by the law and given a fair hearing. There's no place for women, few places for the black population and few opportunities for those who don't have the best start in life. I want to change all that."

"And I'm mighty proud of you for trying. There is another group who get even less consideration, and they were here before any of the rest of us."

"I don't know much about the Indian settlements, except what we were taught in school." William hadn't even thought about how the country's laws might affect these people.

"Just remember, there are two sides to every story and the things you're taught are often the things that suit the people doing the teaching."

How had his father come to be so wise? William was glad Pa had now chosen to make Pierceton his home.

When they arrived at the farm, the rest of the family were gathered to welcome them, as were Dr and Mrs Pritchard. It should have been a night for celebrating, but William still felt aggrieved about the things said by the attorney defending the Reese brothers, and Molly was obviously distracted with worry for Sarah.

As supper progressed it became more a campaign planning meeting, both to ensure every opportunity was given to the court to find the Reese boys guilty and for what now needed to be done in the run-up to October's election. William wondered which would come first and hoped it would be the election. He had sworn he'd sit in court throughout the trial, and that would be hard to do if he was supposed to be campaigning. He certainly didn't want to choose between the two.

CHAPTER 34

Over the next few days Ellie was extremely busy. She'd arranged with James that he would take over some of the childcare, and now that John was able to move around more easily, he was helping. Liza was thoroughly enjoying the dairy work and took over most of that, together with caring for the hens. Between them, the day-to-day work was covered, so Molly could have enough time for the farm books, the house and the twins.

Ellie's first challenge had been to plan a journey that would not be easy for anyone else to follow. Tongues wagged too easily, and she was not planning for Joe Spencer to have any idea where he might find his wife and children. Thankfully, with George Dixon's help, it was far easier to accomplish. No one in Pierceton knew their ultimate destination. Even Cecilia had no idea that Ellie was taking Sarah to Cecilia's parents' house in Iowa City. Ellie felt sure Dr and Mrs Hendry would help, and being several days' travel away made it much harder to find, especially as she planned to break the journey.

Ellie's starting point was to buy tickets which began from earlier on the train line than Pierceton itself.

"After all Cecilia told us about Fort Wayne, George and I might travel out there today and spend some time looking around," Ellie said, at breakfast on the Saturday morning.

"What a lovely idea," Molly said, clearly none the wiser

to the plan.

Ellie left immediately after breakfast and met George in town. Planning to do the return trip in the day would leave them little time for sightseeing, but in reality they didn't need to go further than the station itself to accomplish their goal. Once they arrived at the Fort Wayne station, separately and with a reasonable time interval between, they each went to the ticket office. One of them bought an adult and a child ticket for the train from Fort Wayne to Chicago, whilst the other bought an adult and a child ticket from Fort Wayne to Wanatah, a point at which Ellie had stopped previously. Booking from Fort Wayne with only one child on each, Ellie hoped that if anyone asked whether a woman with two children had travelled from Pierceton, it would be enough of a diversion to put any searchers off the scent. The tickets were for the following Tuesday. Now all she needed to do was to work out how to get Sarah and the children to the station.

She and George still had a couple of hours to look around the town and make the most of their time. As Cecilia had told her, the buildings were much grander than the ones in Pierceton, and as she and George walked arm in arm, Ellie didn't think she'd ever been happier.

"How can I get word to Sarah of what she needs to do?" Ellie asked George as they walked.

"That I can help you with. I do believe Dr Pritchard would be a very willing party in getting a message to her for you." He stopped and turned to her, his face clouded. "Have you considered the possibility that she might not choose to leave on the day? There is a risk she may not be ready to break free."

Ellie nodded sadly. "Yes, I've been talking it through with Liza. She was telling me how easy she found it to convince herself Ned would change, if only she tried harder. In her mind she still loved him and didn't think she was worth better. I find it hard to understand. It's such a dreadful cycle, and one it seems is more common than we realise."

They walked on in silence for a while. Ellie was thinking through the next stages, including how they might cause enough distraction in the store for Sarah and the children to slip out unnoticed. She had an idea.

Sunday passed quietly and, although she attended church, Ellie's thoughts were on the week ahead and not on the pastor. She reckoned his words would be just as much use to her in a couple of weeks' time, and could be managed without for the moment. After church she walked over to the Pritchards' house, ostensibly to see Dorothea, but in reality to leave the note Charles would take when he visited his patient the following day. In the afternoon, she took Liza aside and briefed her on the important role she needed to play.

Ellie could only hope the letters she had sent had arrived at their destinations and that everything was set at the other end. She'd specifically stated no reply should be given, as she wanted nothing to give a clue to the journey. Her one remaining fear, which she could do nothing about, was what might happen to Joe's mother. However, she reckoned that, given her history, Clara Spencer might be better placed to deal with her son than Sarah was.

Monday seemed an interminably long day. George took Ellie's small case, with essentials for the journey, to keep ready at his house. He planned to take it to her at the station and load it onto the train without needing the help of the porter. Later in the day, Ellie received word that the message had been delivered to Sarah, but of course there'd been no opportunity for Sarah to reply and there was no indication of whether she would carry the plan through. All Ellie could do was wait.

On Tuesday morning the train from Fort Wayne, which passed through Pierceton on its way to Wanatah and Chicago, was due at half past ten. Its stop at Pierceton was a brief one and Ellie, Sarah and the children needed to be ready to board without being conspicuous for any length of time.

Ellie walked into town with Liza Hawksworth. Even though she knew the journey well, she'd timed each section to ensure they left nothing to chance. She parted from Liza at the general store and continued down the road to meet George. Liza's role was the most vital. She would go into the store and strike up a conversation with her friend Clara Spencer. At the same time, she would slowly select purchases from around the store. If Sarah was following her instructions, she should be pretending to be suffering from severe morning sickness and so be unable to attend to the store. At a little before ten o'clock, Liza, who was carrying a large basket, would have a fainting fit and swing around, accidentally knocking over the large display in the middle of the store. They were assuming that, if Joe was around, he would work to put the display back together and leave his mother to care for Liza, who would need some female support.

As long as Sarah had been able to obtain the key to the back door of the house, and had no need to go out through the store itself, that would be the moment she would take both children and set off for the station. Liza had even practised a loud wail, in case she felt the need to cover any sounds that might come from Sarah's suddenly getting the children moving.

Ellie would be ready, sitting on a bench with George on the route that Sarah would take to the station.

Even if they got that far, that would only be the beginning of the journey.

Waiting with George was nerve-racking. It took quite a lot for Ellie to be fazed, but there were so many things which could go wrong.

"Will you stop worrying? Your planning would do credit to any spy."

George winked at her and Ellie felt herself blush. There'd been aspects of the subterfuge which she'd found rather fun and thrilling to put together.

Time was moving on and there was still no sign of Sarah. Ellie wished she could walk up and down rather than sitting on the bench. "What if she doesn't come?"

"Charles seemed fairly confident that she will, if she can. He seems to think she's past the stage of believing anything will change, and is more scared for the baby."

Ellie nodded and kept watching in the direction of the store. As the sun came and went from behind the clouds, it was difficult at times to see exactly what was going on. The clouds parted and the street was much brighter. Ellie could see a figure walking briskly, with a child holding her hand one side and another on her hip. "They're coming." She got up quickly.

"Stay calm," George said. "No sudden movements that will set either of the children off, or draw attention."

Ellie nodded. They'd said all that in the note Dr Pritchard had taken to Sarah, but Ellie still felt like running to meet the girl. This was supposed to be like a chance encounter that no one would pay any attention to. Going to meet her would not help in the long run. There was still enough time to catch the train.

As Sarah and the children neared, Ellie fell into step with Sarah, taking Jenny and giving her a big kiss before putting her on her own hip, and greeting Henry as they walked.

George went on ahead of them, with Ellie's little case, to find the right carriage of the train and see that the door was open ready for them to board.

Ellie felt her heart pounding. She would save questions and explanations until they were safely aboard and ideally when the children next fell asleep. Until then, they would pretend it was a day out and an adventure.

There were few people on the platform as they approached the train. Ellie breathed a sigh of relief as they climbed aboard and took their seats. George closed the door behind them and stood back to wave. When the whistle blew and the train began to move, Ellie knew that, although the journey was now in progress, their problems had only just begun.

"Why isn't Pa coming with us?" Henry asked as he looked out of the window.

"Because he needs to work in the shop today," Sarah replied, with a slight wobble in her voice.

"Where are we going?" the boy continued, climbing down from his seat and starting to look around.

"We're going to see lots of different scenery and enjoy a day out on a train." Ellie smiled as best she could at the boy, who from the start she had feared could be trouble. He was in many ways his father's son and had a strong, determined streak that risked being their undoing.

"Can I see the engine?" Henry asked.

Ellie smiled. The immediate danger of his questions and behaviour had passed for a while. "Later, we'll take you right up to the front to see it."

Jenny was asleep almost as soon as the train started moving, but Henry was watching out of the window and asking a whole stream of questions about the things he saw. Sarah was looking around nervously, and Ellie was doing her best to keep her tone light and answer the boy without showing any of the frustration she was feeling.

"I'm hungry," Henry announced after a while.

Although there were stops at stations, and carts on the platform which offered snacks along the length of the train when they stopped, Ellie had brought some provisions with her to try to minimise any upset. She brought out some bread and cheese, with buttermilk and lemonade to drink.

Thankfully the boy was soon placated and, after eating, fell asleep quite quickly.

"Where are we going?" Sarah asked quietly.

Still not trusting Henry was asleep, Ellie asked, "Is Henry reading yet?"

Sarah shook her head.

Ellie took out a piece of paper and showed it to Sarah, who looked at her, wide-eyed. "But that's a long way away."

"Which is why I think you'll be safe, child."

Sarah nodded but Ellie could see the fear in her eyes.

"You know Cecilia is trying to win the right for them" — Ellie nodded at the children — "to stay with you? If she manages, then things can be different."

Sarah nodded, but her eyes were damp, and Ellie was reminded that she had never been the strongest of creatures. At least, when they arrived at their destination there would be someone to care for her.

CHAPTER 35

When he heard the commotion, William came straight out of the back office.

"Where are my children?" Joseph Spencer was shouting at Cecilia.

William noticed he made no mention of Sarah.

Cecilia looked perfectly calm as she answered. "I'm sorry, Mr Spencer, I have no notion to what you are referring. I have no idea of the whereabouts of your children. Have they gone missing?"

Cecilia's smile was as beatific as usual, and were it not for the fact that Joseph was still advancing toward her, William might have laughed.

"Sir, if you cannot be civil you should leave our office, before I call the sheriff to join us." William moved toward Joseph to escort him to the door, but Joe pushed him away.

"I asked where my children are. I do believe you know the answer to that, and you have no right to keep them from me."

His anger was palpable, and William was worried for Cecilia's safety. For the first time, he could see the violence in the man for himself.

This time, Cecilia's voice was as hard as iron. "Mr Spencer, I have told you honestly I do not know the whereabouts of your children. Furthermore, as your wife's attorney, if I did know their location I might not be at liberty to divulge it to you, unless I supposed them to be in any danger, which I do not. Now, will you kindly leave my office?"

"My wife's what? My wife doesn't have an attorney — she has no right to one and she certainly has no need of one." Joe thumped his fist on the edge of the desk.

"That, Mr Spencer, is entirely between Mrs Spencer and me. Now please leave these offices, sir, before I have to throw you out."

Looking at Cecilia for a moment, William could well imagine she would be quite capable of throwing Joseph Spencer into the street, without any assistance from him. However, he felt the need to back her up. "You heard what Mrs Dixon said." He took a step toward Joe, wondering if he was about to be punched, but thankfully, seeing himself beaten, Joseph's shoulders slumped and he turned toward the door.

As he went out, he threw back to them, "You haven't heard the last of this." Then he stumbled out into the street.

"Well, that is one angry man." William scratched his head. "You were incredible. Are you all right?"

Cecilia held out a trembling hand. "I think I may be a little shaken." She gave a weak laugh. "We've just seen some of what poor Sarah has been dealing with all these years. I wonder if he's already been out to the farm, or if we should warn them."

"We won't get there ahead of him. I suspect my sister might take much the same approach as you did. Wisely, Miss Ellie has told none of us where they're going, so we can answer truthfully. I'm not even sure if my father knows the whole plan. If you're all right, then I'll get back to my campaign preparations. I only have a few weeks until the vote and I can't afford to waste any of it."

Cecilia smiled, more genuinely this time and went back

to her desk.

William returned to the other office, shaking his head as he did so.

Over the next few days, William spoke at meetings and joined hustings, debating with those candidates whose names would also appear on the final ballot. The mouse like man had not made it through the Primaries, so was no longer there to take the pressure when things got tough, but William was learning from every experience and was more able to answer without being caught out.

There was no word from Miss Ellie, and although the sheriff dropped by to interview them both on what they knew of the whereabouts of Joseph Spencer's children, they could answer with complete honesty that they had no idea where they were.

When the sheriff called a couple of days later, William was all set to go over what they didn't know about Sarah, but the sheriff stopped him before he got that far.

"I'm not here looking for Mrs Spencer today, although we do think she may have left this town on the train, but we're not getting far with that. No, sir, I've heard from the District Attorney's office and they've set a date for the trial."

William froze. "And when will that be?"

"You're not going to like it, Mr Dixon. No, siree."

"Then I'm guessing it clashes with the election, so sometime between now and October 11th." William sighed heavily.

The sheriff's chin wobbled as he nodded. "Monday 3rd October."

William paced up and down the office, running his hand through his hair. He'd already agreed to speak at a number of events in that final week. How could he campaign and sit in a court in Warsaw each day? "Thank you, Sheriff. I guess I need to work some things out."

Once the sheriff had left, Cecilia said, "Do you think he's lost some weight?"

Her comment broke the atmosphere and William burst out laughing. "The trial and the election are at the same time, and your main thought is that the sheriff might have lost some weight. It's all this work he's having to do. He's not used to it, in our little town."

"Ben would not be happy if you missed the chance of being elected. You can't serve him well in that way." George Dixon was standing behind his son. "I'll sit in on the case over in Warsaw, if you can do without me here. Cecilia can run the office, if that's all right with you?" He looked across at Cecilia, who nodded. "That leaves you free to continue on the campaign trail."

"But I made a promise," William said, frowning.

"And you will keep the promise to see justice done for Ben more effectively by representing his interests in Congress than you can do now as part of the trial. The work you've done means the trial will take place. You can't determine its outcome."

William knew his father was right, but he still felt uncomfortable about having to make a choice. "I'm going over to the farm to talk to Molly." He picked up his hat and went out to untether his horse.

Molly was not in the best of moods when William arrived. "I don't suppose you know where I can sell all this cheese and butter, do you?" She was standing next to the cart, which was loaded with a large quantity of dairy produce. "Besides, I'm going to need money to buy our groceries, if we're going to eat more than corn."

"Do I take it Spencer's General Store has cancelled its

order?" William dismounted and tied his horse.

"It most certainly has. I should have realised that was going to happen. I was so busy worrying about Sarah, I didn't think. Joe hasn't gone as far as barring us from buying things from him, but he may as well do. I'd prefer to take our business elsewhere."

"Couldn't you set up a shop here?"

"Well, I can, but who's going to walk all this way if they can get their produce perfectly well while they're in town?" Molly started taking everything back to the cool of the dairy and William followed her with some of what needed carrying.

"Can't you find a different store to stock Cochrane's Farm produce?"

"I'm guessing I can, but it's not going to be easy. I sure will be glad when Miss Ellie comes back. Have you heard from her at all?"

William shook his head. "I don't even think Pa has. She's taking keeping Sarah safe very seriously."

"I'm glad to hear it. Joe's been out here a couple of times sniffing around. I don't rightly know where he thinks I'm hiding them when he calls. He's not going to give up easily." Molly had finished taking things back to the dairy and was wiping her hands. "Now," she said, passing the towel to William, "I'm guessing you didn't come out here in the middle of the day to listen to my problems, so how can I help?"

Explaining to Molly seemed less important in the light of the immediate issues she was facing and the risk it meant to hers and Daniel's livelihoods.

Once he'd finished, she said, "I think I know what Ben would say. Do the thing that will make the difference. Let others be there to do the rest. Mr Dixon can't run your election campaign for you, but he's more than capable of sitting in on the trial and of speaking if he's called. You can't be in two places at once."

William kissed his sister's cheek. "Thank you. I just needed to hear it from you. I'd best get back to the office, but I'll get Pa to send word to Miss Ellie about the dairy produce, if he knows how to contact her. Maybe she'll have some ideas."

Molly was smiling as she waved him off, and William was reminded how like their mammy she was. It was only when there were echoes of Mammy in Molly's face that he really thought about her, these days. It seemed such a long time since he'd lived in New York. It was almost as though it had happened to someone else.

As he rode back into town, William wondered if that same Irish immigrant boy, who had grown up in a shack on the end of a horse stable, could really go on to win a seat in Washington. If he could, it would prove above all else what a land of opportunity this country could be.

CHAPTER 36

The journey with Sarah and the children started to become more difficult later that afternoon.

"When are we going home?" Henry was bored with sitting in the carriage and was becoming increasingly fractious.

"We're going to visit some friends first." Sarah looked pleadingly at Ellie.

"Why don't I tell you a story?" Ellie said, trying to pick the boy up and sit him on her knee.

Henry squirmed and wriggled out of her grip. "I want Daddy to tell me a story. When will I see Daddy?"

This was too much for Sarah, and tears rolled down her cheeks. Henry marched over to her and hit her. "Stop crying, Mummy, that's bad."

Sarah looked up with fear in her eyes and Ellie realised with a jolt that Henry was copying behaviour he'd seen from his father. With a strong and stern voice, she said, "No, Henry, it is not bad for Mummy to cry, but it is very bad indeed for you to hit her." She took his arm firmly. "Now, you will come and sit in your seat."

The tone she used had the desired effect and Henry gaped at her, and he meekly complied.

For a few minutes, peace was restored.

Ellie started to wonder how they were going to manage Henry, both on their overnight stop and when they arrived at their destination. She had little enough understanding of the workings of young children, even in a normal situation, and this was anything but normal.

At Wanatah, Ellie left the train to buy the tickets she needed for the remainder of the journey, one adult and one child, the others being covered by tickets through to Chicago, where they'd buy the onward portions to Iowa City. Perhaps she was being overcautious, but she'd rather be safe.

Thankfully, Henry was tired and after a short tantrum, placated with some food and another story, he fell asleep. Jenny had so far been positively easy by comparison and was quite clearly a mother's girl, not in the least concerned about where her father was in the proceedings.

Ellie tried to make staying in a Chicago hotel overnight into an exciting adventure for Henry. It was something the child had never done, but he was unsettled rather than excited and it was a long night. They were all tired on the train to Iowa City the following morning and although Henry wanted to know if they were now going home, it wasn't long before all four of the party were dozing in their carriage.

When Henry awoke he started to become more difficult and Ellie was worried he would draw attention to them.

"I want my daddy. When are we going home?"

Ellie didn't think it wise to say he wouldn't be doing that for a long time, and was tempted to think Sarah might have been better to have left her older child in Pierceton.

As the day wore on, Ellie wondered if everything was in place for their arrival. She knew there was a risk they would arrive and find no one to meet them and no preparations made, since she had not been able to risk replies to her letters. She'd already thought about what measures might be needed if the worst-case situation occurred, but thought that was unlikely. There was another half hour to their arrival and, mercifully, Henry was asleep. She hoped they would be able to carry him off the train and away from the station before he created another scene.

As the train pulled into the station at Iowa, Henry woke and Ellie sighed. She lifted her case off the rack and stretched a little. Sarah prepared Jenny, ready to leave the train and Henry was looking out of the window.

"Will Daddy be here?"

Ellie was trying to think of the right words in response when she saw Cecilia's parents, Dr and Mrs Hendry, on the platform, together with a small puppy. She could have laughed out loud with relief. It was a positively inspired thought and she hoped it would do the trick. If nothing else, it gave her a new confidence in dealing with Henry, and she took him firmly by the hand. "There might be a nice surprise waiting for you in a moment."

Henry looked up at her. "Daddy?"

"No — not Daddy, just wait and see."

As soon as the train stopped, Ellie opened the door and Herbert Hendry came forward to lift Henry down onto the platform. "You must be Henry and if that's right, I've got someone here who has been so looking forward to meeting you."

Cecilia's mother passed the dog lead to her husband, who made a flourishing bow and presented it to Henry. "Now," he continued, guiding Henry away from the train so the other passengers could disembark, "he is a very special gift to you. He's going to need you to give him a name. What do you think he should be called?"

As Ellie introduced Sarah to Mrs Nancy Hendry, Henry was already down at the level of the puppy, earnestly talking to the little fellow.

"Whose idea was the puppy?" Ellie asked Nancy, as she made sure they had everything before leaving the station.

"Oh, Herbert's, of course." She laughed. "When I told him what we needed to do, he got one of those twinkles in his eyes and said he knew just the thing. The dog belonging to one of his patients had puppies a few weeks ago, so it was all easy to address. Mind you..." She looked at Sarah with some concern. "...I don't rightly know how big he will grow. The mother is a fair size and they've absolutely no idea who the father is."

"If it keeps Henry happy until we're more settled, I shan't mind what size the dear thing grows to. Although I have no idea how we'll feed him."

"You don't need to worry about that," Ellie said. "I've still got plenty of money put by, so I shall be covering all the costs."

Sarah suddenly looked far less stressed and much younger. "Oh, Miss Ellie, we are so lucky to have you. I don't feel as though I've treated you very well since I married Joe. It's just..."

Ellie put a hand on her arm. "That will do, my girl. You've no need to say anything more. Now, Nancy, will it be all right for me to stay with you for a few days, as well as Sarah and the children, while I get everything else arranged?"

"You're more than welcome, but I don't think there's anything much left to address for the time being."

Nancy smiled confidently, and Ellie raised a questioning eyebrow.

They were distracted, before she could ask anything further, by Henry, who was shouting back to his mother,

"His name is Captain Fido and this nice man says he's mine to keep. Can he sleep in my bed?"

Sarah turned to Nancy, looking alarmed. "I don't rightly know where we are to sleep so what do I say?"

Nancy smiled. "You can say 'yes'. You will all be staying in our house for the foreseeable future. I do hope that's amenable to you. Herbert insisted and I was more than happy to agree. You're in Cecilia's old room and there's a neighbouring room for the children... and Captain Fido, of course."

"I thought you were going to arrange a separate lodging for the family?" Ellie was more than happy to pay for them to have a place of their own.

"Well," Nancy said as they walked, "Herbert and I thought they might need some support, and with Cecilia away, there are times I feel a little lonely. Having Sarah and the children about the place will be company for me. You know what odd hours Herbert sometimes has to keep. Besides, I do worry for their safety. I believe Cecilia will be looking after their case, and hopefully when she wins, it will be well for them to set up their own home. Until then, our home will be their home. No one will think anything of a mother writing to her daughter from time to time. You know, when she was young, one of the games we used to play was to develop codes to communicate. I'm rather thinking she may still recognise them and I won't have to say anything that will be understood by others."

Ellie gently shook her head. "Is it any surprise Cecilia is such a wonderfully successful young lady, when she has you for a mother?"

Ellie stayed a few days while Sarah got settled. Henry spent every waking hour with Captain Fido — and the sleeping ones as well. Whilst his protestations of missing his father continued, they were not as strident as had been the case on the journey. How he'd react when he realised he was not going home, either now or any time soon, Ellie hated to think.

Ellie travelled back to Pierceton a week later. She knew she'd have questions to answer when she got back, but hoped she had covered her tracks sufficiently for her destination to have remained secret. She was almost expecting to find Joseph Spencer waiting on the platform at Pierceton when she arrived, but she hadn't even told George Dixon which train she'd be arriving on, so it was a silly notion.

She stepped down onto the platform with her case and took a deep breath. There was no one there. Just as it should be.

"Miss Cochrane, do you have a moment?"

It was the station master, and Ellie went over to where he was standing.

"Would you mind coming into my office for a moment, please?"

Ellie's heart sank. It hadn't occurred to her that the station master might have been briefed to look out for her. She was sincerely glad she'd at least had the foresight to take the train on to Fort Wayne and then come back on a ticket from there. If nothing else, it had laid a confusing trail. She'd ensured that her original ticket had been destroyed, and she was only carrying a ticket from Fort Wayne to Pierceton, in case she was asked.

"How can I help you?" Ellie put on her most charming smile and tried to appear as most men seemed to expect older women to behave, demure and a little uncertain.

"I believe the sheriff would like a word with you,

ma'am. He asked that we might keep you here when you returned from your trip, until he was able to come himself." The man, who Ellie had known since his childhood, looked particularly uncomfortable.

"And how is your dear mama, Walt?"

The station master seemed uncertain about having to keep her there, and the more so because she was being so friendly.

"She's fine, Miss Cochrane. Can I get you something to drink while you're waiting?"

"Well, that would be mighty kind of you, Walt." Walt appeared relieved to have a reason to leave his office, and Ellie felt sure he would take some time in returning.

It was the sheriff who came in next. He raised his hat to her. "Miss Cochrane. I'm afraid I need to ask you a few questions, please."

Ellie gave him a winning smile. "Why, Sheriff, I'm only just back from a few days' holiday in Fort Wayne and Toledo and I'd like to get home to have a wash and change."

"This won't take a moment, Miss Cochrane. I need to ask you whether you know the whereabouts of Master Henry Spencer and Miss Jenny Spencer?"

"Oh my," Ellie said, "have the children run away? Poor Sarah — she must be beside herself. How long have they been gone?"

"Actually, Miss Cochrane, Mrs Spencer is missing as well. She is believed to have taken her husband's children and we need to find them. Mr Spencer seems to think that, as her guardian, you might have something to do with her disappearance."

"Sheriff, I have not the least idea where they are right now. Sarah is free to make her own decisions; she's an adult, after all."

"Do you have the ticket from your journey?"

Ellie smiled sweetly and produced her ticket. The sheriff nodded, but said nothing. He seemed to think for a while.

"It would be far better you told me anything you know. Mr Spencer is likely to want to ask questions himself. He's a very angry man at the moment."

"Sheriff," Ellie said, "I do trust you aren't threatening me. Besides, if Mr Spencer were to be any risk to me, that would be a very sad indictment of your own work." She got up from the chair. "Good day to you, Sheriff. I do hope the children are safe." Then, taking her case, she set off at a brisk walk in the direction of Cochrane's Farm.

CHAPTER 37

"I can't do it." William was sitting at the breakfast table in the Red House, his head in his hands.

"William, whatever are you saying? Of course you can do it. You had one speech go badly — that's just a small part of your campaign. The election doesn't hinge on that speech. Besides, from what your father said, it didn't go as badly as you think it did."

He looked up at his wife. He was hoping for a little sympathy, but, he thought ruefully, she knew that would not serve his needs. As he looked at her, he couldn't help but think she would be the better candidate.

"Now," she said, as though he hadn't been throwing a tantrum of self-doubt, "your father is going to be attending the trial in Warsaw from next Monday, so we need to make sure everything is up to date in the office. With you on the campaign trail and George unavailable, I'm going to have quite a lot to be getting on with. If you've finished feeling sorry for yourself, I'd like you to take Thomas over to the farm so I can get an early start."

William smiled. He knew when to give in gracefully and he had to acknowledge that Cecilia was right. "Did I see a letter from your mother? How are they?"

"They're well, thank you. They send their love. I haven't read all of it. I shall take it to the office to finish later."

William looked closely at his wife. Her complexion

291

looked a little more ruddy than normal, but she looked well enough. As Thomas had finished eating, he lifted the boy out of his high-chair and carried him from the breakfast room, ready to go to the farm. Thomas loved the times he accompanied his father on the horse. William went much more slowly on those occasions, but his mare was reliable enough and he could hold Thomas with one arm while he had the reins in the other.

By the time William arrived at the office, Cecilia was already at her desk. She seemed to be concentrating hard, and was making occasional notes on a legal pad beside her. He thought it looked like the letter from her mother she was reading. William frowned, but said nothing.

The following few days passed in a whirl of speaking engagements, hustings and work. William barely saw Cecilia, except at mealtimes. Despite the long hours she was working, he couldn't help thinking she looked remarkably well.

He'd managed to keep Monday free for the opening of the trial and, whilst he would have to leave on an earlier train than his father, if the hearing continued to the end of the afternoon, he would at least be there for the start.

He was quiet on the journey to Warsaw, putting the final touches to a speech he was giving that evening. With only a week until the election he had few chances left to make a positive impression on those voters who were yet to decide how to cast their votes. Pa seemed happy enough to read the newspaper.

The weather was still reasonable for early October, and William and his father decided to walk to the courthouse from the station. "Do you think they'll take long to swear in the jury?" William was anxious that he should still be there for the opening of the case itself and not just the administrative part of the trial.

"I hope they can find twelve men not connected to the Reese brothers in some way. That's the advantage of the trial being here rather than Pierceton. I guess there is more likelihood of them doing so. I'm not aware those boys had many connections to this town."

William nodded. He certainly hoped that was true, but knowing that Justice Warren himself had a connection to old Mr Reese when he was alive didn't fill him with a great deal of hope. It would be down to the District Attorney to make the necessary objections and he had no idea how independent that man would prove to be.

Whether the Reese boys knew any of the jury who were sworn in that morning, or not, William had no idea. However, one thing was clear — the twelve men looked an awful lot more like the Reese family than they did like Ben. Any hopes the jury might include black representatives were thwarted.

Opening statements were adjourned until after the lunch break. William felt almost as nervous as if he were the one arguing the case, and could eat little.

They were back in their seats long before the District Attorney was ready to set out the case for the prosecution. There were few in the public gallery, although William did notice a reporter from the newspaper in Pierceton and another man who he presumed represented the Warsaw paper.

When proceedings began, Justice Warren, as the presiding judge, scrutinised all those sitting around his court but gave no sign of recognition. The Reese brothers were brought into the dock and William sighed, seeing them scrubbed and smartened to show their best appearances. They could almost have passed for gentlemen, though he suspected they would find that deception hard to maintain for any length of time, if the District Attorney was worth his reputation.

Just as William thought the trial was about to begin, the defence lawyer went forward to Justice Warren to have a quiet conversation, and the District Attorney was summoned to join them. William was straining to hear, but was much too far away and had no lip-reading ability. Justice Warren then addressed the court to say he would be seeing the two lawyers on a point of law in his chamber before the trial could commence, and they would reconvene in half an hour. The Reese boys were led out of the court and the jury returned to the jury room.

William sat rooted to his bench.

George touched his arm. "Don't worry, I'm sure it's nothing major. We're not going to see the case thrown out. I've gone over every last detail of how the sheriff has handled things so far, and there are no loopholes that I can see."

William nodded and relaxed slightly. He looked at his pocket watch. He probably ought to leave.

"I'll update you this evening, after your speech."

William took his leave from his father and walked back to the station. Right and wrong seemed such confused issues. He was wrestling with so many things right now, and hoped in some small way he could make a difference.

With only one week to the elections, William's time became fully occupied with campaigning. Dr Pritchard helped where he could, but had little opportunity to attend the out-of-town appointments with him. William missed his father's presence.

His father reported that the early part of the trial was uneventful. The arguments were laid out and the jury asked to consider the opposing points of view. On Wednesday, both Daniel and Molly were called as witnesses, and Miss Ellie and Mrs Hawksworth were left at the farm to keep things going. James was also being called, but not until the following day. Wednesday evening, William wished he could sit at the farmhouse table for supper and hear how each of them had fared, but as he was speaking out of town, he had to wait to hear from Cecilia when he returned.

She was asleep in a chair when he let himself into the Red House, the candle still flickering by her side. Whilst he longed to hear all the news, she looked so beautiful by the candlelight that he simply knelt down before her, marvelling at the gentleness of her face and the smile playing across her lips even in slumber.

He had no notion how long he'd been before her, when she awoke with a start to find him there.

"I'm sorry, my darling. I didn't mean to disturb you."

The smile spread across her face to her eyes and she reached her hand out and touched his cheek. A shiver of pleasure ran through William and he took her hand and kissed it.

"I saw Dr Pritchard today," Cecilia said, as she continued to smile at him.

"He couldn't make the meeting tonight. He had a prior commitment."

Cecilia shook her head. "I'm not talking about your campaign, silly. I mean I saw him as his patient."

William's face clouded. "Why, is something wrong? Is everything too much? I'll withdraw from the campaign now. We can stay here."

Cecilia laughed. "You dear, dear man. No, nothing like that. It's good news. I'm expecting another baby."

William brought her hand back to his lips. "Oh, my darling girl, what wonderful news. I love you so much."

"I guess this one will be born in Washington," she said.

He lifted her up out of the chair and held her close. "I would be just as happy to stay here in Pierceton with you."

She drew her head back and looked at him. "Well, that's a lovely thought, but I know that's not the case. And don't you want to ask me about the trial?"

He looked hesitant for a moment, not wanting to appear too eager to leave the subject of their second child behind.

Cecilia adopted her no-nonsense voice. "Now, just put me down William Dixon and let's get back to business." She grinned at him as he placed her back in the chair and drew a chair over for himself.

"Your sister was outstanding. Anyone would think it ran in the blood."

"Go on." William wanted all the details.

"She gave her testimony before Daniel and no matter what their attorney asked her, your father said she didn't waver once. She was thorough in her account and could have done no more to make what happened clear to the jury."

"Did the District Attorney ask her about the other things that happened on the farm before the fire?"

"According to your pa, he was careful not to annoy the judge. He did make reference to its being the last in a long line of actions against the farm — well, except for the traps — but he hasn't mentioned those, as far as I can tell." He asked everything in a manner that didn't give any grounds for their lawyer to object, and Molly was careful not to make general accusations in reply. I rather suspect your pa has been going through things with them when we weren't there."

"And how did Daniel do?"

"Your father said he found it hard. It brought back too much of his own trial and he was shaking when he was being questioned. He kept his answers brief. As he wasn't there when it happened, his was not the main testimony and there were fewer questions for him. He didn't join us for dinner. He was out chopping wood. I think he needed to be alone."

William nodded and looked at the clock. "Is it too late for me to go over there?"

"Good heavens, yes." Cecilia thought for a moment. "Why don't we get up early and you could go over then? We could both go and tell them my news."

William smiled and nodded. "Very well, Mrs Dixon. I shall do exactly as you instruct." Then he swept her up into his arms and carried her toward the stairs.

Cecilia couldn't stop laughing. "Put me down, you silly thing. Besides, you've not told me about your speech yet."

"In comparison to all your news, that simply isn't important. It was fine."

The following morning, he and Cecilia went to the farm, only to find Molly standing in the doorway to the kitchen, her hands on her hips.

"Now what's the dark face for, sister?" William called, as he helped Cecilia down from the carriage.

"That husband of mine's not come in for his breakfast and I'm wondering where he's got to."

"Well," said William, thinking quickly, "I did want to talk to him, so I could go and find him. Are my overalls still on the peg?"

Molly grimaced, but nodded. "You mind you don't start billing us for cleaning your suit. That's a cost we can ill afford."

William laughed. "Have you any idea where he'll be?"

Molly shook her head. "Harvest's done, so it's not easy to judge. I'd try the furthest field. There were some fences needed repairing so he may be there."

Cecilia went into the house with Molly, and William made his way down to the barn.

Once he'd changed, it took him nearly three quarters of an hour to find Daniel. When he did, his friend was sitting on a tree stump at the edge of the copse where John and Junior had been caught in traps. William went and sat next to him, but said nothing.

"Whatever they've done to me, whatever they've done to Ben, I can't accept any man being hanged." Daniel was pulling apart an ear of wheat that he'd picked up as he spoke, and was looking straight ahead.

William nodded. "That's what the law says the punishment should be for arson, where you kill a man."

"I damn near killed a man when I was running away from Hawksworth. Would you have had me hanged?"

"But you acted in self-defence. That's different." William was trying to find the words to calm Daniel. He'd never seen him like this.

Daniel got up and started to pace. "You saw it as self-defence, the court didn't. I was running away and that put me in the wrong in their eyes." He wheeled around. "The Reese boys are guilty all right. They are guilty of jealousy, guilty of stupidity, but I don't believe they meant to kill someone. I know I lost my first son because of them, and I lost Ben because of them. God dammit, I could have lost my wife and daughter, my son and my dog, but that doesn't give me the right to take their life. When I stood in that court yesterday, it brought back my own imprisonment. I was terrified. I don't wish that on another man, and I don't wish death on them. If the law hangs those brothers, it will be on my conscience for the rest of my days."

Having come to give his friend comfort and reassurance, William had no idea what to say. He could live with the fact that the law said the Reese boys would lose their lives if found guilty, but now he was worried what such a verdict might do to his friend. He sat in silence and asked himself who was right.

CHAPTER 38

Liza was up long before she needed to be on the Wednesday morning. She fumbled as she tied her boot laces and, despite the cold of the day, she doubted she would need her coat. She would have been happy never to have set foot in a courtroom again. It had been an ordeal testifying against her husband when Daniel was on trial for defending himself while running away. She shuddered. How far her life had come since those days.

For a moment she wondered what Ned was doing now, and whether he'd taken another woman to his bed. Another poor soul he could bully and beat when she displeased him. She thought how much happier she'd been on her own; then she thought of Franklin and smiled. While she was happier now than she'd ever been with Ned, she did still hope, if things could work out with Franklin Marsh, she might have even better years ahead of her.

She travelled to the station with James. As with Franklin, it was his day to give his testimony against those boys. By comparison, she imagined James being questioned would be swift and straightforward. It was the fire and its aftermath he was witness to, and not the Reese brothers themselves.

They were both quiet on the journey, lost in their own thoughts. It was only when they alighted from the train in Warsaw that they realised George Dixon had been on the same train, although Liza assumed he would have travelled first class. Franklin didn't want to be waiting around for longer than essential and was travelling by a later train.

The three of them walked to the courthouse together, with George making polite conversation and Liza trying to respond. Once George had shown James where he needed to go, they parted and he led Liza to the public gallery so they could watch proceedings.

She was anxious as she tried to make herself comfortable on the wooden bench. Seeing Daniel's distress when he returned from giving his testimony the previous day had left her shaken. He'd left the house even earlier than she had that morning, and Liza knew Molly was worried about him. Whilst there were no questions for her to answer, her heart was still pounding as she sat beside George and waited.

It might have been better for Franklin Marsh not to know she was present. For all that, she had to support him. He was risking everything to give his testimony today and she knew how that felt.

It was James who stood in the witness box first. He calmly recounted the events of the night of the fire and answered the questions put to him. His testimony was clear, and he would not be confused or side-tracked by the attorney representing the Reese boys.

The point at which Liza gasped was when the attorney asked him, "If this man, Ben, went on ahead of you, was it possible he could have started the fire?"

Even George gave a sharp intake of breath at the suggestion. James, however, remained calm.

"No, sir, it is not. He had been alerted to the problem by his dog, Junior. I was only a moment or two behind them, having gone back for a lamp. By the time I rounded the bend the whole house was ablaze and Ben had not yet entered the building."

The questions he was asked, by both prosecution and defence, led to James going over the same information several times. He told how Ben had dragged Molly out of the house and had then gone back in search of Mary. He recounted how Ben had managed to throw Mary down into James's waiting arms, before trying to get out of the building himself.

"And why didn't Ben jump from the window, rather than return into the burning building? Was there a possibility he wanted to die?"

This time the gasp ran around the courtroom at the suggestion. James's voice was steady and clear as he replied. "No, sir, there most certainly was not. Ben was a good man, but like myself he was not a fit young man anymore. Jumping from that height would have been a great risk. I might be strong enough to catch a baby, but I couldn't catch a full-grown man." He gave a self-deprecating shrug and this time murmurs of ascent followed. James turned serious. "Besides, sir, Ben had witnessed his own brother falling from a rock face as a child. Jeremiah died in that fall, sir and it left Ben with a lifelong fear of such things."

There were murmurs of understanding. Even after all the years she had known Ben, Liza had had no idea he'd ever had a brother. She wondered how much more about that good man he had kept largely to himself.

James left the stand and Liza looked around to see if he would join them to watch the rest of the morning's proceedings. She remembered how she had felt after giving her own testimony against Ned, wanting to get as far away from the courthouse in Iowa City as it was possible to go. Part of that had been driven by fear, but she'd been exhausted too. Utterly wrung out by the experience.

She had little more time to think about it, as the next witness was called to the stand. This time the name called was Mr Franklin Marsh and Liza sat up a little straighter, clasping and unclasping her hands.

She smiled when Franklin appeared. He'd obviously tried to make himself presentable, but there was no sign of a woman's touch. She wanted to go down and brush the specks off his jacket shoulders and straighten his neckerchief.

They ran through the formalities of who he was and his place of residence, and moved on to how he knew Jacob and Reuben Reese.

"Well, sir, I've known them all their lives, but these days it's mostly from them frequenting Marsh's Saloon in Pierceton."

"And how often would you say they come into your saloon?"

Franklin scratched his head. "It's maybe easier to tell you the times they haven't been there, sir. If the saloon's open, they are generally to be found seated at the bar."

"And when they are there, Mr Marsh, are they drinking lemonade?"

There was a ripple of laughter. George Dixon shook his head and sighed. Liza could see where they were taking Franklin with the questions and she hoped he was prepared.

"No, sir, they've never been known to drink lemonade."

"What is their normal drink, Mr Marsh?"

"Beer, sir."

The attorney for the Reese brothers nodded slowly. "Would you say my clients drink a lot of beer?"

"Yes, sir, a great deal."

Liza hoped Franklin could see the picture the attorney was painting of his clients being little short of alcoholics.

"And are Jacob and Reuben very often drunk when they leave your establishment?" The attorney made it sound as though Marsh's Saloon was the sleaziest, most disreputable place in all of Christendom, and Liza shuddered.

"Yes, sir, they are often drunk."

Liza sighed. The picture the jury had received of Jacob and Reuben was exactly the one the attorney wanted them to have. It would fit completely with the story of them dropping the lamp when they were lost. All of this might still be in vain.

It was the District Attorney's turn to ask Franklin Marsh some questions. Now they would really see which side the attorney was on.

"Mr Marsh…"

Liza held her breath.

"… Strangely, my colleague has only asked you some general questions and not about the night of the fire."

Liza relaxed slightly and realised George was doing the same thing.

"Were the Reese brothers in your bar on the night of the fire?"

"Yes, sir, they were."

"How can you be sure they were there on that particular day, Mr Marsh?"

"Because they weren't drinking, sir."

"When you say they weren't drinking, do you mean

they didn't consume anything on your premises that day?"

"No, sir. I mean they were not drinking alcoholic drinks. That's how I know what day it was, because it was so unusual."

"Was it possible they'd been drinking elsewhere, either before or after they entered Marsh's Saloon?"

"No, sir, that would be very unlikely. They came in when we opened in the morning and they left when I threw them out at night. I don't rightly think there's another bar in Pierceton open for longer hours than mine. They were sober at the time they left my bar."

"What happened when they left your bar, Mr Marsh?"

"I didn't follow them, sir, but they said they were going to finish the job, and the timing would have been right for them going directly to Cochrane's Farm for the start of the fire."

"When they said they were going 'to finish the job', Mr Marsh, what did you understand that to mean?"

"Objection, your honour." The attorney for the Reese brothers was on his feet.

Justice Warren paused a long moment and Liza held her breath. "Overruled, but please stick to the facts, Mr Marsh, and not to any supposition on your part."

"Yes, your honour." Franklin took a visible deep breath before he began. "They'd been talking for weeks…"

"Objection, your honour." The defence attorney was on his feet before Franklin Marsh could answer further.

Justice Warren hesitated and looked uncomfortable. He looked across at Jacob and Reuben Reese and then back to the District Attorney. "Overruled. Please continue with your answer, Mr Marsh."

Marsh dabbed his face with a handkerchief and returned it to his pocket before starting his answer again.

He cleared his throat nervously. "They'd been talking for weeks about how they might ruin the farm owned by Mrs Flynn. They said it was their daddy's land and she had no right to be there."

"Thank you, Mr Marsh. I have no further questions for this witness, your honour." The District Attorney sat down, but even before he had done so, the defence attorney was clearing his throat to speak.

Justice Warren asked, in a voice which acknowledged that the man was already on his feet, "Any further questions for Mr Marsh?"

"Yes, your honour." The defence attorney wasted no time in beginning. "Mr Marsh, how could you know Jacob and Reuben Reese were not carrying their own alcohol with them?"

"They were sober when they left my bar."

"Mr Marsh, please would you answer my question. How could you know they were not carrying their own alcohol with them?"

"They never had before."

"But you don't know they weren't, on that particular day?"

"No, sir, I don't." Franklin looked down and Liza felt his sadness.

"Mr Marsh, do the Reese boys owe you money."

Franklin Marsh looked up, frowning. "Yes, sir."

"What is that money for?"

"Their drinks in my bar. They've not paid for a while."

"And have you threatened to stop serving them unless they pay off some of their tab?"

"Yes, sir, but I don't see…"

"So then, Mr Marsh, is it possible they would bring their own alcohol for fear you wouldn't serve them any?"

"Well, I suppose so, but…"

"In which case, Mr Marsh, is it fair to say you cannot be certain they had not been drinking alcohol on the day of the fire?"

Franklin Marsh looked up with a fierce light in his eyes that Liza had never seen before. He looked directly at the jury as he said. "They walked out of my bar in a straight line that night. That's something they've never done before."

He turned to look back at the defending attorney, with a bearing that suggested he was ready for any further fight, and waited.

The man looked startled and checked back on the notes in front of him. "No further questions, your honour."

Franklin Marsh was released from the witness stand and walked slowly out of the courtroom, his head held high. Liza quickly excused herself from the public gallery, took her leave of George and hurried out of the courtroom.

She was too late to see where Franklin had gone and went outside to look for him. She looked both ways along the road, but there was no sign of anyone walking away. She had no idea if he'd be heading straight back to the station, but she had to find him. Liza didn't know Warsaw, so had little idea where to start. She walked around the court building and found a small square. Franklin was sitting on the ground, his head in his hands. This was not quite as she'd envisaged any reconciliation with him. Not many men wanted a woman to see them cry, and Liza wondered if she should walk away and wait to see him later. Then she remembered how she had felt after giving her testimony, and the feeling that she hadn't done enough.

"Franklin," she said gently.

He looked up, frowning, at the sound of his name, then scrambled to his feet and took a step back. "Liza, I... you..."

She held her hands out to him.

Hesitatingly he came forward and took them. "I don't know if I've helped," he said miserably. "And I may have risked my business into the bargain."

Liza smiled. "You're a greater man now than you ever were with a flourishing business."

"But..."

She put a finger to his lips, then wiped a stray tear from his cheek. "Will you walk with me to the station?" She didn't wait for him to answer, but linked her arm through his, and he fell into step beside her in silence.

CHAPTER 39

"You seem to be getting many more letters from your mother at the moment — is everything all right?" William perched on the edge of Cecilia's desk. She carefully refolded the letter as he did so.

"Yes, everything's fine." She seemed to think for a moment before adding, "I wrote and told her about the baby. She's delighted."

William frowned. He knew there was something his wife wasn't telling him, and he wasn't used to that. "You would tell me if there was something wrong, wouldn't you?"

Her shoulders slumped. "I suppose you're going to work it out sooner or later, and if I tell you as my fellow attorney rather than as my husband, it will at least be covered by client confidentiality."

"What?" He was completely confused now. He thought he knew about all the cases Cecilia was handling.

She pursed her lips before speaking. "That's where Sarah's staying."

"Iowa? I thought Miss Ellie headed out to Fort Wayne."

"That's what everyone's supposed to think. Oh, it's complicated, but they actually went to Iowa. Sarah and the children are at my parents' house and will stay there for as long as it takes for me to win custody of the children for Sarah."

"They could be there for a very long time. There's no

way Joseph Spencer will agree to that."

"I know." Cecilia sighed. "They'll probably have to stay in hiding until the children are adults. I think her biggest fear is that, in time, Henry will find a way to contact his father. She's hoping there'll be long enough for his early life to fade from memory, before he does something like that."

"Somehow, I doubt that." William shook his head. "You need to be careful the sheriff doesn't see any of those letters when he comes in."

Cecilia laughed. "He can see them as much as he likes, as can you, but he won't find anything very useful. They're written in code. That's why it's been taking me so long to read them."

William took her face in his hands and kissed her. "You are one special lady, Cecilia Dixon. I would never have thought of that." He picked up one of the sheets and began to read, gently shaking his head as he did so. It read as any normal letter from mother to daughter might.

"There have to be some advantages in being an only child and being home-schooled for a while." She took the letter back from him and smoothed it flat.

"Don't ever let me get on the wrong side of you. Has the sheriff been in recently?"

"No, I think they're mainly keeping an eye on what Miss Ellie's doing, which is why my mother is only writing to me. Your father passes information to Miss Ellie when needed."

William pouted, realising he had been the only one who didn't know what was happening.

"Now don't look like that. I would have told you sooner, but you've been a little busy of late."

William laughed. "Yes, and if I don't get moving I shall

miss where I'm supposed to be today. Pa says the case is likely to wrap up in Warsaw today or tomorrow. I just wish I could be there."

"We'll hear soon enough. Now, you run along and leave me to decoding my mother's message." She shooed him away.

William had to go to a lunchtime meeting, so he picked up the papers from his own desk, put on his coat and set off. As far as he could tell, his election bid was going well, but until the votes were counted one could never be certain.

The lunchtime meeting ran on into the afternoon and William found his mind wandering to whether the trial had drawn to a close. He had hoped there might be time to go over to Warsaw, but by the time he got there it would all be over for the day, one way or another. Besides, he had a dinner to attend that evening.

When he eventually got home, Cecilia was sitting up in bed waiting for him.

He kissed her and began removing his tie. "Any news from Pa?"

"Yes, he came back to the farm. There's the final summing up to go and then the jury will retire. That's the good news."

"And?" He sat on the side of their bed to remove his shoes.

"The Ku Klux Klan have taken up a position to demonstrate outside the courtroom. He thinks they're trying to intimidate the jury."

"Did no one stop them?" Even though William was still wearing one shoe, he began to pace the room. "Surely that can't be allowed to happen."

"Pa spoke to one of the court officials, but the man

shrugged. William, sit down, before you do yourself an injury." Cecilia patted the bed beside her.

"At least that's made my mind up. Tomorrow morning I'm going to Warsaw first thing. Do you know which train Pa will be on?"

Cecilia sighed and passed him a note from her bedside table. "He said you'd probably say that, so he got you a ticket and said he'd see you on the train. There was one other thing."

William looked up from his father's note and saw her worried expression. "Are you all right? Is it the baby?"

She sighed. "No, silly, I'm fine. We're fine. It's Sarah. I think that son of hers is going to prove a liability."

"How so?"

"Well, Mama was out with him a few days ago when he insisted on telling a lady in the shop that he had been taken away from his father and wanted to go home. Thankfully, it was someone who knew Mama and she accepted the explanation that the child had a vivid imagination. I think Mama may have led them to believe Henry's father had died and it was his way of coming to terms with it. The boy is going to be seven years old in only a few months. If he starts talking to the wrong person, it won't take long for the story to be pieced together."

William sighed. "Anything else?"

"Dr Pritchard said to remind you we are all dining there tomorrow night. I think he wants to give you some final encouragement before Tuesday."

"I may need a lot of encouragement if tomorrow's closing of the trial doesn't go well." William finished getting ready for bed, expecting to lie awake thinking about how the next week was going to unfold, but that was the last thought he had until he felt Cecilia gently kiss his cheek in the morning.

Pa was waiting to board the train when William got to the station.

"I thought you'd want to be here if you possibly could." Pa shook his son's hand. "We could do with there being a few more of us, ideally, to make a clear path through the Klan protesting outside."

"Maybe it's time for me to give an impromptu election speech. I could use them as an example." William grinned at his father. "What do you reckon?"

His father sighed. "If you aren't careful, they'll damage both the case and your election chances."

They fell into silence, each reading a copy of the newspaper as they travelled.

William felt as though he was readying himself for a street fight when he got off the train. His heart was pounding as they walked toward the court. In a strange way it threw him back all those years to New York, and to knowing which routes he needed to take to avoid the gangs. This time he could be walking straight into trouble, but as far as he knew, the Ku Klux Klan would be set on intimidation rather than being likely to draw a knife on him.

Despite being prepared, William was still surprised when he saw the number of the Klan who were outside the courtroom. There was no sign of the sheriff's men and no court staff making passage into the courtroom easy. William wondered how the jury might fare, as he walked forward to try to pass through the protesters who barred his way.

His father raised the cane he was carrying. "Follow me."

William marvelled at how he used the cane to move the

men aside, with a confidence that you would not expect from someone his age when faced with such a mob. He did nothing to cause injury, just confidently moved forward in a direct line to his destination. William followed. He would have felt like swinging the cane to either side to disperse the mob, but his father maintained his calm exterior and secured passage. Once inside, George Dixon did not head straight for the public gallery, but went instead to an official who was sitting in a small office inside the building.

"What arrangements are being made to afford the jury safe passage into the courthouse?"

The man looked up at George Dixon and blinked.

"Are they already safely arrived?" George asked.

"No, sir."

"Then I suggest you get some men outside to escort them through the protest — or, better still, have them enter the building by a different entrance."

"I don't have the authority to do anything about it, sir."

William had never seen his father look so angry. "Dammit, man, you can't expect them simply to come through that mob on their own. Where's the judge?"

"He's in his chambers, sir, and not to be disturbed."

"You either get outside and make it possible for the jury to gain entrance safely, or you disturb Justice Warren right now. Which is it to be?"

William stood in total awe of his father. The man behind the desk was already on his feet. His eyes were darting around as though looking for his own escape route. Then he nodded to George Dixon and headed out of the room.

"Until proved otherwise, I am going to assume he is making it possible for the jurors to enter by a different door," Pa said. "Shall we go and take our seats?"

William was astounded at how calm his father seemed to be. For his own part, he still had much to learn. He followed Pa to the public gallery and waited.

There were no others on the benches. Not even the reporters had made it through the protesters. Which story would they report, the trial or the presence of the Klan?

Eventually, Justice Warren took his seat and the jury were brought in. William's heart was pounding. They were all there. That was something.

The final summing up by both sides was brief. The whole case hinged on whether or not the brothers had been drunk and therefore whether it could be believed to be an accident. William thought of Franklin Marsh and hoped he'd done enough to convince the jury.

Once the twelve men left the courtroom for their deliberations, William decided to take the opportunity to stretch his legs and see if the protesters were still outside. He went as far as the steps to the courthouse, but the doors were closed so he assumed the protest was continuing. He returned to sit with his father.

It felt like a long wait. William thought about how the debate between the jurors might be playing out. He doubted whether, after the demonstrations, they would all feel confident of their safety, if they decided the Reese brothers were guilty. Were those men brave as well as good and true? William got up and walked around the gallery for the fourth time. His father simply looked at him, sighed and shook his head.

William eventually sat again, but this time his thoughts turned to Daniel. How would he cope if it were a guilty verdict? The Reese brothers would surely be hanged. Could Daniel live with the burden that would cause for him? William wondered if a conviction would be the end of the matter, in any event. Those boys seemed to have so many relatives in Pierceton, any one of the others might take up the fight.

He began to walk around again.

"William, sit down. You really aren't helping matters."

Meekly, William sat. He was about to speak when Zac Harrison came into the gallery, with the man William had assumed was from the newspaper here in Warsaw.

"You got through then?" William said, by way of greeting.

"We finally got the court to let us in the entrance they'd used for the jury. It doesn't look like the protestors will be disappearing just yet."

William sighed. He was about to say something further when Justice Warren returned to the courtroom and the jury were ushered back in. As he looked down at the Reese brothers, William felt his hands tense. What he'd give for the chance to wipe those smiles off their faces. The sight of them brought out the worst in him. How was he going to fare if he won public office? He'd need to maintain a controlled appearance at all times. Sometimes, even now, his red hair seemed to get the better of him. He took a few deep breaths and looked away from the boys and in the direction of the jury.

The foreman of the jury was a heavily whiskered man who looked as though he'd have been more comfortable in Marsh's Saloon than the courtroom, although William couldn't help thinking he wouldn't have looked out of place in the dock.

Justice Warren peered at the foreman. "Have you reached a unanimous decision?"

"Yes, sir, we have."

William sat up straighter. He feared this meant they were going to find the brothers not guilty.

"On the charge of arson, do you find Reuben Reese guilty or not guilty?"

The foreman looked across to the dock and then back at the judge. "Guilty, sir... er... your honour."

"Yes," William said quietly.

"And on the charge of arson, do you find Jacob Reese guilty or not guilty?"

"Guilty, your honour."

William brought his fist down on the seat in front of him. Justice Warren looked up to the gallery and frowned, then turned his attention back to the foreman, who was still standing.

"Is there anything you wish to add?"

"Er, yes, your honour." He looked at his fellow jurors, one or two of whom were nodding. He cleared his throat. "It is our opinion..." He looked around again for reassurance, and the man next to him gave a decisive nod. "... That whilst Mr Reuben Reese and Mr Jacob Reese are guilty of the offence of arson, they should not be held responsible for the death of a man who went into the building when he already knew it to be on fire. Er..." He looked around and blinked. "That's all, your honour."

"It could have been my sister." William was on his feet. Pa Dixon took his arm firmly and pulled him back.

Justice Warren brought his gavel down. "Silence in my court. If I hear so much as one sound from you, I will have you locked in the cells."

William's heart was pounding. He wanted to hit the wall with his fist. How could they say the boys were not guilty of killing, when Ben had died — and, if he hadn't, Molly and Mary could have done? He felt as though the pulsing in his ears was drowning out all else.

Justice Warren was speaking. "This court finds Reuben and Jacob Reese guilty of the charge of arson at Cochrane's Farm." He paused. "However, I agree they should not be held responsible for the death of a man known simply as..." He looked down at his notes. "... Ben, who went into the building of his own accord."

"To save my sister," William hissed through his teeth.

Pa gave him a stern look.

Justice Warren didn't seem to have heard. "They will be sentenced to a term of five years' imprisonment."

William was struggling to contain his anger. He was doing his best to hold his fury in, and wanted to get out into the fresh air. The moment Justice Warren left the courtroom, he was on his feet and heading for the door. "Five years! They kill Ben, damn near kill my sister and niece, burn down the farmhouse and everything in it and all they get is five years. How dare they? How dare the jury and Justice Warren collude to give them such an easy time?" He pushed his way through the protestors, quite ready to swing at any who got in his way.

Pa hurried after him and took his arm, directing him away from the crowd to a quiet corner. "William, if you want to be elected to Congress next week you have to stop right now. How do you think your behaviour is going to be reported in the newspapers? You cannot afford to lose votes because of this."

William pulled himself free and thumped the wall with his fist. Pa was right, he knew that. But this wasn't justice. This, and a thousand things like it, were the reasons he wanted to go into politics. He wheeled around. "Are the reporters still here? I want to talk to them."

CHAPTER 40

Zac Harrison and the reporter from Warsaw, Bud Grant, were still talking on the steps of the courthouse when William walked back. The protestors were starting to disperse and all seemed quiet.

"Gentlemen," William began, "you've both seen what has happened here today and I'd like, if I may, to comment on it for your newspapers."

Zac, who was still supporting his campaign, readily agreed, and Bud fell into line.

"Shall we find somewhere more comfortable, gentlemen?" William led them away from the court.

By now Pa had joined them, and they went across to the Kirtley Hotel and found a lounge where they could be served coffee while they talked.

As William began, he could have been speaking to an audience of hundreds, instead of the two reporters in front of him. "Gentlemen, what we have seen today is not justice. That a man can die in a fire saving a woman and child, but count for nothing because he is black, does no credit to our country. That a woman's business can be undermined by men, while she is given little support by the laws of this land, is not something we should accept. That women are denied a vote and a say in our government and are not afforded equal opportunities in education or business is not simply a scandal but deprives our country of much which could make it great. That the reforms our fellows fought for during the Civil War are being undone, even as we speak, does nothing for our position in the world. When we broke away from the British Empire in 1776, it was because we saw ourselves as more civilised than a country which still favoured a hereditary monarchy from whom to take its orders. But what have we done with the freedom and democracy we claimed in its place? The British abolished slavery long before we did, and without a civil war. Have we really created the fairer and more democratic process we think we have? We are a society where a man may progress, whatever his background, but we are a long way from being a just and fair country. Gentlemen, if I cannot change that through the legal system, then I intend to do so through our Congress. In the name of Ben, I will continue to fight for equality for all, whoever they might be."

William sat back. It felt odd to give such a speech and receive no applause, but the warmth of his father's smile was enough for him to know he'd spoken well. He would not know until he read their reports the following day, if the newspapers reported his words favourably.

"At least the Reese brothers will be behind bars," Pa said, as they walked back to the station.

"For a while. Five years without an early release is still a small price for what they did."

Pa nodded. "I guess at least Daniel won't have to deal with his conscience, as he would have done if they'd been hanged."

William nodded. That surely was a thought to hold on to.

"Keep the fire you spoke with this morning and use it for your remaining speeches. Anyone listening would find it hard not to be moved by your passion." Pa opened the carriage door of the train and William stepped up into their compartment.

"Thank you. I take that as a real compliment, sir."

Pa smiled. "And I take it as a real compliment that the work Ma and I did in bringing you up hasn't gone to waste. You'll make a fine Representative for this district when you're elected."

"If, sir."

"No, William, when. Even if it's not this time, I do believe you'll get there. Of course, I'm hoping, as much as any, that you make it this time around, but there's no certainty." Pa was quiet for a while. "There was one other thing." He ran his finger around his collar. "I was going to wait until next week to ask you, but now seems as good a time as any."

William looked at him and thought his father looked extremely uncomfortable. He frowned.

"William, how would you feel if I were to ask Ellie to marry me?"

William looked up sharply. Had he heard his father correctly? Walking out with Miss Ellie was one thing, but surely at their age they didn't need to marry?

"She's a good woman and I enjoy her company. I think it might suit both of us rather well as we get older."

"But what about James?" It was the first thing William could think to say, odd as that was. "Won't he miss having her in the neighbouring cabin?"

"Well, he probably would. I'm not sure that's something I can do much about, although I dare say Liza Hawksworth might choose to move into Ellie's cabin, unless she finds a way to get around still being married to Ned, or overcomes her conscience. Apart from worrying about James, which wasn't what I was expecting you to say, would you give us your blessing?"

William was quiet. How could he say 'no', when he knew how much Cecilia's support meant to him? How could he deny something similar to his own father, just because Ma had died? It had been hard enough to come to terms with Pa seeing another woman, but even then, he had not expected him to want to marry. It was feeling like a very long and gruelling day, and he still had a great deal to get through.

As the train rattled on through the countryside, William looked out of the window. Both he and Pa said nothing. Suddenly, with overwhelming clarity, an image came into William's head. It was the hall in Dowagiac where he had been taken from the train as an orphan to find an adoptive home. He remembered Ma and Pa Dixon extending nothing but love to him and asking if he was on his own. He had denied Daniel then, for fear that extending their love to Daniel would in some way dilute what was available to him. As a result, Daniel had a dreadful childhood, while he had everything. He'd been selfish then. He saw his own reflection in the train window. Had he changed so very much? Could he still be scared that if love were extended to others, there wouldn't be enough for him? He sighed.

He turned to Pa and said quietly, "You have my blessing."

Pa put a hand out to his son, and William shook it and smiled.

"Will you be my best man if she accepts me?" Pa looked very young as he asked.

William laughed. "I will indeed. I just hope it's less eventful than my own wedding. Maybe putting the Reese brothers behind bars beforehand wasn't the best idea."

They were both in much better spirits by the time they alighted from the train in Pierceton and headed to the farm, having first checked whether Cecilia was still in the office.

Molly greeted them in the yard. "If you're going to tell us all at the same time, someone needs to go and find Daniel. He's been out since dawn again. Is it good news?"

"Daniel will be fine," William said. "Should I go and look for him?"

"No, James said he'd go as soon as we knew you were here. I'll go down to the cabin and ask him to find Daniel." Molly turned, before William had a chance to say more.

He called after her. "Tell James to say it's good news. He's safe to come back indoors."

Molly disappeared and William turned to find Cecilia and Thomas coming from the house to greet him. Cecilia looked at him quizzically, and he used his hand like a balance to show it could tip either way. She nodded. He lifted Thomas up and with his free arm embraced Cecilia. "I've given Pa my blessing to ask Miss Ellie to marry him."

Cecilia pulled back and looked him in the eye. She was smiling. "And you're all right with that?"

He nodded. "I did some soul searching. When I saw the selfishness that lay behind my reasons for denying him, I thought of everything I have with you. Then I thought what you would say. You've become the voice in my head." He grinned. "The selfish me pouted a bit, but realised you were right."

She kissed him. "I'm proud of you."

"Which makes me the luckiest man alive." He began a jig across the yard, with Thomas laughing in his arms.

They were soon gathered at the table, waiting for James to bring Daniel into the room. Molly was holding

Mammy's wooden rosary in her lap.

That the trial would not be discussed until all were present did not need to be mentioned, and they talked of other things, including the remaining couple of days of campaigning. When James and Daniel came into the room, James joined them at the table, while Daniel paced the length of the room like a caged wild animal.

William hastened to deliver the news before Daniel could do another circuit of the table. "No one is to be hanged."

To William's surprise, Molly crossed herself. He'd not known she was as worried about the prospect of the hangings.

Daniel stopped in his tracks and turned to them. The anguish was clear on his face. "Does that mean they're free again?"

"No, it does not. They've been sentenced to five years' imprisonment." William saw the tension drop from Daniel's shoulders as he slumped into a chair.

"How so?" Molly asked, covering Daniel's hand with hers.

"Well, if I'm honest, I don't really know where in all this the truth lies." William looked across to his father. "You have more experience in these things — do you have any idea?" His father shook his head and shrugged.

William continued. "The foreman of the jury said they didn't think those boys should be guilty in relation to Ben's death, because he went into the building of his own accord. No one mentioned the fact that he only went in to save the two of you." He looked to Molly. "The Ku Klux Klan were protesting outside, making it difficult for anyone to go in. The judge knew the Reese family, when old Mr Reese was alive. Ben was black. I just don't know. If Ben hadn't gone into the house it would have been a white woman and child who were dead. Maybe they'd have hanged then."

"And maybe I'd have been happy for them to do so," Daniel said quietly.

"Or it would have been me," James said. "I'd have gone in there myself, if Ben hadn't been ahead of me. I wonder what losing my life would have been punished with."

A sombre mood settled on the party.

"For what it's worth, those boys will be out of the way for a while. We've still got no place to sell the butter and cheese, but that's not down to them. Mr Marsh may have lost his business too." Molly looked across to Mrs Hawksworth, who blushed.

"Franklin will be just fine. We've had some ideas about that bar of his. I don't think you'll need to worry there. Maybe we could find a way to sell the farm produce too, but it's early days." Mrs Hawksworth had a beaming smile and William felt pleased that some good had come out of the last few days.

"If you'll excuse us, we need to be getting back into town." William raised an eyebrow to Cecilia to see if she was ready, and she nodded in reply.

"Before you go..." Molly got up and addressed everyone. She was turning the rosary around in her hands as she spoke. "I know we had his funeral, but with the fire and all, we never had a celebration for Ben's life. I'd like to have a little memorial for Ben, now the trial is out of the way, as a means of putting all this to rest. Would you all be free on Sunday afternoon? I'm not really sure what we need to do." She looked to Miss Ellie. "Would you help me to prepare something?"

"I'd be honoured to do that. Maybe we could each say a few words." Miss Ellie looked around the table to them all and they silently gave their ascent.

Sunday was the one day before the election when William was not booked to speak anywhere, and a trip out to the farm would be a welcome way to spend it. He lifted Thomas onto his shoulders, and together with Cecilia, went toward the door.

"Might I get a lift into town with you?" Mrs Hawksworth said, looking slightly sheepish.

"How will you get back later?" Molly asked. "Would you like Daniel to come out to bring you back?"

"Er, that won't be necessary, thank you." Mrs Hawksworth blushed.

As William held the door for Mrs Hawksworth to accompany them, he grinned back at Molly, who smiled and gently shook her head.

CHAPTER 41

Molly put together some food to take down to the cabins. There was a chill in the air, but it seemed more appropriate to remember Ben outside the place he'd been happy to call home, rather than in the new farmhouse.

James had made a wooden cross that would stand at the foot of the apple tree by the cabin. Of course, there was something in the graveyard in town, but it was here they wanted their lasting memorial to him. James had carefully carved the words 'Ben — Our Good Friend and Hero — Died 1868'. No one knew when Ben had been born. Mrs Hawksworth said he'd seemed old even in his early days on their farm in Iowa. Molly suspected that was as much from the hardness of his life as the passing of the years.

Even the newspapers, in their reporting of the trial, barely made reference to Ben. It seemed unfair, but Molly thought he would have preferred it that way.

She, with John and Mary's help, had spent much of Saturday gathering what wild flowers, branches with berries, and attractive foliage they could find. She had then tied them into small posies for each of them to lay by Ben's cross. Molly had them all ready as the small crowd gathered. Daniel had carried one of the cradles down to the cabins so that the twins would be safe close by.

Liza Hawksworth spoke first. "I knew you longer than any other here, and yet I hardly knew you at all. Ned wouldn't stand for me to spend time at the bunkhouse and

I'm sorry I couldn't do more to ease your life. I'm mighty grateful to you for all you did for Daniel. I was always glad to see you back for harvest and sorry to see you leave again." She laid her flowers and stood back.

James stepped forward. "We may not have been neighbours in these cabins long, but they were some of the best times I've known. Rest easy and know you did a great thing." He laid the flowers and wiped his eyes as he walked away.

One by one they took their turns, Mary and John going forward together. John only knew Ben by the stories they all told and yet he was clearly moved.

Molly followed close behind them. How could she find words for the man who'd saved her life and without whom she never would have found Daniel? She knelt and kissed the cross. Holding her hands in prayer, she recited the Hail Mary, crossed herself and stepped back. The tears streamed down her cheeks and she made no attempt to stop them. Miss Ellie put her arms around Molly and held her.

Finally, Daniel went forward, with Junior by his side. "You were as close to a father as I ever had, after I lost Da. You and Duke saved my life and kept me believing there could be better times. You shared everything you had with me and I tried to do the same for you in return." He sank to his knees. "I will never forget you."

As Daniel leaned forward to lay the last posy, Junior moved around and faced Daniel. Standing on his hind legs, something he had not done since the accident with the trap, he reached up and licked Daniel's face.

"You've certainly earned your stripes as Duke's son. Thank you." Daniel smiled at the little dog.

William had been carrying a large bag, but had so far

not taken anything out of it. He went across and untied the top. "I've been working on this for a good while, to Cecilia's despair. I thought it was about time one of us Irishmen learned to play the fiddle. I wanted to keep it secret until the time was right, and I do believe that time is now. I think," he said, drawing a violin out of the bag, "it would be a good way to honour Ben with a song. "If I were to play, would you sing for us, Daniel?"

Molly clapped her hands. "However did you keep that quiet? Oh, Daniel, John, sing for us. Ben used to love to hear you sing."

William began to play the fiddle as though he'd been born to it. He started with one that Ben had loved.

Michael row the boat ashore, Hallelujah!
Michael row the boat ashore, Hallelujah!
Jordan's river is deep and wide, Hallelujah.
Meet my mother on the other side, Hallelujah.

Then he played *The Star-Spangled Banner* so they could all join in. After that he began on some of the Irish tunes that Daniel had sung since they were children.

"Ben would have enjoyed our little party," Molly said to Cecilia, who was happily bouncing Thomas in time to the music, while Mary was trying to dance with James.

As William finished playing a jig, Mr Dixon raised his hand for quiet. He stepped forward and went toward Miss Ellie. Molly wondered if he was going to ask her to dance. Instead he stood awkwardly in front of her and got down on one knee.

"I'm not sure if this is the right time and place, but something tells me Ben would have liked to be part of it."

Molly looked at William, who was grinning, and she suddenly realised what was happening. She gasped and covered her mouth.

George Dixon continued. "Ellie Cochrane, I may not be so much of a catch these days, but would you do this old man the very great honour of being my wife?"

Ellie didn't speak immediately but took a step back and pulled a chair forward, then sat down on it heavily. "Did I just dream that last part?" she asked Molly, who was standing close by.

Molly laughed. "No, Miss Ellie, you most certainly didn't. Not unless we're all dreaming."

"Then I'd better answer this wonderful gentleman." For a moment she looked concerned and turned to William. "Would you mind awfully if I were to say 'yes'?"

William grinned broadly. "My father has already asked for and received my blessing. I would be delighted if you'd say 'yes'."

As Miss Ellie nodded to Mr Dixon and they stood together hand in hand, William began to play another jig and the party continued.

When William stopped playing and they all sat down, Molly said to Miss Ellie, "I wish I'd not used the material you put by for a wedding dress. It should have been yours to wear."

"No, child — at my time of life that would never have suited me anyway, and you did look beautiful wearing it. I'm sure we can find something that would be appropriate for my age. I would like it if Sarah could be here for the wedding, but I don't suppose that could happen." She turned to Cecilia. "Is it looking any brighter, in the eyes of the law, that she will be able to keep the children?"

Cecilia shook her head.

Mr Dixon, who was sitting by his fiancée, said, "We'll go to Fort Wayne and find the finest material there is for sale. Better still, we'll have your dress made. Perhaps it would be best for Cecilia or Molly to go with you. I can't say I know a great deal about dresses. If you wanted to, we could always go to where Sarah is and be married there."

Miss Ellie sighed and shook her head. "I'm afraid that would raise too many questions and would likely give away where she is. No, we'll marry here in Pierceton, if it's all right with you. I'd like to be close to where my daddy is. I might be an old lady now, but I'd still like to think he'd be proud of me. Is William to be your best man?"

George Dixon nodded.

"In which case," Miss Ellie said, "I'll need to ask James if he'll give his old cousin away. What do you say, James?"

James laughed. "About time too, cousin. I thought I'd never have the chance to send you on your way."

To Molly, Mr Dixon had never seemed happier, and she hoped William was as pleased for the couple as he said he was. If the week went well, then William's life would be looking very different by the end of it, and his father being happy and settled might be to everyone's advantage.

CHAPTER 42

"It seems strange to think there's going to be another Mrs Dixon," William said to Cecilia as they headed back to the Red House that evening.

"We really are a funny little family. Your sister's adoptive mother will become your adoptive step-mother, and for Molly the other way about." Cecilia was resting her head on his shoulder and holding Thomas on her knee.

"I hadn't thought of that. So, what does that make Thomas and Mary?" William tried to work it out in his head, but got confused.

"I think they're still cousins, whichever way you look at it."

"Did I ever tell you that Molly and I don't have the same father?"

Cecilia sat up. "No. It seems to be quite the day for revelations. How so?"

"We never really knew much about it, but my father was a heavy drinker and often went off, leaving Mammy on her own. If I'm going for the full confession, I think she may have sold herself to bring in a little extra money. I've never told a soul. Even Molly and I have never talked about it."

"Do you know who her father is?"

William nodded. "A man called Patrick Mahoney. Mammy had known him when we were back in Ireland, but we knew him in New York too. His son, Patrick

Mahoney junior, saw to it that we were thrown out onto the streets when Mammy died. I wonder where he is now. For years I bore him a grudge, but the irony is, if it hadn't been for what he did, we'd never have ended up on that orphan train. Fate can play a strange hand."

They pulled into the yard of the Red House.

"Well, Mr Dixon, you may need to remember the role fate plays, depending on the election result this week." Cecilia kissed his cheek.

William climbed down from the cart and gave her his hand to help her down.

"Thank you, kind sir," she said, before carrying the sleeping Thomas into the house while William uncoupled the horse and put her into the stable for the night.

William spent the whole of Monday talking to people ahead of the election. The outcome of the trial had given him renewed determination to change things for the better. He might look like the many others who governed the country, but he'd known enough of adversity to appreciate the opportunities afforded to him. None of this privilege was his of right and he saw no reason why so many others should be excluded from those opportunities. He'd learned the hard way that closing the door behind him to maintain his own position didn't make him a better person. Holding the door open for others to benefit gave him far more pleasure and satisfaction than ever privilege and money could for their own sakes. He only hoped that he'd convinced enough of the voters to put their trust in him with their votes.

Tuesday October 11th was polling day in Indiana. After that, all he could do was wait. As with the Primaries, it would take a while for votes to be collected together and counted, right across the District. William went into the office on the Wednesday, but was no use to anyone, and instead went for a long ride on Brandy. It calmed him for a while, as he had to concentrate, but when he got back he was as unsettled and anxious as he'd been earlier.

"Go and help Daniel on the farm," Cecilia said to him when he went back, stalking the length of the office rather than settling to his desk. "Either that or start helping me with the paperwork for those of our clients whose voting rights have been denied."

A number of Cecilia's women clients who met the voting criteria in all but sex had presented themselves to cast their votes and been refused. They were now bringing actions against the State for having been denied. "Let's hope you don't lose by six," Cecilia said, as she showed him the files she was working on.

He sighed. He couldn't settle to paperwork so he took up her original suggestion and headed out to Cochrane's Farm. The overalls were still hanging in the barn and were beginning to feel less alien to him. He went in search of Daniel.

"Fence repairs," Daniel said, passing him some wooden posts to carry.

William had felt he was getting the hang of harvesting, but he knew nothing of repairing fences and only hoped Daniel wasn't going to leave him to it. What he hadn't been expecting was to find himself in the cow field at the same time as the cows. He eyed them suspiciously as they grazed, and for his own part stayed very close to the edge of the field. When the cows came over to see what they were doing, William climbed over to the neighbouring field, much to Daniel's amusement.

"You'll never make a farmer."

"I'm rather hoping these aren't skills I'm going to need

if I'm in Washington."

"When will you hear?" Daniel was completely unfazed by the cows watching him.

"Tomorrow, I hope, otherwise I'm going to have to get a bit more used to livestock." William passed one of the new posts to Daniel, but stayed at more than arm's length from the cows.

"You're not going to be here for milking in the morning, then?"

William knew Daniel was teasing him, but despite his normal reaction of accepting any challenge, this was one he felt comfortable to pass on. "I'll arrive a little later, if it's all the same to you. That way I can bring Thomas over and save Cecilia the journey. She's got her hands pretty full with cases right now."

Daniel laughed. "I'm sure the girls will be sorry not to have the chance to get to know you more intimately. I'll break it to them gently."

William might as well have agreed to do the milking, as he hardly slept on Wednesday night. He was up and about long before Daniel would have gone out to the cowshed. He went out to the stables and spent an hour grooming Brandy. "I don't suppose those cows are so very different to you. But when I look into your eyes, I see a friend." He brushed down the length of her flank. "Mind you, it took me a while to get the hang of Cady, but now look at us." The little dog was curled up on the straw beside where he was working.

"Are you enjoying yourselves out here?" Cecilia was standing in the doorway in her dressing gown.

"I'm sorry, did I disturb you?"

"No, silly, I'm as anxious as you are."

Cady ran to her mistress, wagging her tail.

"Let's hope we hear the result today. I don't think Brandy will appreciate my getting her up so early tomorrow as well." He presented the horse with a hay net, kissed her nose and went back to the house with Cecilia.

There was no point changing, if he was going to be working on the farm for the day, so he tried to eat some breakfast and, as soon as Thomas was ready, set off for the farm. "Let me know if you hear something," he said as he kissed Cecilia goodbye.

William was so full of nervous energy that he thought of walking to the farm. However, as he might need to get back into town quickly, riding seemed the better option. "Me again," he said to Brandy as he saddled her. "We'll have to take it steady, girl. We have Thomas as well."

Thomas laughed at his father talking so earnestly to Brandy as they set off. It wouldn't be long before he would be wanting a pony of his own, and William wondered what their stabling might be like if they were in Washington.

He left Thomas with Miss Ellie and went to find what work Daniel had in mind for the day. He found him sitting on a large tree stump with some tool or other in his hand. William had no idea what it was used for.

He sat next to his childhood friend.

"We've come a long way since our days in New York," Daniel said, looking away into the distance. "I know for a while we…"

Daniel seemed to be searching for the right words, and William waited. He didn't want to fill in the reality that he had deserted his friend when he was most needed.

"… We lost touch, but it has meant a great deal to me and Molly having you back with us and here in Pierceton. I shall be sorry if you leave again now. Promise me one thing."

"Anything," William said, without hesitation.

Daniel rolled his sleeve up a little way, revealing not the deep scars on his back and legs inflicted by Mr Hawksworth, but the fine white line of a scar where the skin had long since healed.

"That you will stay true to the blood-brothers' oath we swore as children, and even more importantly, whatever happens, you'll stay true to yourself."

William rolled back his own sleeve and looked down at his matching scar. He thought back to the many times he'd denied Daniel when they were younger, and the behaviours in his life he was not proud of. Then he took Daniel's hand in his, their arms pressing together once again. "I promise."

Daniel nodded and smiled a sad smile, leaving William wishing dearly he could undo some of the past, but he couldn't. He could only hope to make amends in the future.

"So, what's to do today?" William folded his shirt sleeve back down and got up, ready to work.

They could hear the sound of horses coming into the yard.

"Given you're already here, I don't think we're expecting anyone else." Daniel got up and started walking back toward the farmhouse.

"Representative Dixon! Representative Dixon!" Zac Harrison was now running across the yard, shouting at the top of his voice and waving a piece of paper. "This has just come in from Fort Wayne. You've done it!"

Whilst Zac was jumping in the air, Cecilia and Pa were standing quietly by the carriage, smiling broadly. William walked forward in a daze. Zac slapped him on the back as he passed and went to Cecilia.

"Is it true?" he asked.

Cecilia nodded and took his hands. "It's true. You have been duly elected to the House of Representatives, Mr Dixon. Washington awaits."

He turned to Pa.

"Well done, son. Ma would have been exceedingly proud of you. I'm only sorry she didn't live to see this day. I'm proud of you too, of course."

"Will you take care of things here while I'm away?"

"You know I will, son. It will be my pleasure."

"We need to get you into town. I've got the photographer ready for a victory photograph." Zac was still bouncing up and down on the balls of his feet.

William turned to him. "That will need to wait. There's something I need to do first. Will you all excuse me for a short while? I shall be back, but there's something I need to fetch. There's one last thing I need to do."

They looked confused as he walked to the stable, saddled Brandy and mounted. He patted her flank and set off across the field route to the Red House. Once there, he left her in the yard while he went inside to fetch his fiddle. Then he remounted and headed back to Cochrane's Farm.

He looked into the kitchen, where everyone seemed to be talking at once but stopped when they saw him.

"I won't be much longer," he said, plucking a single flower from the vase on the table and going back outside down to the cabins.

He walked past the cabins to the cross remembering Ben. He laid the flower at the base of the cross.

"I didn't know you well, but your dignity when facing prejudice and your determination not to let the bad guys win has done as much to inspire me as has any other single person. You were there for my friend when I failed him. You saved my sister and niece and lost your own life doing so. As I go on to Washington, may everything I do honour your memory." He lifted his fiddle to his chin. "There was one tune we didn't sing for you last Sunday. My singing's not up to much, but I can at least play it."

As William lifted his bow, he heard footsteps behind him and turned to see Daniel and Molly hand in hand, Daniel raised his voice in song as William began to play the haunting melody beloved by Ben.

Amazing grace how sweet the sound
That saved a wretch like me!
I once was lost, but now am found,
Was blind, but now I see.

THE END

FAMILY TREE

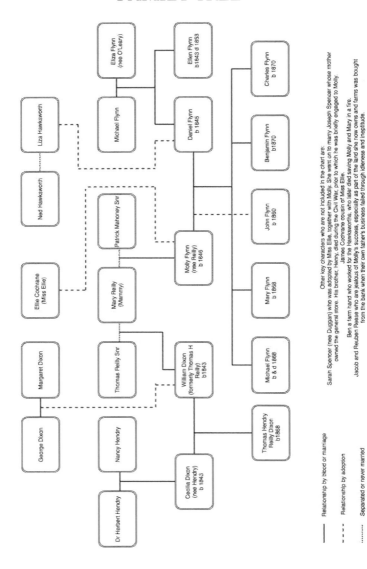

Eliza Flynn (nee O'Leary)

Ellen Flynn b 1843 d 1853

Charles Flynn b 1870

Liza Hawksworth

Ned Hawksworth

Michael Flynn

Daniel Flynn b 1845

Benjamin Flynn b 1870

Patrick Mahoney Snr

John Flynn b 1860

Ellie Cochrane (Miss Ellie)

Mary Reilly (Mammy)

Molly Flynn (nee Reilly) b 1846

Mary Flynn b 1868

Margaret Dixon

Thomas Reilly Snr

William Dixon (formerly Thomas H Reilly) b1843

Michael Flynn b & d 1868

George Dixon

Nancy Hendry

Cecilia Dixon (nee Hendry) b 1843

Thomas Hendry Reilly Dixon b1868

Dr Herbert Hendry

——— Relationship by blood or marriage

- - - - Relationship by adoption

·········· Separated or never married

Other key characters who are not included in the chart are:

Sarah Spencer (nee Duggan) who was adopted by Miss Ellie, together with Molly. She went on to marry Joseph Spencer whose mother owned the general store. His brother, Henry, died during the Civil War, prior to which he was briefly engaged to Molly.

James Cochrane cousin of Miss Ellie.

Ben a farm hand who worked for the Hawksworths, who later died saving Molly and Mary in a fire.

Jacob and Reuben Reese who are jealous of Molly's success, especially as part of the land she now owns and farms was bought from the bank when their own father's business failed through idleness and ineptitude.

PLEASE LEAVE A REVIEW

Reviews are one of the best ways for new readers to find my writing. It's the modern day 'word of mouth' recommendation. If you have enjoyed reading my work and think that others may do too, then please take a moment or two to leave a review. Just a sentence or two of what you think is all it takes.

Thank you.

BOOK GROUPS

Dear book group readers,

Rather than include questions within the book for you to consider, I have included special pages within my website. This has the advantage of being easier to update and for you to suggest additions and thoughts which arise out of your discussions.

I am always delighted to have the opportunity to discuss the book with a group and for those groups which are not local to me this can sometimes be arranged as a Skype call or through another internet service. Contact details can be found on the website.

Please visit http://rjkind.com/

SOURCES OF INFORMATION

In addition to the reference sources listed in The Blight and the Blarney, New York Orphan and Unequal By Birth, the following additional information has been consulted:

http://www.wiseoldsayings.com/justice-quotes/

A History Of Pierceton Indiana by George A. Nye Pierceton

Missouri Law Review's 'Metamorphosis of the Law of Arson' - Volume 51 Spring 1986 John Poulos

The Intellectual Origins of Torts in America - G. Edward White, The Yale Law Journal, Vol. 86, No. 4 (Mar., 1977), pp. 671-693

History of Indiana
https://en.wikipedia.org/wiki/History_of_Indiana

Steinson, Barbara J. "Rural Life in Indiana, 1800–1950." Indiana Magazine of History 90, no. 3 (1994): 203-50. www.jstor.org/stable/27791761.

The Agricultural Development of the West During the Civil War Author(s): Emerson D. Fite Source: The Quarterly Journal of Economics, Vol. 20, No. 2 (Feb., 1906), pp. 259-278 Published by: Oxford University Press Stable URL: https://www.jstor.org/stable/1883656

https://kosciuskohistory.com/

https://www.in.gov/history

ALSO BY ROSEMARY J. KIND

Unequal By Birth (Tales of Flynn and Reilly 2)

1866 - Daniel Flynn and Molly Reilly's lives have been dogged by hardship. Finally, the future is looking bright and Indiana is the place they call home. Now they can focus on making Cochrane's Farm a success.

The Civil War might have ended but the battle for Cochrane's Farm has only just begun. The Reese brothers are incensed that land, once part of their family farm, has been transferred to the ownership of young Molly. No matter that their Daddy had sold it years previously, jealousy and revenge have no regard for right. Women should know their place and this one clearly doesn't.

How far will Daniel and Molly go to fight injustice and is it a price worth paying?

New York Orphan (Tales of Flynn and Reilly 1)

Orphaned on the ship to New York in 1853, seven-year-old Daniel Flynn survives by singing the songs of his homeland. Pick-pocket Thomas Reilly becomes his ally and friend, and, together with Thomas's sister Molly, they are swept up by the Orphan Train Movement, to find better lives with families across America. For Daniel, will the dream prove elusive and how strong are bonds of loyalty when everything is at stake?

The Blight and the Blarney (Prequel to Tales of Flynn and Reilly) – *see Free Download information for how to obtain the ebook, including additional material on the series absolutely free*

Ireland has suffered from potato blight since 1845. Friends and neighbours have died, been evicted or given up what little land they have in search of alms. Michael Flynn is one of the lucky ones. His landlord has offered support.

With the weakening brought about by hunger, there are some things he is powerless to protect his family from. Is it time for the great Michael Flynn to take his family in search of a better life?

The Appearance of Truth

Her birth certificate belonged to a baby who died. Her apparently happy upbringing was a myth. Does anyone out there know – who is Lisa Forster?

The Lifetracer

Connor Bancroft is more used to investigating infidelity than murder, and when he's asked to investigate a death threat he's drawn into a complex story of revenge. He uncovers a series of, apparently, unlinked murders. He is nowhere close to solving the crimes but now his eight year old son, Mikey's life is in danger and Connor has little time left to find out – Who is The Lifetracer?

Alfie's Woods

Alfie sets out to befriend a money-laundering hedgehog when he is recaptured following his escape from the Woodland Prison. Hedgehog is overwhelmed that any other creature should care about him, finds the strength to change his life. Alfie's Woods is a story of the power of friendship and the difference it can make to all of us.

Embers of the Day and Other Stories

From the movingly beautiful, to the laugh-out-loud funny. This collection of short stories covers the breadth of Rosemary J. Kind's fiction writing in her usual accessible style.

Lovers Take up Less Space

A humorous review of the addictive misery of commuting on London Underground.

Pet Dogs Democratic Party Manifesto

Key political issues from a dog's point of view by self-styled political leader Alfie Dog.

Alfie's Diary

An entertaining and thought provoking dog's eye view of the world.

From Story Idea to Reader

Whether brushing up your writing skills or starting out, this book will take you through the whole process from inspiration to conclusion.

The Complete Entlebucher Mountain Dog Book

This book provides a complete insight into the Entlebucher Mountain Dog. Whether you are looking to add an Entlebucher to your family, get the best out of your relationship with a dog you already own or are interested in the story of the breed itself and its development in the UK, this is the book for you.

Poems for Life

A collection of poems including the inspirational 'Carpe Diem'.

You can find out more about the author's other work by: visiting her website http://www.rjkind.com

ABOUT THE AUTHOR

Rosemary J Kind writes because she has to. You could take almost anything away from her except her pen and paper. Failing to stop after the book that everyone has in them, she has gone on to publish books in both non-fiction and fiction, the latter including novels, humour, short stories and poetry. She also regularly produces magazine articles in a number of areas and writes regularly for the dog press. As a child she was desolate when at the age of ten her then teacher would not believe that her poem based on 'Stig of the Dump' was her own work and she stopped writing poetry for several years as a result. She was persuaded to continue by the invitation to earn a little extra pocket money by 'assisting' others to produce the required poems for English homework!

Always one to spot an opportunity, she started school newspapers and went on to begin providing paid copy to her local newspaper at the age of sixteen.

For twenty years she followed a traditional business career, before seeing the error of her ways and leaving it all behind to pursue her writing full-time.

She spends her life discussing her plots with the characters in her head and her faithful dogs, who always put the opposing arguments when there are choices to be made.

Always willing to take on challenges that sensible people regard as impossible, she set up the short story download site Alfie Dog Fiction which she ran for six years. During that time it grew to become one of the largest short story download sites in the world, representing over 300 authors and carrying over 1600 short stories. Her hobby is developing the Entlebucher Mountain Dog breed in the UK and when she brought her beloved Alfie back from Belgium he was only the tenth in the country.

She started writing *Alfie's Diary* as an internet blog the day Alfie arrived to live with her, intending to continue for a year or two. Thirteen years later it goes from strength to strength and has been repeatedly named as one of the top ten pet blogs in the UK.

For more details about the author please visit her website at www.rjkind.com For more details about her dogs then you're better visiting www.alfiedog.me.uk

ACKNOWLEDGMENTS

Thanks must be given to the following people for their help in putting this book together.

Sharon Whetstone, Librarian, Genealogy Research Library, Warsaw, Indiana, for her help with some of the questions to which I could find no answers.

Katie Stewart who has once again produced a spectacular cover and I really cannot thank her enough for her work.

Sheila Glasbey, thank you for your wonderful proofreading skills.

As ever, my writing buddies - Lynne, Patsy & Sheila - without you, my work would be much the poorer.

My parents and my husband for thinking I'm marvellous, but not so marvellous that they don't tell me how I need to improve.

Alfie Dog Fiction

Taking your imagination for a walk

visit our website at www.alfiedog.com

Printed in Great Britain
by Amazon